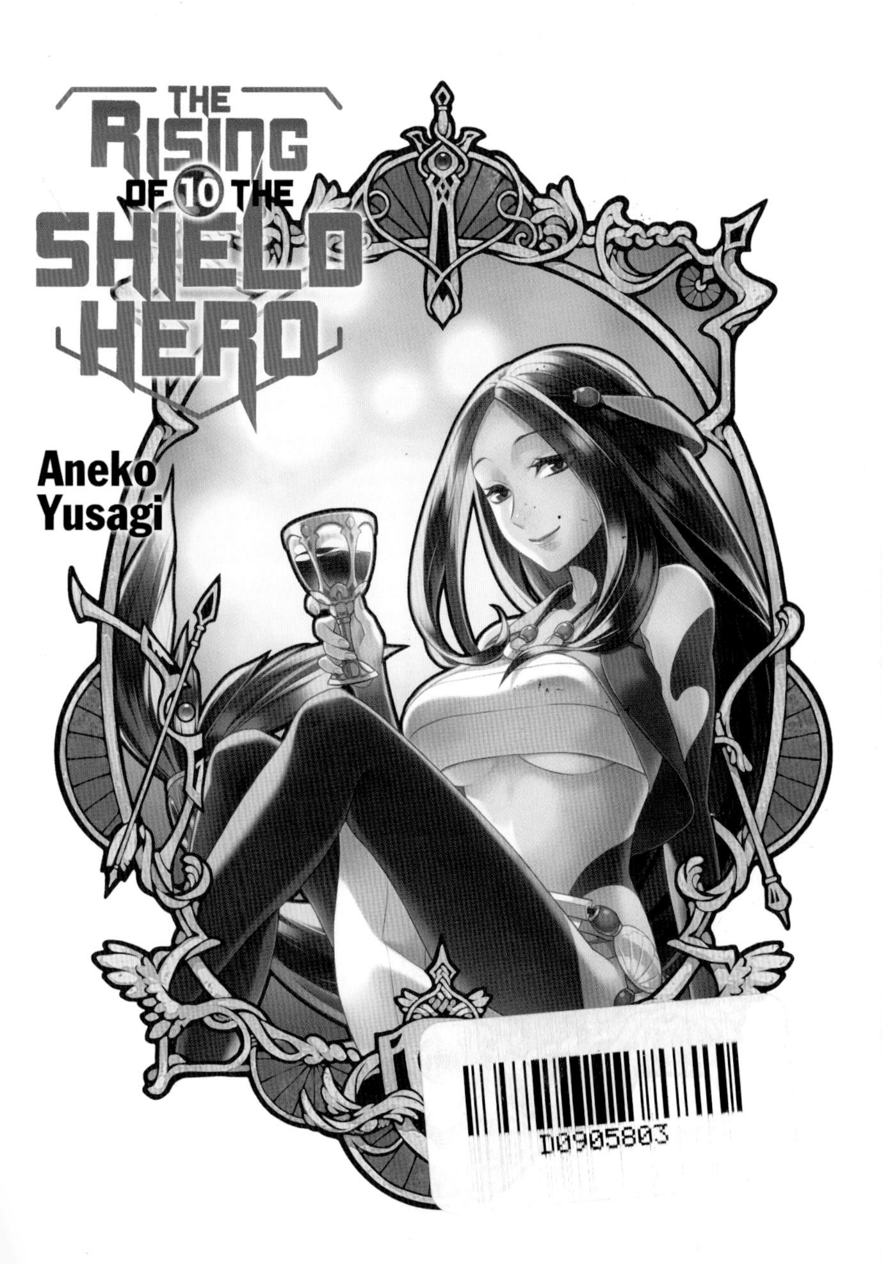
THE RISING OF 10 THE SHIELD HERO
Aneko Yusagi

Nadia
Raphtalia
Keel

Eclair
Rishia
Melty
Naofumi Iwatani
Filo
THE RISING OF 10 THE SHIELD HERO

“Now, now . . . I’ve got nothing against children being a bit feisty, but you boys are just plain naughty, aren’t you?”

Table of Contents

Prologue: The Spirit Tortoise's Barrier

After saying our goodbyes to Kizuna and the others we were transported, and just like when being summoned to a wave, our surroundings instantly changed. We were in . . . Yes, these were familiar fields, along with their view of the Melromarc Castle Town.

"We made it back."

Raphtalia's voice was overflowing with emotion. I guess it did feel a bit like a homecoming.

"Looks that way."

"Fiiinally!"

Filo seemed to feel the same way.

"We've returned at long last!"

Even Rishia was getting emotional. Just as I felt a sense of relief begin to settle in, a brilliant light shot out of my shield and high into the sky . . . and then faded away as if it had dissolved into the atmosphere.

"Whoa!"

"Wh . . . what was that?!"

"I'm guessing that was the Spirit Tortoise's energy returning to this world."

The whole Spirit Tortoise ordeal hadn't lasted that long.

Even so, there was something deeply emotional about it all. Thinking about it, it seemed short, but it had actually been a long battle.

The Spirit Tortoise was something that existed to create a barrier that would protect the world, but someone seized control of its body, and so Ost reached out to me for help. It turned out it was Kyo that had manipulated the Spirit Tortoise and inflicted great damage upon this world, and we ended up chasing him all the way to another world.

In that other world, we met Kizuna, who was one of the four holy heroes just like me. Kizuna joined us to fight Kyo, and together we made Kyo pay for what he'd done. Then we took back the Spirit Tortoise's energy and returned to this world.

The Spirit Tortoise was one of the guardian beasts, which were monstrous creatures meant to consume the souls of living things to create a barrier that would halt the fusion of worlds—a phenomenon known as the waves.

Apparently once enough of this energy used to produce the barriers had been collected, it would be possible to make the waves stop. But even if less than the full amount of energy had been collected, it would still be possible to stall the waves for some time . . . or so I had been told.

We had taken back that energy, and now it had been released out into this world to serve its original purpose. It was a magical sight, and I had a feeling it had probably been visible from far off in the distance.

I had been staring at the Spirit Tortoise Heart Shield on my arm and lost in thought when suddenly I realized something. The very last of the light had left the shield. I guess all of the energy that was stored inside had been released. Even the faint glow that had remained for a moment had now faded away.

I noticed that the Energy Blast special effect was at zero percent now. The other stats had fallen a bit, too. It was as if the shield was saying it had served its purpose and its work was done.

"Well then, I suppose we should check up on things here."

"Agreed, Mr. Naofumi."

That was Raphtalia.

Raphtalia was a demi-human girl and former slave that had been fighting by my side for so long that I recognized her voice instantly without having to turn around. Even though I considered myself something of a surrogate parent to her, it wasn't uncommon for me to be the one relying on her in certain situations these days.

She had been chosen by the katana of the vassal weapons to be its owner in the other world, which meant that she could no longer be a slave. She possessed a beauty that felt Japanese somehow, and miko clothes suited her strangely well. Maybe it was because of her tanuki-like ears and tail?

"Alright then, let's see how long until the next wave."

I glanced over at the hourglass numbers that hovered in my

field of vision. I could see . . . the red hourglass numbers had come to a halt. I also noticed that the blue hourglass icon had become active.

Was that an 8?

I was pretty sure I remembered Ost saying something about a delay before the next guardian beast appeared.

The Phoenix, was it?

That made sense. The blue hourglass was showing how much time we had left before the Phoenix's seal was broken. It looked like we had around three and a half months before the seal would be broken. Only three and a half months after a battle that intense? Or maybe, should I have been happy that we even had that long?

"Looks like we have three and a half months until the seal is broken on the next guardian beast."

"Oh . . . I see. Seems like we have less time than expected."

"Not necessarily. Compared to how it's been up until now, that should be plenty of time."

The first wave came one month after I'd been summoned here. The next was a month and a half later. Pretty much right after that was the whole Church of the Three Heroes mess, meeting the other heroes to exchange information, the wave at the Cal Mira islands, and then the Spirit Tortoise incident.

The next Melromarc wave would have been right around the corner, which means . . . it had been right around four months since I'd first arrived in this world.

"That's just about the same amount of time I've been in this world, combined with the month spent fighting in Kizuna's world."

"Reeaallyyy?"

"Considering how old you are, Filo, three and a half months should be more than enough."

Filo was a young girl who was actually a type of monster called a filolial. Filolials were strange bird-like monsters that delighted in nothing more than pulling carriages, but Filo was a certain type of filolial that was considered superior among their kind, and she had the ability to transform into what looked like an angel. If she kept her mouth shut, you might think she was just a cute little girl with blonde hair and blue eyes.

Her actual age was one month less than the total amount of time that had passed since I'd been summoned to this world. In other words, the three and a half months was about the same as the total length of time that Filo had been alive.

"Fehhh . . . No time for a break, I guess."

That was Rishia that just made that whiny "feh" sound. Rishia's abilities fluctuated based on her emotional state, but the girl had the potential to be a real heroine. I had to give her credit for contributing more than anyone else in our fight against Kyo.

I took her in after Itsuki, another one of the heroes, tossed her aside for having nothing to offer the team, but her performance had made it clear that she had plenty to offer. She still couldn't manifest that strength without becoming extremely emotional, but I was sure that would change once her abilities had really blossomed. I figured she was just a late bloomer and her stats would only improve going forward.

"Yeah, not really. We need to figure out how to get stronger before it's too late. Not to mention, we'll be fighting the Phoenix next, so we better train hard. Time is limited."

"Okay!"

"Rafuuu!"

Raph-chan responded along with Rishia.

Oh yeah, Raph-chan was a shikigami that had been created using a lock of Raphtalia's hair. She was a cute little thing that looked kind of like a tanuki or a raccoon. I imagined it's what Raphtalia would look like if she were turned into an animal. Raph-chan was surprisingly sharp and had proven useful in all sorts of situations.

I noticed my shield was reacting to something. What's this? Familiar Shield?

When I checked the flashing shield icon, it indicated that the Familiar Shield had been unlocked. It was pretty much the same as the Shikigami Shield. I must have needed it to use Raph-chan and that's why it appeared.

I sure was glad that Raph-chan hadn't disappeared or something due to differences between this world and Kizuna's world. It seems things that weren't compatible with both worlds ended up with their names garbled in the status screen and ceased to function after crossing over. I'd thought about how depressing it would be if the Shikigami Shield ended up with some unrecognizable name and Raph-chan turned into a stuffed doll or something, but thankfully nothing like that happened.

"Mr. Naofumi? You're thinking about something weird, aren't you?"

"I was just thinking about how happy I am that I can use Raph-chan in this world, too."

"Oh . . ."

It seemed like Raphtalia wasn't really sure what to think about Raph-chan.

"Although, it looks like all of the powering up that I did has been reset. I'll have to do that over again, but this time it will be in a more familiar world. I'll make you more powerful than you were in Kizuna's world in no time, Raph-chan!"

"Rafuuu!"

I loved how Raph-chan always knew just how to respond. She was standing up on two legs as if to show a sense of determination.

"Oh, it looks like someone from the castle is coming to pick us up."

While Raph-chan and I were busy gazing into each other's eyes, a familiar-looking carriage appeared, heading in our direction from Melromarc Castle Town.

And oh yeah, that was the corpse of the Spirit Tortoise that lay towering behind us. We had ended up right in front of it when we were transported back. A month had passed since we left, so the remains had been cleared away to a certain extent. The flesh and some other portions had been removed, and the flora from the mountainous areas had begun to spread . . . or at least it looked that way.

Ost . . . we made it back.

For a split second, I thought I could see a soft light radiating from the corpse of the Spirit Tortoise, as if in response to my sentiment . . . but surely it was only my imagination.

"Well then . . . I guess we should start getting caught up on things with whoever it is headed this way."

"Agreed."

"We have a lot to discuss, and all kinds of souvenirs, too."

"You think Mel-chan will be happy?"

"Who knows?"

Filo was wearing pajamas that had been designed to resemble her own filolial form. She wanted to give them to her good friend Melty, the second princess of Melromarc, as a souvenir.

"Things are probably going to get busy from here on out, so be prepared for that, Raphtalia."

That's right. Much like Kizuna and her friends, we had all

sorts of issues waiting for us that needed to be addressed, like dealing with the other three heroes that had lost to the Spirit Tortoise and been captured, for example. I really wanted to believe that they would finally listen to me after that.

"Understood."

"Other than that . . . Yeah, I guess we'll go if we can still manage it, after taking care of what needs to be done before the battle with the Phoenix."

"Go? Where are you planning on going?"

"That . . . You'll find out soon enough."

"Umm . . . okay."

"Fehhh . . ."

I had winked at Raphtalia suggestively, and for some reason Rishia responded with a frightened whimper. How rude could she be? Was it really so strange for me to wink?

After a few more moments passed, the approaching carriage and the knights escorting it came to a halt before us. The Queen of Melromarc stepped out of the carriage and gave a salutatory bow.

"I'm glad to see you made it back, Mr. Iwatani."

"Long time no see."

It had been a month since I'd last seen the queen, but she seemed pretty much the same as before. Her outward appearance hadn't changed anyway.

"And were you successful?"

"I'm sure you already have a pretty good idea, don't you?"

"We received confirmation of a bright light dissolving into the sky before heading this way. Am I right to assume that was proof you were able to successfully recover the Spirit Tortoise's energy?"

"Yeah. It looks like we won't have another wave for a while, thanks to the Spirit Tortoise's energy."

The surrounding knights responded with gasps of excitement.

"We should be safe until the seal is broken on the Phoenix—the next guardian beast of the four benevolent animals."

"And how long is that?"

"Around three and a half months. That may not seem long, but . . . we'll just have to make do."

"Understood. I'm sure you are all exhausted after such an arduous battle in another world—in enemy territory, no less. Please, this way."

"Sounds good. I'd like to hear how things have been going here, too."

I nodded, and the queen stepped aside and motioned us toward the carriage she had prepared for us. We boarded the carriage and headed for the castle.

Chapter One: The Seven Star Staff Hero

"Come, Mr. Iwatani. The people of Melromarc are offering you their ungrudging appreciation. Please, give them a wave."

"Yeah, yeah. Sure."

Such an exaggerated show of appreciation had the opposite effect. It made it all feel so contrived.

"Thank you, Shield Hero!"

"Hero!"

It was like a real hero's welcome, with the crowds waving to me as we headed toward the castle in the carriage prepared by the queen.

What a conniving bunch they were!

Then again, stuff like anime and history had taught me that this kind of thing was just a natural part of how the collective consciousness worked. I humored them and waved back as much as I felt comfortable with. But if it had been just two or three months earlier, my welcome would have likely been something like a piece of trash thrown in my face.

I was the Shield Demon, after all.

After we defeated the first wave, there were people glaring at me like I didn't belong here. I knew I should be happy that I was finally getting my due appreciation, but it still really bothered me.

I wondered how much time had passed in this world since we had crossed over.

"By the way, Queen . . ."

"Yes?"

"How much time has passed here since I left?"

I had made a point of keeping track, but I still wanted to check to make sure. It was always possible that an exceedingly long amount of time had actually passed, like in the tale of Urashima Taro—the Japanese Rip Van Winkle.

"Two and a half weeks."

"Oh really?"

Strange. Apparently time passed quicker in Kizuna's world. You could see the surprise on Raphtalia's and Rishia's faces when the queen said it had only been two and a half weeks.

"What is it?"

"Around a month had passed in the world we followed the enemy to."

"I see. To think there would be such a difference . . ."

I wasn't sure if it was a good thing or a bad thing, but I figured it meant we had saved some time . . . maybe?

We finally arrived at the castle and were taken to the throne room.

"What happened with the coalition army?"

"All of the members are working hard to rebuild their own respective countries."

The damage done by the Spirit Tortoise had indeed been awful. I had seen the scars left by the battle. We had managed to defeat the Spirit Tortoise here in Melromarc, but its massive corpse was still lying out in the fields with an expansive wasteland of wreckage extending out behind it.

"Let us review the current situation. At present, all of the dragon hourglasses across the world have come to a halt."

"The red hourglass on my status screen has stopped, too."

"I see."

"But the other hourglass shows a time of three and a half months."

The room took on a somber atmosphere.

"That three and a half months is our cutoff. We need to complete preparations for the battle with the Phoenix before then."

We already knew that the Phoenix would be reawakened.

"There's more. We learned something in the world we ended up in after pursuing Kyo, the enemy who stole the Spirit Tortoise's energy."

I told the queen what we had found out in Kizuna's world.

In Kizuna's world, legends told of the waves as being a phenomenon resulting from the fusion of two worlds. It was said that if the current fusion were to reach completion then the limits of what a single world could contain would be exceeded, ultimately leading to the destruction of the worlds.

To prevent that from happening, heroes known as vassal weapon holders were slipping into other worlds through the dimensional rifts created by the waves and attempting to kill the other worlds' heroes that possessed the holy weapons, since those heroes were the pillars of the worlds.

A commotion broke out among the queen's advisers.

"And is all of this a fact?"

"Honestly, I think it's all pretty questionable," I went on. "They hadn't actually pulled it off, and one of the holy weapons over there . . . one of their four heroes lacked the ability to fight against other people. If it really were true, surely the four heroes would need to excel in combat against other people, don't you think?"

Although, it actually might very well have been true. For some reason, though, Kizuna refused to accept it.

"We did find something in that world that seems to offer a different explanation of the waves. Rishia."

"Y . . . yes!"

Rishia pulled out the manuscript that Kizuna and the others had given her and showed it to the queen.

"We're not sure what the text means, but many of the drawings seem to be related to the waves. If we can decipher the text, we might learn something."

"Understood. I shall request the dispatch of those that decipher such things from all of the other countries so that we commence the task using all available resources."

"I want you to put Rishia on that team. She's already learned the language of that world, and she seems to be really good at this kind of thing."

Frankly, she seemed like she'd be better at it than she was at fighting.

"Fehhh . . ."

"Glass and the others are counting on you. Do your best."

I had to prepare her to be able to take on any challenge.

"In addition to that manuscript, I also talked with one of the four heroes over there and we worked things out. Glass and L'Arc agreed to a truce, too, albeit a temporary one. So even if we happen to run across them again, the likelihood of us fighting is extremely low."

"Understood. It does indeed seem that there would be little value in being any more cautious than we already are, in our current situation, with the waves having ceased for the time being."

"We also brought back several items from the other world. I'm not sure if they'll function properly here, but there's quite an assortment."

I showed the queen the bag of items that we had received from Kizuna and the others. If everything worked out, not only would the items help us deal with the waves, but they were all things we could easily make a fortune off of, too. There was equipment that could emulate the drop function of the legendary weapons, as well as the Scroll of Return, also known as Return Transcript, which was equivalent to a teleport skill and could summon the user to an hourglass just like during the waves.

"Now then, there's something important I'd like to address before anything else."

I took a step toward the queen to make a suggestion, or perhaps I should say request.

"During the next three and a half months, it's imperative that we recover from the curse that came as a toll of our battle."

That's right. Right now, Filo, Raphtalia, and I all had drastically reduced stats due to the aftereffects of the All Sacrifice Aura. Even worse, full recovery was still a long way off.

"I had no idea . . ."

To be honest, we were in pretty bad shape. We wouldn't be able to really push ourselves until we had fully recovered from the curse. Even a normal battle would likely be pretty tough right now.

According to the doctor in Kizuna's world, full recovery would take around three months. I planned on trying out various methods of recovery on my own, too, but we would still have to get by with reduced stats one way or the other until we had fully recovered.

Still, it was too bad, because I knew that at one point I had become ridiculously strong after meeting with the other heroes to discuss our power-up methods. Luckily my defensive power had been spared from the effects of the curse, so we could probably still manage somehow.

"In three and a half months, the Phoenix's seal will be broken, and the battles we'll face after that will probably grow more difficult as well."

I'd heard that the monsters being stronger in Kizuna's world had something to do with the waves. The situation was slowly getting worse, so the heroes had to be considered indispensable. There was no way I could handle everything on my own, and Raphtalia couldn't be expected to take up all of the slack, even if she did possess the katana of the vassal weapons now.

I had given Fitoria my word, too.

At the very least, we needed more solidarity among the four heroes.

"Considering what lies ahead, I think the heroes need to get together and have another discussion. The four heroes *and* the vassal weapon . . . err, the seven star heroes, I guess?"

I figured that the term "vassal weapon holders" probably corresponded to the seven star heroes in this world. I wanted to talk with them and learn about their power-up methods, if possible.

". . ."

The queen covered her mouth with her folding fan upon hearing my words.

"I have taken your words into consideration, Mr. Iwatani. As for the meeting with the seven star heroes . . . I will contact Faubrey and the other countries and do my best to make it happen."

The queen's response confused me. Just the seven star heroes? What about those three idiots—the remainder of the four heroes?

"Wait a minute. The four heroes . . . what happened to the other three?"

The queen averted her eyes when I asked.

"Hey!"

"I . . . I'm very sorry, but . . . just several days ago . . ."

In addition to myself, the four heroes consisted of the Sword Hero, the Spear Hero, and the Bow Hero—Ren Amaki, Motoyasu Kitamura, and Itsuki Kawasumi, respectively.

The three of them were convinced that they had ended up in some kind of game world and ran wild, relying solely on their knowledge of games from their own worlds. They had confronted the Spirit Tortoise and been defeated, after which they were captured by Kyo and used as a power source to control the Spirit Tortoise. I remembered seeing Eclair and the old Hengen Muso lady carry them off just before we set out for the other world.

Anyway, this is what had happened according to the queen.

The heroes had yet to awaken and remained unconscious at the hospital until several days ago, when there were reports from the hospital that each of them had regained consciousness. According to the examining doctor, each of the heroes was told what had happened and finally came to the realization that they had confronted the Spirit Tortoise and been defeated.

"And then?"

"The same day that they woke up . . . I've been told that later that night, all of the heroes suddenly disappeared . . ."

I could feel my cheek twitching.

Those half-wit heroes! They must have run away using their teleport skills! I had no idea why they would run. It wasn't like they had done anything bad . . . Although it was true they had made themselves *look* really bad.

"We have implemented an information blockade, but there are still rumors among the people that the defeat of the other three heroes is one of the reasons for the Spirit Tortoise's increased violence. The heroes' situation is concerning."

"Ugh . . . I don't know where they went, but please try to see to it that they are protected, if possible."

"I will do my best. However, it is possible that if they feel they're being blamed for the spread of destruction, they might behave rashly. I have ordered that they be handled with caution."

Jeez . . . Just how much trouble did they need to cause before they would be satisfied? Those fools!

"We must consider the possibility that another country might attempt to take advantage of the heroes' emotional vulnerability resulting from defeat to gain their favor and secure the country's position as the leading world power."

"Ah, so there are groups that might try something like that after all."

"Of course, such an act would be criticized harshly. We would not stand by quietly, nor would Faubrey, I am sure."

"Umm . . . That's the huge country that first attempted to summon the four heroes, right?"

"Yes. The country is closely involved with the four heroes. If another country were to attempt such a thing without the consent of Faubrey, war would likely be unavoidable."

I'd thought that war and all of that mess was less of an issue here than in Kizuna's world, but I guess that kind of thing was always just right around the corner.

So if the heroes were to flee to a country attempting to gain their favor, they would risk being used as political instruments. I had refused such an invitation without even realizing it and so nothing ever came of it, but those guys were definitely liable to fall for something like that. What a bunch of good-for-nothings! Of course, I didn't really have room to talk since I was part of their group.

So for the time being, all we would be able to do is call together the seven star heroes. I wasn't sure whether I should consider them friends or foes, but I needed to meet and speak with them either way. It was critical that we shared our power-up methods.

Of course, there was the issue of whether or not they would be willing to talk. There could always be someone like Kyo from Kizuna's world, so I wasn't sure if the seven star heroes could be considered allies yet. Still, I had to get them to share their power-up methods somehow to make up for my stats being lowered by the curse.

"Understood about the heroes. Other than that, with the extent of the damage . . . is recovery even possible?"

Upon hearing my question, the expressions of the queen and her advisers grew even grimmer. So it really was that bad, after all.

"The coalition army itself suffered significant losses during the incursion into the Spirit Tortoise's body and also while distracting it outside."

"Sorry I couldn't protect them."

As the Shield Hero, it was my job to think about how to prevent casualties and act accordingly. And yet, there had still been considerable losses.

"Oh, no . . . They were there because they wanted to be, I am sure. Everyone that participated in the incursion has indicated that it was thanks to the Shield Hero that any of them were able to escape alive."

"Well, I'm happy to hear that."

"Our neighboring countries have also been dealt a heavy blow and recovery will likely require quite some time."

"I see."

"To be honest, providing you aid will also be a bit more difficult now, Mr. Iwatani."

I couldn't argue with that. If they had been able to continue providing massive amounts of aid even after suffering such heavy damages, I would have been suspicious about where the money was coming from.

"We will provide what aid we can, but compared to what we had initially planned . . ."

"Yeah, I understand. If I need money, I'll work it out on my own."

On the contrary, I should probably have been helping gather reconstruction funds. I decided to bring up the plan I had been considering.

"Hey, aid doesn't have to be money, right?"

"Indeed. In fact, other forms of aid would certainly be preferable considering our current situation."

This was related to an issue I had noticed while leading the coalition army and something that I had been thinking about for a while.

"In that case, how about you grant me a territory?"

That's right. Seeing Kizuna and the others made me think about how the waves should be dealt with. At the same time, I figured it was the best I could do to show my thanks to Raphtalia. Assuming the world achieved a state of peace, I wasn't planning on sticking around like some kind of fool. I'd return to my own world without hesitation. But what about Raphtalia?

For Raphtalia, this world was her home. She had believed in me and stuck with me in both good times and bad, so she deserved a place where she could live out a happy life.

"A territory? That's not a problem, but may I ask why? Until now, you have been . . . Pardon my rudeness, but you seemed indifferent about such things."

I figured I should give her the official reason.

"The hero in the other world had trained a group of acquaintances to deal with the waves without the assistance of heroes. After careful consideration, I believe it will be necessary for us to do something similar."

Ultimately, it had been us that defeated the Spirit Tortoise, but since I was limited to defense, it only made sense that the company I kept would become more and more important.

"I believe I understand your reasoning, Mr. Iwatani."

"Without the coalition army, we would have lost to the Spirit Tortoise. I want to be clear about that. That said, surviving the coming waves will prove difficult with the coalition army as it is now. To be honest, they're weak."

"Ugh . . ."

Being a proud bunch, knights could be difficult to deal with.

"I'm saying the overall military power of the army is weak. Considering the Spirit Tortoise's connection to the waves, there's a very high possibility that even more powerful monsters will appear going forward. That's why I want to build a private army that is prepared to deal with the waves. I'll need money, too, and a territory would provide a basis for all of this."

"That makes sense. I am beginning to understand your line of thinking, Mr. Iwatani. We needed to reward you anyway, so this is a good chance."

The queen closed her folding fan and pulled out a map.

"Somewhere close to the castle town would probably be best. Do you have a place in mind?"

"Here."

Without hesitation, I pointed to a coastal area near the port. The port was the one we had departed from when heading to the Cal Mira islands.

"Wha . . . ?"

Raphtalia had started to say something but held back.

"Hmm . . . That area . . . Yes, that's where Miss Seaetto is currently serving as governor."

"You mean Eclair? She's got more going on than I expected."

"Yes. I had been planning to assist with the reconstruction of the territories in that area as well, but according to reports, the current situation . . . doesn't sound very promising."

"I see . . ."

I'd heard that the area had suffered extensive damage in the first wave, the one that occurred before I had been summoned. I'd passed by it several times. It had been a desolate area filled with abandoned buildings. I wasn't sure if it was because of the wave, but even the plant life seemed to lack vitality. Reconstruction would be a difficult task.

It had only been two and a half weeks since the most recent disaster, too.

"I would like to recommend another area, if possible. That area suffered extensive damage in the first wave and is in ruins."

"I'll be developing the land, anyway. It will be easier to do things my way there than somewhere that's already been developed, like the areas near the castle. It works out perfectly."

"Understood. Now, if you are going to have a territory, you will need to be given an appropriate rank."

"I plan on returning to my own world once the waves have ended anyway. I don't need a successor. In fact, you should just return the territory to Eclair at that point. Actually . . . If she'll let me do things my way, I wouldn't mind if she just stays the governor."

It's not like Eclair was a stranger, and I figured she'd do

just fine, considering she had shown an exceedingly earnest determination to get along with the demi-humans.

"I cannot allow that. Mr. Iwatani, you are not giving yourself the credit you deserve. If we did not reward you appropriately, we would be giving other countries cause to attack Melromarc."

I was being lectured by the queen for some reason.

"I shall grant you the rank of Count."

"Wait a minute . . ."

Wouldn't the fact that my shield had translated her words as Count mean that the rank was hereditary?

I knew about the noble ranks and titles from some manga about nobility that I had read fanatically a long time ago. The manga had been set in the early modern period and not the Middle Ages, but still . . .

Duke, Marquess, Count, Viscount, and Baron.

These were known as the five ranks of nobility and were ordered from the highest rank to the lowest.

Noble titles were generally divided into two categories: hereditary and territorial. In my world . . . In Europe, owning territory usually meant having a title, and those who ruled over territories were collectively referred to as the aristocracy . . . or something like that.

That meant that members of the aristocracy who owned multiple territories would, of course, have multiple titles as well. And having a title meant that you were a member of the aristocracy who owned at least 10,000 acres of land.

I wasn't sure if all of that held true in this world, though.

"There is always the possibility that you will have a child, Mr. Iwatani. We must keep that in mind. Perhaps, for example . . . with Melty."

"Not happening."

Did she really want to have me and Melty get married that bad? That girl was still a child. There's no way I was going to feel any kind of sexual desire for a 10-year-old kid.

"Just a moment, please. We must perform the conferment of title ceremony."

"What a pain . . ."

"Perhaps, but the dignity of our country is at stake. The formalities and the reward must be fitting of your performance."

I couldn't really argue that just simply handing over some money to the hero, who had defeated the chief villain that had caused so much damage, wouldn't look too good.

"To think that the Shield Hero—worshipped by the demi-humans—would request the Seaetto territory, which is known for its acceptance of demi-humans even in Melromarc . . . Well, Miss Eclair's father was quite popular, and a man that I trusted dearly."

The queen had completely seen through my plan. She kept glancing over at Raphtalia.

"This could be good for publicity, too. I'm counting on you."

"Don't get your hopes up."

The queen handed me a ceremonial sword.

Normally, it would have been rejected by the shield, but that wasn't a problem as long as I had no intention of fighting. I was supposed to unsheathe the sword and hand it to the queen, who would then tap each of my shoulders with the sword and attest the conferment of title. That would complete the ceremony.

"We hereby commence the conferment of title on the Shield Hero, Naofumi Iwatani!"

The castle knights sounded their bugle-like instruments.

I marched confidently through the doorway and into the throne room toward the waiting queen. I then assumed a blatantly pretentious pose and lowered my head before unsheathing the sword at my side and handing it to the queen.

"In accordance with the customs of this land, I hereby grant you the rank of Count in recognition of your most recent noble efforts."

The queen returned the sword to me.

"I look forward to your continued success."

I returned the sword to its sheath and stood up.

"And that's it. Truthfully, I would prefer to perform the ceremony on a much grander scale, but . . ."

"Too much trouble."

"I expected that would be your response, so I kept it simple. Regardless, I do plan to make this known to the people."

"Yeah, yeah."

I had a feeling that my days of openly roaming the castle town streets were now over.

That reminded me, where was Trash? It felt like I hadn't seen him in forever. Was he still around?

Trash was the queen's husband and had been serving as the Crown by proxy in her absence. He'd had another name, but it had been changed to Trash as punishment for his actions. He had been one of the culprits responsible for framing me for religious reasons.

There he was. He was glaring at me with disgust in his eyes.

He couldn't say anything since the queen was keeping a close eye on him. Or so I thought . . . Looking more closely, I noticed he was wearing a collar.

"—!"

Oh? He was touching the collar like he wanted to say something. It seemed to be tightening. Now this was funny. I laughed at him.

"——!!"

He seemed super mad now, but every time he tried to scream out, the collar tightened and silenced him before he could make a noise. Talk about quality entertainment!

"Mr. Naofumi . . . ?"

Raphtalia called out as if to reprimand me. Apparently she hadn't noticed Trash's collar.

"What can I say? It's funny! Look at that."

"Sigh . . . That's just like you, Mr. Naofumi."

Raphtalia's voice was tinged with disapproval.

"Ah, yes. Mr. Iwatani, you mentioned that you would like to speak with the seven star heroes."

"Huh? Yeah, that's right."

The queen looked over at Trash, as if to imply something. The knights surrounding Trash dragged him over in front of me and forced him to his knees.

"Allow me to tell you about a certain seven star hero."

Why was she saying this after dragging Trash over here?

"This hero was an extraordinary character formerly known as Lüge. When Siltvelt made an attempt at world domination twenty-something years ago, it was this hero that attacked them head-on, saving Melromarc and many other countries in the process."

"Sounds like quite the reputation."

Twenty-something years ago meant that the hero had to be pretty old now. Thinking about the people I knew, that would probably limit it to the old lady, the slave trader, or the accessory dealer. The last two were out of the question, but I wouldn't be surprised if it turned out to be the old lady. She'd made a dramatic turnaround and gone on a rampage after I gave her that medicine, after all. Still, something about her didn't quite fit.

"Despite being the Staff Hero, this hero came to be known instead for his formidable intelligence, and the people referred to him as 'His Excellency, the Wise' when telling stories of his deeds."

"—!!"

Trash was really starting to struggle for some reason.

Hmm . . . His Excellency, the Wise? Must have been a pretty impressive guy. If he was that smart, then . . . I looked over at Rishia.

"Your father?"

"Fehhhh!"

Rishia shook her head emphatically. So it wasn't her dad, then.

"Do you know who she's talking about, Rishia?"

"Yes, I do. It's that man. The king is the Seven Star Staff Hero."

"Huh?"

Dumbfounded, I pointed a questioning finger at Trash, who was still struggling for some reason.

"It's thanks to the king that Melromarc and the other countries still exist today."

Hold on. She was saying that Trash—that this stupid, power-hungry fool—was a seven star hero? No way! I had never seen him holding any kind of staff. And His Excellency, the Wise? Seriously? More like His Foolishness, the Daft!

"Good one, Rishia. You almost had me there for a second."

"!"

Trash snorted and glared at me.

"It wasn't a joke. I'm sure that this all must be some kind of strategically planned act. Mom and dad always said that Melromarc would remain peaceful and secure as long as the king were here."

"And that right there is why your mom and dad ended up ruined nobility."

"Fehhh . . ."

"Mr. Naofumi!"

Raphtalia reprimanded me again. But it was probably true.

So from what she was saying, if we were talking about my world, was he like some kind of famous military strategist? Was he the kind of character who couldn't be underestimated because he was always several steps ahead, and even if he acted foolishly, it was sure to be some kind of trap? Yeah, I wasn't falling for that.

"I get it. The guy exists, but this is some kind of political decoy, right?"

I pointed at Trash defiantly. Unable to stand it any longer, he made a fist and lunged at me.

"I will not allow it! Icicle Prison!"

"!?"

Now encased in a cage of ice, Trash glared at the queen.

"Or maybe the real Trash died, and this is some kind of replacement?"

"Not at all. This is all true. Right, Trash?"

"!"

"Ah, yes. You can't speak because of that collar. Think about it, Mr. Iwatani. Why do you think I made Bitch my slave but didn't do the same to Trash?"

She had a point. Trash seemed to have given up relatively quickly and I figured that's why she had let him be, but now that I thought about it, maybe his punishment had been a bit underwhelming.

"I am sure you already know this, Mr. Iwatani, but it is not possible to enslave a holy hero or a seven star hero."

"Ah . . . So what you're saying is that you can't make Trash a slave and that's why you're keeping him quiet with a collar. But does the collar really work?"

"Yes. Of course, he could easily break it if he wanted to, but he doesn't because he knows he would be punished for doing so."

As soon as the queen finished her sentence, Trash ripped the collar off.

"I can't take it anymore! Shield!!"

He was as annoying as ever.

"I will let that slide this time. So there you have it. Aultcra—Trash, I mean. Tell Mr. Iwatani how you power up your staff."

"I'll never tell him! I . . . I refuse to accept this! The Shield, a Count?! Absolutely unacceptable!"

"Oh my, what shall we do? I'd like to request that you spare his life at the very least."

As she said this, the queen delivered repeated blows to Trash's face. Being my twisted self, I'd begun to enjoy the whole spectacle a bit, but realistically speaking, it would be difficult to get Trash to share his power-up methods. In that case, killing him, waiting for a new staff hero to appear, and asking the new hero would be quicker. But the queen was asking me to show leniency and overlook his behavior. This was proving to be a real predicament.

"Queen. Use every means of torture available to make him speak. A hero that has no intention of fighting for world peace does not deserve to live."

"Insolence! I'll—?!"

The queen ordered Trash gagged and quieted.

"Understood."

"The deadline—"

The queen interrupted me just as I was about to decide how much time to give him.

"My daughter Bitch presents another problem for us."

Oh? Had there been some kind of development?

The power-up methods were certainly important, but they could wait for Bitch. I had a feeling the queen had purposefully changed the subject, but I could always just bring it back up again later when I got another chance.

"According to the account of events given by Mr. Kitamura upon regaining consciousness, it seems very likely that she survived."

"That *is* a problem. You must find and capture her at once."

According to Kyo, Motoyasu had been abandoned by the rest of his party upon facing the Spirit Tortoise. I had no doubt that she'd survived.

"As you wish."

I had no idea if she would return to Motoyasu. Then again, maybe she should be executed for deserting him in the face of the enemy?

"I will need to speak with her before anything else. Depending on how that goes, you may find the outcome quite pleasing, Mr. Iwatani."

"That would be most excellent. Heh heh heh . . ."

The queen and I laughed together as we sneakily probed each other's true intentions.

"Mr. Naofumi!"

"Yeah, yeah. I know."

Jeez, was she ever going to let me get away with a bit of mischief? Raph-chan never seemed to mind.

"Rafu fu fu . . ."

Speaking of Raph-chan, she had been imitating me for the

past few minutes and had a sinister grin on her face.

"In any case, I have many questions for you, as well, Mr. Iwatani."

"I know, but I have some things to take care of first."

We'd just gotten back from the other world, and we needed to get started on preparations.

"Later, Trash of the world. From here on, you shall forever be known as His Foolishness, the Daft, Framer of Heroes. Isn't that nice? You're famous!"

"—!!!!"

As we made our way out of the throne room, Trash was pointing at me and struggling violently in an attempt to destroy the cage of ice. I had no doubt he wanted to attack me, but the surrounding soldiers wouldn't allow it. The queen sure knew how to handle things.

But all of that aside, was that piece of trash seriously a seven star hero?

Chapter Two: Whereabouts of the Slaves

I lay down on the bed in the guest room and rested. Yeah, I really was exhausted. Lying down made it all the clearer. The effects of the curse were heavy, and I could feel them taking their toll on me. In the end, I had spent the whole day discussing future plans with the queen and her advisers.

"That reminds me . . ."

I hesitantly checked my equipment status. Sure enough, my armor's name was unrecognizable. The Barbaroi Armor had ceased to function.

"Raphtalia? Rishia? Filo? Check your equipment."

"Ah, yes, I did. The name listed is garbled, and the effects are null."

Raphtalia had already changed into her previous armor from this world. Damn! She had changed so quickly!

"Why do you look disappointed?"

"Do I?"

Because it looked so good on you! Because it looked so much better than your old armor!

Raphtalia looked at me suspiciously as childish responses flooded into my head.

"Oh! My breastplate name is unrecognizable now, too."

"Do you prefer a kigurumi?"

I seemed to remember having another Pekkul Kigurumi left over somewhere. Where did I put that? Had I left it in the castle storeroom?

"Fehhh . . ."

"Now, now, Mr. Naofumi. I'm sure Rishia has outgrown her kigurumi phase."

"Heeey, Master! Where is Mel-chan? She wasn't in her room."

Filo unfolded her pajamas as she asked about Melty, so I inspected them, too. Oh? Apparently the Filo Pajamas were compatible between worlds.

"Melty? I'm pretty sure the queen said she had gone to help Eclair."

"Oh, really? Will we see her tomorrow, then?"

"Maybe."

We were planning to head that way, after all.

"That aside, Mr. Naofumi . . ."

Raphtalia suddenly drew near to where I was lying on the bed.

"A territory! And you're a Count! You're a real hotshot now!"

"I was already a hero, you know. Doesn't feel like much of a change."

"What is it that you're after, Mr. Naofumi?"

Raphtalia looked at me with uncertainty in her eyes as she asked. That reminded me, she had almost said something when I told the queen which territory I wanted.

"Are you talking about the territory business? It's just like I said. Considering that the battles are going to start getting rough, I think it would be best to build a private army like Kizuna, Glass, and L'Arc have done."

"But why did you choose the area that was damaged by the first wave for your territory?"

I wasn't sure if I should just be honest with her or if that was a bad idea. I started to feel like it might seem patronizing, so I decided to just gloss over the issue for now.

"It's an area I'm already familiar with and I should be able to do things my way there. The area has strong ties with Eclair's father, and it's unlikely that anyone would have a problem with me getting involved there."

Raphtalia and I sat there in silence for a few moments. Finally, she let out a sigh of resignation.

"Understood. We'll just leave it at that."

"We'll round up some slaves starting with those that you know, Raphtalia. It will be easier to fight with people you're already familiar with. After that, we'll move on to other, ordinary slaves. Once we've established a respectable amount of fighting power there, we can consider training the castle soldiers or something."

I wanted to train the slaves and develop enough fighting power that we would be able to easily defeat Glass and the others should it come to that.

"At the same time . . . muhahaha . . ."

This meant that Raphtalia's friends would have to join my private army if they wanted to return to their precious village. I was basically holding the territory hostage.

"You're trying to act all bad again. Let me guess—something about hostages?"

Yikes. She had completely seen through me.

"Hehe . . . You two are like an old married couple."

Rishia went and dropped a real bombshell. Although, it was true that I had spent more time with Raphtalia than anyone else in this world, so she probably did understand me better than anyone. We were nothing like a married couple, though.

"Wh . . . wh . . . what is that supposed to mean?!"

Raphtalia's face turned red in embarrassment as she shouted at Rishia. Just like I thought, any talk of love or romance really ruffled Raphtalia's feathers. Rishia had stepped on a landmine.

Raphtalia may have started out as a child and a slave, but she had an exceptionally kind heart and always looked out for others. She'd lost her family and her village had been taken from her, so it was easy to imagine the sorrow she might have felt. That was why she was fighting—to ensure that no one else would have to end up in a situation like hers.

Driven by such a noble goal, Raphtalia undoubtedly had no interest in things like love and romance. Not to mention that, even though she may have looked like an adult, she was still a child in terms of age. She wasn't even old enough to be interested in boys yet. I guess since Rishia was in love with Itsuki, for better or worse, her female mind would be sensitive to stuff like that.

"That's right, Rishia. Raphtalia doesn't like those kinds of jokes. Best be careful."

"M . . . Mr. Naofumi . . ."

Raphtalia's face returned to a normal color as she began to regain her composure. That was much better. I didn't want Raphtalia getting too upset.

"Oh . . . okay . . ."

Rishia cocked her head to the side in confusion while staring at Raphtalia and me.

"Now then! Tomorrow is going to be a busy day."

I was going somewhere with that, but thinking about what was to come suddenly reminded me of something.

"That reminds me, Rishia. We were talking about whether or not you should reset your level, right?"

"Yes."

"I want you to consider going without the reset."

"Wh . . . why is that?"

"But Mr. Naofumi, didn't you say that starting over from level one would improve her abilities?"

"I've been thinking about that. I observed Rishia's performance to a certain extent while we were in Kizuna's world. You know that much, right?"

"Yes."

I made sure to keep an eye on how Rishia developed while we were there.

"Honestly, there's not much of a difference between her abilities right now and what they were like over in Kizuna's world. It's practically nil."

"Really?"

"I mean, there is a small difference, but compared to Raphtalia or Filo . . ."

"Fehhh . . ."

"So, Rishia, I estimate that your abilities will likely have a growth spurt coming. Your class-up could be a problem, though."

Raphtalia and Filo both improved drastically after their class-ups. Fitoria's feather had made it possible for Filo to have a special class-up that paved the way for a lot of her abilities to really blossom. Depending on the person and their abilities, a class-up could have long-lasting effects. Rishia was a jack-of-all-trades and master of none, but for all I knew the right class-up might make her more adept at a certain kind of magic or something.

"Oh . . . huh?! Ah, I suppose you're right. But . . . Itsuki chose this path for me. That's something that I treasure and wouldn't want to change."

"I see. Understood."

She may have been tossed aside by Itsuki, but her heart hadn't changed. That was all the more reason to make him regret it. That sounded good to me.

We continued to just hang out for a while, resting up for the coming day.

"Okay then."

After eating breakfast at the castle, we spoke with the queen briefly before getting ready to head out.

"Where are we headed?"

"To visit the slave trader."

"Mr. Iwatani."

The queen raised her hand as if there was something she wanted to say.

"Might you be going there to purchase slaves from the same village Raph . . . Miss Raphtalia is from?"

"Yeah, why?"

"Regarding that, we may have complicated matters a bit. I must apologize in advance."

". . ."

What was that supposed to mean? I had a really bad feeling about this. My cheek started to twitch. Actually, I didn't even want to know what it meant. But there was no way around asking.

"What do you mean?"

"Well . . . After the Spirit Tortoise incident, I reinstated Miss Seaetto's status as nobility and issued a proclamation ordering all Melromarc citizens—including nobility—to release any demi-human slaves from the Seaetto territory immediately."

"I see . . ."

"Since that would include the others from Miss Raphtalia's village, I had hoped the proclamation would allow us to quickly find any survivors."

I had already figured out what the queen was trying to say, but I didn't want to hear the words, honestly. Even Raphtalia was turning pale.

"Our investigations show that the results have been less than favorable. It would seem that before the emancipation proclamation was even made, the slaves were sold off and their whereabouts largely remain a mystery."

Shit! Would the filth of this country ever stop dragging me down?! I mean, it's not like I couldn't understand their motivations. If I found out an item was going to be nerfed in an online game, I would sell it off in a flash. But come on! Ugh . . . this really sucked.

"Our investigations continue, and the . . . monster trainer . . . that you patronize is currently searching for Miss Raphtalia's friends."

In other words, they hadn't found them. That's why they were still searching. I steadied Raphtalia, who started to look like her legs might give out on her. And the fact that my plan had already hit a brick wall from the very get-go started to sink in.

"Fortunately, Keel and three others have already returned to the Seaetto territory."

So there were four in all, counting Keel. That was it? Considering the kind of development I had in mind, we would need a lot more than that. I was left with no other choice.

"For the time being, it looks like we'll just have to round up some demi-human slaves without being too picky."

"Mr. Naofumi!"

"We can't build a territory with four people. We need more."

There were all kinds of things that needed to be done.

"It is what it is. We'll just start off by buying some cheap but useable slaves."

"Un . . . understood."

"I'm sure they'll probably end up being children."

Younger slaves would have more room for growth, among other things. I continued to mull over the situation as we parted ways with the queen and headed for the slave trader's tent.

We threw on cloaks and made our way through the back

alleys toward that oh-so-familiar tent for the first time in a long while.

"Oh?"

There sat the slave trader—a man I would have preferred not to associate with—looking bored, waiting for the next customer. Wasn't he supposed to be searching for the slaves from Raphtalia's village? I doffed my hood to show my face and gave him a salutatory wave.

"Well if it isn't the Shield Hero! It's been a while. I've heard the news of your recent successes."

"Long time no see."

"I thought you might have forgotten about me."

"I doubt anyone could forget someone like you."

How should I put it? The guy had a unique air about him that would make it difficult to forget him. He seemed far more adept at his trade than your average merchant. This kind of business was all about making sure your customers remembered you, after all.

Come to think of it, we hadn't been back since we came to buy Filo's claws. Not since the time we hadn't been able to class up at the dragon hourglass. The slave trader had coaxed us into heading for Siltvelt or Shieldfreeden back then.

Wait a minute . . . Judging from his earlier comment, could it be that he had secret ties to the queen?

"You've played your own little part, too, haven't you? To think you had secret ties with the monarch . . ."

"I wasn't lying when I told you I liked you from the moment I saw you."

"Yeah, yeah. We'll just leave it at that."

"And what can I do for you today?"

"I'm here about your actual line of work."

"Oh!"

The slave trader's eyes twinkled conspicuously. I wasn't sure what he was getting so excited about, but I wasn't going to let things go his way. I could imagine he was probably secretly delighted over the fact that I was still buying slaves even after my rise to fame.

"I'm looking to buy some cheapish demi-human slaves for now. The lower their level, the better."

"What kind of budget are we looking at?"

I had 5,000 silver pieces that the queen had given me before the Spirit Tortoise incident.

"Around 5,000 silver. Including the slaves you're currently searching for, too, of course."

"An investment for a new project, I presume?"

"I've told you before—don't ask me contrived questions you already know the answer to."

Just how much did this guy know, anyway? I had a feeling I might just believe it if he told me he could see the future or something.

"This way."

The slave trader motioned us toward the inner depths of his tent. We began to follow behind him, but Filo came to a halt.

"What is it?"

"I don't wanna go . . ."

She must have picked up on the grim atmosphere and signature stench that lay ahead. I had gotten used to it, but it certainly wasn't pleasant.

"How about you just stay put, then."

"Okay!"

Filo nodded as she sniffed at the lottery monster eggs. Did she realize that was where our paths had joined? I warned her not to eat the eggs and then chased after the slave trader. After catching back up to him, we approached the cage where I had met Raphtalia.

"This is the place where my fate was forever changed," Raphtalia murmured.

It wasn't that I couldn't understand her sentiment, but . . . thinking about it now, it had really only been a short amount of time, even though it felt so long. It hadn't even been six months yet.

"I'll make you a special deal today."

"How generous of you."

"I'm very excited about this intriguing little project you're starting. You're going to become a regular customer now, I presume?"

"Yeah, I guess so."

"Business is good thanks to the Shield Hero!"

"What's that supposed to mean?"

"I'm sure you'll understand if you just think of it as the same phenomenon that occurred with the bird god."

Ah . . . Raphtalia had played a big part in our success, after all. I'm sure the coalition army held her in high regard, too. If people knew that a slave like that had been purchased from this guy, his business was sure to benefit.

"But that's pointless if you don't have any slaves from Raphtalia's village in stock."

"Oh, no. That's a completely different issue. Yes sir."

"Let's start with . . ."

I figured I would just pick several slaves that caught my eye.

"This one, this one, and that one. Also, that one over there, that one under the blanket, and that one, too."

I picked two boys that looked relatively healthy, a couple of trembling slaves that were holding hands like they were friends, another that was wrapped up in a blanket and trembling near the back of the cage, and lastly one who was standing near the cage door, staring at Filo. Eclair already had four slaves at the territory, so that made a total of ten. That seemed just about right to kick things off.

"Oh yeah. I'll be applying the slave curses at my territory, so we'll need to take someone who can perform the ceremony with us. It'll be necessary to enhance their abilities."

"Such a seemingly random selection, and yet you choose such fine specimens—the Shield Hero has a good eye! My hat's off to you! Yes sir!"

"Fehhh . . ."

"Mr. Naofumi? Perhaps you should choose a bit more carefully?"

"I just went back and forth between the healthy-looking ones and the ones that looked problematic. Hey, you in the blanket—come over here."

I was sure this one would be weak and feeble. I could tell it was trembling in fear, too. The slave trader gave an order and a brawny man opened the cage and tore the blanket away from the child.

"No . . . don't!"

"Oh?"

With the blanket gone, I could see the slave resembled a mole.

"That's a lumo, a type of therianthrope known for its nimble hands. Their eyes are sensitive to light, which makes them a good choice for nighttime security duties. This one is a child, of course."

"Ahh!"

The lumo slave was cowering in fear in the corner. Raphtalia looked concerned.

I took a closer look at the appearance of the lumo child. If I had to describe him in one word, I'd have to go with "mole." He was kind of like the mole version of a werewolf or something. And he was short—only about as tall as my waist. Was that because he was a child?

So it was known for its ability to do detailed work, huh? I had all kinds of work for them in my plans, so that was fine.

"Speaking of detailed work, racoon types—like your associate here—are also quite dexterous, you know."

I looked at Raphtalia. Now that I thought about it, I'd never taught her to do work like that. I'd had her help tan some monster hides, but that was about it. Maybe the fact that she didn't express interest in doing that kind of thing meant that she was naturally clumsy.

"You're thinking about something rude, aren't you?"

"Not really . . ."

"But yes, lumo types tend to be well suited for delicate work that requires dexterous hands. They also tend to be rather reserved. A good choice. Yes sir."

I took another look at the trembling lumo slave.

"Is it just me or does this country have a lot of scumbags that are into physical abuse?"

Every slave I'd seen was covered in scars from being whipped.

"This country has a long history of being at war with the demi-humans, so it's only natural. Yes sir."

"Meaning people like the nobility that fought in those wars use physical abuse to make themselves feel better about the past?"

The nobleman that Raphtalia had gotten tangled up with had done just that.

"We even have a special low-priced option for borrowing a slave just to physically abuse it a bit before returning it. Yes sir. We require the slave to be purchased outright at a hefty sum when it's not returned in usable form."

The shadiness of this country was astounding. Watching on as I reconstructed the demi-human village would probably leave a bitter taste in the mouths of the nobility.

"Physical abuse is punishable by law, of course. Yes sir."

"So it's illegal? The way it's treated sure makes it seem legal."

I couldn't help but feel that way thinking about this tent tucked away in a back alley.

"And that's why my business is thriving. Yes sir."

Thriving, huh? The slave trader's way of proudly flaunting it made him seem seriously shady. Tell me then, why was he selling slaves that had been physically abused, anyway?

"Now that you mention it, he does look better than most, I guess."

Raphtalia's response was practically a whisper.

Was this really better than most? I looked at the wounds

on the lumo slave's back. They seemed surprisingly deep. It was a blotchy mess of layers upon layers of scars from being whipped repeatedly.

"Zweite Heal!"

I cast some healing magic and the lumo slave's open wounds began to close. Still, the wounds were deep and far from being fully healed.

"Huh?"

"I hear you've got dexterous hands."

"I don't know."

The lumo slave looked away when he answered. That was certainly a better response than claiming he could do something that he couldn't.

"Will you put them to use if I teach you?"

"If that's an order then I will. So please, don't beat me."

The lumo slave shrunk away, his voice strained as if he were about to cry. I guess I couldn't blame him, being a slave and all.

"I'm not interested in that kind of thing. If it's a beating you want, then ask someone else."

"Huh?"

Okay, now he was starting to get on my nerves.

"I'll leave you some medicine, so treat their wounds. After that, go ahead and take care of the slave registration."

"I look forward to seeing how the Shield Hero makes use of the slaves. So very exciting! Yes sir!"

"Enough with that, already! I have to take care of some other preparations in the meantime, and then I'll be back. Don't let me down."

"Heh heh heh . . . Exciting times ahead. Yes sir."

I left things in the slave trader's hands and headed back toward the entrance of the tent with Raphtalia in tow. Filo caught sight of me and came running over.

"Finiiiished?"

"Yeah. Still some formalities that need to be taken care of, but we have other things to see to while that gets done."

I stepped out of the tent. I still had plenty of other places to stop by, after all.

Chapter Three: Acquaintances

We threw our cloaks back on and roamed the town a bit, observing. The damages really had been severe. The scars left by the Spirit Tortoise ran deep, and countless signs of the onslaught of its familiars still remained.

Shortly after, we arrived at the shop that we had been headed for. Oh, thank goodness . . . The shop hadn't suffered any noticeable damage and was open for business as usual. I stepped into the old guy's weapon shop.

"Welcome!"

"Glad to see you're okay."

"That voice . . . Is that you, kid?!"

I doffed my hood and greeted the old guy. He seemed to be in one piece—not a single scratch to show, thankfully.

"Why are you wearing a cloak?"

"Don't want to stand out."

"Ah, that's right. You're an overnight sensation, kid."

That was the real problem. I was no Itsuki, but the happy greetings . . . "Shield Hero!" just gave me the creeps. I suppose I could have basked in feelings of superiority, but being well loved by the riffraff of this country wasn't really something to be proud of. Not to mention, I had way too many things

I needed to take care of now. I didn't have time to waste on meaningless affairs.

"People tagging along in droves would only cause trouble, right?"

I replied to the old guy while giving the inside of the shop a look-over.

"Doesn't seem to be any damage of note from what I can see."

"Yeah, not really. I chased off any monsters that showed up here."

"That's good to hear."

"I guess I had you all wrong. Here I thought you looked disappointed or something when you showed up."

"You're so full of it."

The old guy had done so much for me, but we still went back and forth like this.

"This thing is all covered in dust now since you never came to pick it up, kid."

The old guy brought a small sword over.

Pekkul Rapier

quality: good

imbued effects: agility up, magic power up, blood clean finish

Oh yeah . . . This must have been the weapon I'd requested for Rishia so long ago.

"Did you come to order something else?"

The rapier seemed just about right for Rishia. Or maybe I should have Eclair use it?

"Support from the castle isn't going to come so readily anymore. I figured I'd have you put my orders for weapons and gear on hold for now."

"I guess that's to be expected. The castle town wasn't hit that hard, but this has been a major disaster for us and the surrounding countries, too."

"How's business been?"

"Having just had a disaster like this, everyone wants a weapon, so they come and buy them here."

"So business is booming?"

"You could say that. With all the sales, I'm actually a bit worried about stock."

"That's booming, alright."

"Thing is . . . I'm not quite sure how I feel about a bunch of amateurs running around and buying up all of the weapons."

That couldn't be helped. Amateurs or not, people would want weapons if they felt like they were in danger. It was that same mindset—just like when there's a natural disaster people start buying up water and food rations. There had been a battle, so now people wanted weapons. It didn't seem like there had been any looting as far as I could tell, so the situation could have been worse.

"Is that all for today?"

"Well, there is something . . ."

I was trying to decide whether to have the old guy make a bunch of weapons for the slaves. I had already discussed things with the queen and I knew she could supply some used weapons, but the available resources would make anything more than that tough. I wasn't sure if we really needed anything more than that, but the fact that they were used meant they would have plenty of issues.

With that in mind, I decided to go ahead and approach the old guy.

"I had the queen give me a territory, and I have a large-scale project in the works."

It would be useful to have the old guy around to make weapons for the slaves, among other things. I figured it wouldn't hurt to ask.

"And what does that have to do with me, kid?"

"You could say I came here as a headhunter, if you catch my drift."

If the old guy set up shop at the territory, that could be a source of income. I had confidence in his skills and I was sure he'd get plenty of business.

"I've already got this shop, you know."

"I know that. I'm not trying to force you to do anything. I just figured . . . maybe you could take an apprentice or two. Think about it."

"Ah, so that's what you meant. Sure thing, kid. That said, I don't really think I'm good enough to be taking on apprentices or anything."

Alright, he'd given me his word. Now I'd be able to have one of my more dexterous slaves become an apprentice of the old guy and learn his trade. Skill in a trade would mean money. Of course, I didn't plan to bite the hand that feeds me or anything like that.

"Stop being so modest. I'm confident in your skills."

"Ha! I'll do my best not to let you down."

"Anyway, I've got a lot in the works, so spread the word among your associates for me. The location is . . ."

I told the old guy where my territory was and explained how the village would be my base of operations. I figured there would be plenty of people wanting to get in on a new project. If I only chose the ones I could trust from that group, I could expand my operations and that would lead to more profits. My territory was relatively close to the castle town, too.

"Got it. Well, we were all worried about you, kid, and it's a good opportunity, so there very well may be some takers."

"I have a debt to pay, so I plan to treat them well. And that's especially true in your case, so think it over."

"Got it."

After a bit of lighthearted conversation, the old guy gave me a long look.

"There's something else, isn't there?"

"You can tell?"

"You always show up with a million things at once, kid."

"I guess so."

I didn't really want to show him, but I took off my cloak. With one look, the old guy understood.

"What in the world is that?"

The old guy was staring at my Barbaroi Armor with his head cocked to the side. I took the armor off and put it on the counter.

"I chased the culprit that caused the Spirit Tortoise to go on a rampage to another world. When I got there my Barbarian Armor had ceased to function, so I had a local blacksmith modify and reforge the armor. The result was this Barbaroi Armor, but now that I'm back it has stopped functioning, too."

The old guy stared at the Barbaroi Armor long and hard. He started poking at different parts of the armor as if to see how it responded.

"There's no problem with the core, but I can't say one way or the other about the rest without doing some testing."

"Can you fix it?"

"It's possible. Give me some time."

"Sure. I'm counting on you."

"This shop is here just for you, right kid? By the way, they're practically handing out materials from that beast now. If things work out, we might be able to make something out of them."

There were more Spirit Tortoise materials than anyone could use, after all. I guess if I just thought of it as a thank you from Ost . . . No, I still felt a little bad.

"I'll go ahead and throw a few things together for you as long as you can pay me later."

"Would you?"

"If it's a request from you, kid—the one and only—sure. Besides, working with strange, new materials never gets old. This armor is really something. That blacksmith must have been quite the artisan, no doubt."

"Oh?"

Such generosity despite my dubious financial circumstances . . . The old guy had a big heart that made me genuinely want to repay his kindness. To be honest, I really did want to recruit him to be my territory blacksmith. I wouldn't push the issue right now, though, but once I finished developing the territory I'd try approaching him about it again.

"We should probably make the armor our top priority for now. Once that's finished, I guess we can't go wrong with making a shield, right kid?"

"Agreed. If nothing else, I can just make a copy of the shield."

"You understood exactly where I was going with that. Alright then, leave the armor and get out of here."

"I'm counting on you."

"Righto!"

The old guy removed the core stone from the armor and handed it to me.

"You hold on to the core stone for now, kid."

"You sure?"

"I'll make it so that we can embed the stone afterward. You can pay me when it comes time for that."

"Thanks."

"What will you wear in the meantime, kid?"

"I'll just use some old armor from the castle stores, so you do whatever needs to be done."

"Righto! What next? There's more, right?"

I nodded in response to the old guy's question.

"Next up is . . ."

I laid the Angel Breastplate on the counter along with the miko outfit that Raphtalia had been wearing. I wondered if I should show him the Filo Pajamas, too, but I decided to leave those for later.

"What's this? A breastplate and . . . a miko outfit?"

"That's some of the gear we were using in the other world. It stopped functioning just like the armor. Is there anything you can do?"

It was pretty exceptional equipment if only we could make use of it, and considering how well the outfit looked on Raphtalia, I had to ask even if it was unreasonable.

"This one was originally made out of the Filo kigurumi. The Filo Pajamas that Filo has been wearing were, too, but those are functioning fine, so we don't need to worry about them."

"You bring me all of the tough ones! Who was wearing a miko outfit, anyway? The little miss?"

I nodded and then whispered to the old man so that Raphtalia couldn't hear.

"The outfit looks super good on her, so I want to have her wear it in this world, too. Is there any way you could make it seem like she has no other choice for equipment?"

"So that's your plan?"

Apparently Raphtalia had heard me. I should have asked the old guy when she wasn't around. Fail!

"Oh, kid. Did you really like the way the miko outfit looked on the little miss that much?"

"Pretty much. I could tell you all about it if you're interested, but we might be here until midnight."

"I'll pass."

"Regular clothes might have worked great as armor in the world you went to, kid, but they have their limits here. Actually, this is the kind of thing a seamstress or tailor would handle."

Ah . . . That would be the lady who made Filo's clothes—the one who looked like she would write doujinshi or something. I bet she was chipper as ever.

"I'll hold on to it for now, but don't get your hopes up."

"Understood. Just do whatever you can."

"Mr. Naofumi, haven't you been treating me a bit like a dress-up doll lately?"

"Call it a father's adoration for his daughter."

"Mr. Naofumi, what is that supposed to . . ."

I beat around the bush a bit to avoid answering Raphtalia's questions. I was sure the old man wouldn't let me down.

"That should do it for now. I'll be back once I manage to make a bit of money, so see what you can do until then."

"Righto! Studying this equipment of yours should keep me busy for a while, kid."

"I'll be expecting something good."

We wrapped things up and left the weapon shop.

Chapter Four: E Float Shield

"Now then . . ."

I figured it wouldn't be a bad idea to talk to the queen about my plans going forward. I was already planning on getting some old equipment from her anyway. We returned to the castle and asked where she was. She had just finished a meeting and was still in the room, wrapping up some paperwork. That's where we found her, behind a desk with mountains of paperwork piled up on top.

"Queen."

"Mr. Iwatani. What is it?"

"It's alright if I take some equipment out of the storeroom, right?"

"Yes, that's fine. Just be aware that much of it is damaged from the recent battle."

"I know. I just figured I could use it at my territory if you don't need it."

Now we just needed to go and see what was there.

"Alright. Raphtalia. Filo. Rishia."

"Yes?"

"Start loading up some things onto a carriage. We'll be using it at the territory, so look for lighter equipment, preferably.

Filo, I'll be counting on you to make regular trips to transport the stuff by carriage."

"Okaaay!"

Raphtalia and the others nodded and headed for the storeroom, leaving me behind. Filo was still in a weakened state due to the effects of the curse, so I wasn't actually sure if she could carry anything too heavy. That made me think that maybe I should raise another filolial.

"Ah, yes. I was actually just about to summon for you, Mr. Iwatani. I've had the Spirit Tortoise materials rounded up at the training grounds in front of the storeroom, so please take what you need."

"Understood."

I left the queen and headed to the grounds in front of the castle storeroom. When I got there, I started going through the mountain of Spirit Tortoise materials that literally did cover the entire training grounds.

"Oh, come on!"

Eyeballs and brains came tumbling out of the pile, startling me. I mean, this had basically been a friend of mine, so . . . it just felt wrong. And then, all of a sudden . . .

"Wh . . . what?!"

A pale light emanated from the Spirit Tortoise materials before they were absorbed into my shield, seemingly of their own accord.

Spirit Tortoise Carapace Shield conditions met!

Spirit Tortoise Skin Shield conditions met!

Spirit Tortoise Flesh Shield conditions met!

Spirit Tortoise Bone Shield conditions met!

Spirit Tortoise Blood Shield conditions met!

Spirit Tortoise Body Fluid Shield conditions met!

Spirit Tortoise Immune Cell Shield conditions met!

Spirit Tortoise Muscle Shield conditions met!

Spirit Tortoise Cardiac Shield conditions met!

Spirit Tortoise Myocardium Shield conditions met!

Spirit Tortoise Blood Vessel Shield conditions met!

Spirit Tortoise Eye Shield conditions met!

Spirit Tortoise Pupil Shield conditions met!

Spirit Tortoise Sacred Tree Shield conditions met!

Spirit Tortoise Familiar (Bat Type) Shield conditions met!

Spirit Tortoise Familiar (Yeti Type) Shield conditions met!

Etc. . . .

Merging with Spirit Tortoise Heart Shield!

Forcibly unlocked!

An absurd number of shields scrolled by—probably enough to complete the Spirit Tortoise series. They all had high defense ratings. Wait a second . . . The Spirit Tortoise shields had all unlocked on their own . . . That Spirit Tortoise Heart shield was really something. An image of the Spirit Tortoise appeared as a backdrop to the Spirit Tortoise series listing on the status screen floating in my field of vision.

Now to check their stats . . . Oh? I noticed a shield that had been unlocked had a usable skill.

Spirit Tortoise Carapace Shield 0/40 C

<abilities unlocked> equip bonus: skill "E Float Shield"

equip effects: gravity field, C soul recovery, magic defense up (large)

mastery level: 0

E Float Shield, huh? Was that related to the Air Strike Shield? What kind of skill was it? I tried changing to the new shield and called out the skill.

"E Float Shield!"

The letters "ON" showed up in my field of vision and a shield appeared in mid-air. So it was something like Air Strike Shield, after all? Thinking so, I walked toward the shield, but it moved away the same distance that I had walked.

Huh? Was it a shield that appeared with me as its axis? Distance-wise, the skill seemed to place somewhere between Air

Strike Shield and Shooting Star Shield. I was timing how long the skill lasted while I analyzed it, and it still hadn't disappeared. It lasted a long time.

Hmm . . . As I stood there, deep in thought, the E Float Shield started to spin around right in front of my face. What was going on? And why was it in my face? Get away!

The instant the thought crossed my mind, the shield moved away. So it was a magical shield that moved wherever I wanted it to? Now that would be convenient. It would be even more convenient than Chain Shield. That one had a restraining aspect that differentiated it from this skill, but still . . .

The effect's range was around one meter. Considering it could be turned on and off, it would classify as a semi-passive skill. As for my SP . . . It was dropping a small amount every thirty seconds. Not bad fuel efficiency at all. As long as I didn't use any other skills, it wouldn't even outpace my natural SP regeneration. I guess I should have expected as much from a shield that came from Spirit Tortoise materials.

"Change Shield!"

I used Change Shield and the E Float Shield changed its form to match. Oh! This was a convenient skill, for sure. Only being able to produce one would be the limiting factor.

As for the other shields . . . They were all good, numbers-wise, but most of them just increased stats or resistances. Being linked to the Spirit Tortoise Heart Shield seemed to have

upgraded all of their stats. On the other hand, the stats of the Spirit Tortoise Heart Shield itself had dropped a bit, as if to say it had served its purpose and was finished. Then again, I couldn't complain after all it had done for us.

"Mr. Naofumi."

Raphtalia and the others came running over to where I was taking a break after I finished experimenting with the shield.

"You get everything ready?"

"Yes. All that's left is to stop by the slave trader's place."

"Alright then. Let's head out."

"Okaaay!"

Filo joyfully pulled the cart while in her filolial form. I could tell she was struggling just a tiny bit. Her reduced stats probably did make the carriage feel heavy, after all.

"Oh? Finished already?"

The queen wandered over as if she had just been out for a walk.

"For now, yeah. Can you have what's left delivered to my territory? I'll use the meat to feed us for the time being."

Food expenses would skyrocket for a while once the slaves started leveling up. It wasn't like I had no other ideas for securing provisions, but I had a lot of things to take care of and I wanted to start with getting the territory set up.

"I'll have some of the soldiers sent over to help out, then. Feel free to use them as you see fit."

"Will do. Thanks. We're going out for a bit to take care of some other things."

"Let me know if you need anything. I'll do whatever I can to help."

"Understood. We'll start with gathering building materials and implementing security measures to take care of thieves. We'll be heading over tonight, so have things ready on your end by then."

Having rumors circulate about a hero loading up a bunch of slaves into a carriage and taking them away somewhere would be bad, so it made sense to leave during the night. I originally thought Filo might have trouble seeing in the dark, but her vision worked just fine at night, so there would be no problem with making our move then.

"Understood."

I nodded to the queen upon hearing her response and we headed out of the castle and toward the slave trader's tent.

The slave curse preparations had been completed and the slaves were trembling with apprehension. I figured now was a good time to be stern with my orders. Raphtalia had started out cowardly in the beginning, and Filo had been selfishly obstinate. I was getting a whole bunch of new slaves all at once, so I planned on making good use of my past experiences.

"From now on, you're all my slaves. But don't worry. I won't do anything terrible to you—as long as you do what you're told. That said . . ."

I couldn't make it sound like I was too lenient or they would take advantage of me.

"I can't stand laziness. If you're not a hard worker, I'll sell you off without a second thought. Don't you forget that!"

The slave trader gave an order to his assistant, who then rang something that looked like a gong just as I finished my little spiel. No one asked for that! Look, now the slaves were cowering in fear. No, wait . . . That was probably my fault.

"Ahhh!"

Nice! There's the trepidation I was looking for!

"Oh, jeez. There you go again, causing misunderstandings . . ."

"Fehhh . . ."

"Also, I plan to continue peddling, so I'll need some monsters that can be used for transport."

"I'd be happy to give you some filolials! Yes sir!"

"No, not just filolials. I'll take one of those, but I want some different kinds of monsters, too."

"You don't like filolials?"

"I want monsters that are easier to handle so that the slaves can use them, too. Also, something that can work the land."

Aside from the usual horses and filolials, I had seen plenty of monsters that resembled cows and caterpillars pulling carts around the town. Besides, if I raised a bunch of filolials, I might very well end up with a whole crowd of Filos. I could hear the chorus of Filos all shouting . . .

"Maaasteerrr! We're hungry!"

Just the thought of it sent shivers down my spine. Oh god, spare me!

Supposing I were going to raise more filolials, it'd have to be one at a time. I had to be especially careful when dealing with filolials. It might have made sense from a fighting power perspective, but we were still just laying the foundations. With that monstrous appetite, raising more than one filolial at a time would be difficult. Even if we did have the Spirit Tortoise meat, it's not like we could just hang around the castle town all day feeding it to them.

I had to start with what I could handle and build up from there or things would get out of control and I'd end up buried in debt. It was a future all too easy to imagine.

"I see. In that case, leave it to me."

"Will do."

"Would you prefer eggs? Or would you rather purchase adult monsters? The eggs would be cheaper, by the way."

"Eggs should be fine for now."

"Understood. Yes sir."

The slave trader walked off toward the tent where he conducted the monster side of his business. I opened up the slave curse settings. Oh? Looking carefully, I noticed you could set work-related rules, too. I'd have to think about what work I'd have them doing later. Looking out of the tent, I could see the sun beginning to set.

"Rishia, I have a job for you."

"Huh? What job is that?"

"I want you—along with Raphtalia and Filo—to help raise the slaves and monsters I just bought."

"Umm, okay."

"And I want you to take the lead."

A jack-of-all-trades and master of none like Rishia would excel at a leadership position once she'd gotten used to analyzing the situation. Raphtalia and Filo would probably tag along as protection, but I wasn't planning on just creating a bunch of high-level slaves that didn't know how to fight. There was value in simply experiencing battle, so I'd gradually move Raphtalia and Filo away from the front lines. It was the perfect chance to have Rishia experience a strength of her own that couldn't be measured by levels.

"Of course, you'll still be continuing your Hengen Muso Style training with the old lady."

"Okay! I'll do my *besht*!"

There she went again with the weird pronunciation! Jeez . . . This girl was hopeless.

"I've selected some eggs that should satisfy the Shield

Hero's requirements. Yes sir."

The slave trader returned with several eggs in hand.

"You have my thanks. Now then . . ."

Hmm . . . I guess there was no avoiding it.

"First things first . . ."

I looked back at the slave trader, who was rubbing his hands together, and made an announcement.

"I'm going to cook us a meal."

I used the Spirit Tortoise meat that Filo had brought to prepare and serve several dishes in the tent. There was your standard grilled meat, as well as a soup and a stew. Having been made using Spirit Tortoise meat, the dishes tasted a bit strange.

"Oh! This is good!"

"What is this?! It's better than my mom's cooking!"

"Yeah, what is this?!"

"Mr. Naofumi is an excellent cook."

"Yup! I love Master's cooking!"

The slaves were all getting along and devouring their food.

"This is superb! The Shield Hero's cooking is simply delectable! Yes sir!"

During the commotion of getting everything ready, the slave trader and his assistant had slipped in with the slaves and were helping themselves to the food. I couldn't let it get to me. It wasn't my intention to feed them, but they had provided the space, after all, so I decided to let it go.

"Do as you're told, and this won't be the last time I cook for you. I expect you all to work like you mean it!"

The slaves continued eating and nodded in response. They could just consider it celebration in advance, since things were going to get busy from here on out. They needed to be well-nourished or they wouldn't last.

After finishing our meal, we set out into the night with the slaves, the slave trader, and his assistant in tow, making our way through the castle town and then departing for the territory.

Chapter Five: The Seaetto Territory

We made our leisurely march through the night with Filo pulling the carriage, and we reached the part of the territory near Raphtalia's village by morning.

"Master, we're heeere!"

According to the queen, Eclair and the others were not staying in the village that Raphtalia had lived in, but rather in a neighboring town. We kept going, and after a short while, we arrived at a town that looked a bit run-down.

"Oh!"

A Melromarc solider . . . The same young soldier that had asked to join me during the second wave, actually, was standing near the entrance to the town.

"Shield Hero!"

"Long time no see."

"Indeed! I was there during the Spirit Tortoise incident but didn't get a chance to talk to you."

I had to give him some serious props for making it out of that alive. It was a close fight with heavy losses, so the fact that he had been there made me shudder.

"We received word that you would be coming. I assume you want to meet with Lady Eclair and Princess Melty?"

"Yeah. I figured I should at least say hello before anything else."

"This way, then."

We followed the soldier into the town. It had been reduced to ruins. The streets were lined with a variety of buildings, including houses that had been destroyed—perhaps by the wave—as well as others that still looked usable. It didn't seem like it had been a very big town. Even the town mansion looked pretty average and wasn't as big as the ones I'd seen in other towns.

The young soldier said something to the gatekeeper, who then opened the gate without hesitation.

"Ya! Hiya!"

I could hear some kind of shouting coming from the mansion courtyard. I climbed down from the carriage and made my way in that direction. Eclair, the old lady, Keel, and three other kids that I didn't recognize were training in the courtyard.

"Mr. Iwatani!"

Noticing she had guests, Eclair stopped the training and waved to us.

"Ah! I smell Mel-chan!"

Filo let go of the carriage and ran off into the mansion.

"How is everything?"

"Bubba Shield! Long time no see! I heard all about it! You went to another world and defeated the bad guy, right?"

"Yeah, we took him out. I'll tell you all about how he died later."

"Ugh . . . I wanted to be there, too!"

Keel stamped his foot in regret. The reason he couldn't come with us was because he'd fought recklessly and had to get his injuries treated.

"Keel, are your injuries all healed up?"

"I'm all good! They weren't that bad thanks to you, bubba!"

"It's been a while, Keel."

Raphtalia smiled as she approached Keel. The other kids that had been standing at Keel's side backed away several steps, speechless.

"Surprised, right? That's Raphtalia!"

"No way . . ."

"Is that really Raphtalia?"

"She looks completely different!"

"Rafu!"

Just then, Raph-chan jumped up onto Raphtalia's shoulder and howled.

"Ah! That was Raphtalia's voice!"

"This little thing?"

"What is that? It sounds like your voice, Raphtalia."

"Umm . . . Just ignore this little thing."

"It's a shikigami that was made using a lock of Raphtalia's hair. They're known as familiars here. Her name is Raph-chan. Be nice to her!"

"Oh? So she's kind of like Raphtalia's alter ego?"

"Keel! Don't say that!"

I left Raphtalia and the others to rekindle old friendships and went to talk with Eclair and the old Hengen Muso lady.

"How have things been progressing? You're working on rebuilding the territory, right?"

"Umm . . . About that . . ."

Eclair's mood suddenly darkened.

"My student Eclair here has been training quite hard. The reconstruction, on the other hand, has not seen much progress," interjected the old Hengen Muso lady.

"Oh?"

So it was so bad even the old lady could tell. Hadn't the queen said that Melty was helping out?

"I fully intend to follow in the footsteps of my late father and rebuild the territory, but . . . I haven't been able to find much help. It seems it will take quite some time," Eclair explained.

"Well, your father's connections can only take you so far, I'm sure. The Church of the Three Heroes made things a lot worse, too, from what I hear."

". . ."

Raphtalia's family had died along with many of the villagers. On top of that, I'd heard that many of the survivors had been captured and sold into slavery.

"After all, you can't expect the people that originally lived here to return if most of them are dead. Not to mention, the residents that were made slaves were all sold off before the queen could secure them. You're trying to locate them now, right?"

"That's right. We're working behind the scenes to do everything we can to bring them back."

"And what happens when you do? Let's say you find ten, maybe twenty of them. Are you just going to throw them into the ruins of a town and say, 'Alright! Rebuild your town!' Is that your plan?"

". . ."

Eclair fell silent. So that was seriously her plan? Try thinking ahead a bit! I couldn't help but sigh. Eclair had an overly serious personality that made her an excellent knight, but she lacked the qualities that made for a good governor.

"Hey, where is Nice Guy, the guy that was taking care of Keel? Or even one of the country's leaders will do. We need someone to drill you in the basics of reconstruction!"

I pointed at Eclair and spoke bluntly.

"How dare you!" she snapped.

Just then, Filo came running up, pulling Melty along behind her.

"Mel-chan, Master is over here!"

"I know! Calm down, Filo!"

"Melty! Perfect timing. What were you thinking letting this

knucklehead govern a territory? Are you stupid?"

"We meet again after all this time and that's what you have to say to me?!"

"Just what do you think makes me unfit to govern?!"

Eclair's furrowed brow made it clear she was upset.

"Seriously? I'm sure Melty has noticed this, too, but Eclair . . . You obviously understand absolutely nothing about what governing a territory entails."

"What?!"

"I'm certainly no expert, but I still understand what's necessary to manage a territory and make it livable."

I looked at Eclair and pointed to a chair. Melty subtly instructed her to sit down for me. Raphtalia and the others . . . I'd just leave them to getting caught up for now. We were going to be busy with other things soon, after all.

"First of all, governing a territory is about more than just owning the land. The people that live on that land are important."

"I understand that much. That's why I'm trying to bring the people that lived here back."

"I'm saying that just bringing them back isn't enough!"

I drew a picture of some people on the ground. That would represent the population.

"To rebuild the territory, you'll need people, clothes, food, and housing."

Securing food would come first. In a world like this, hunting monsters and using them for food would be quickest. Next would be a base of operations for daily life—housing and the like. And then there would be clothing. That would include equipment, too, in this world.

"As for the people, I totally get wanting to prioritize the people that originally lived here—those that were lost. But it's not realistic. It's not about how much we can prioritize them. There simply aren't enough of them."

"I . . . I know that! Princess Melty is working on that."

"I am, but there haven't been many people interested in taking part in the reconstruction. My mother seems to believe that your involvement, Naofumi, will make residents of Siltvelt and elsewhere want to cooperate, though."

"That may very well work in our favor, but let's be realistic. Time is limited. We need to be snatching people up greedily."

Sigh . . . Of course, this wasn't Raphtalia's village, so it's not like I needed to say anything, but still . . .

"I don't really know what being nobility in this country entails, but establishing a safe living environment is what you need to be focusing on right now. Oh, but isn't it just horrible to be stuck with rebuilding some ruined territory with no future?"

Eclair hung her head upon hearing my words.

"What were you doing during the two and a half weeks I was gone? Training?"

"I'd say that's pretty accurate," said Melty.

"No! I was working with Keel and the others to gather more people!"

"We did make some suggestions to my mother. She also sent one of her best to help out here at the mansion. We've made some progress with repairing the buildings, too."

Melty gave me a quick report of the situation. I guess they were doing something, at least.

"And I guess you planned on moving on to the neighboring village once you finish rebuilding this town?"

Melty and Eclair nodded in response. I sighed.

"Well, do whatever you want. I'm technically the governor now, but I'll leave the reconstruction of the town to you two."

"Huh? Are you not going to help us, Naofumi?"

"I plan on rebuilding the neighboring village as I see fit. I'll need to coordinate with you to do that, so it's not like I'm just leaving everything to you and disappearing."

There was no need for me to play boss and order Melty or Eclair around. We could all go about our own projects simultaneously. If my reconstruction plans went well, then people would naturally begin to gather here in this town, too.

"Now that that's decided . . ."

I snapped my fingers, and the slave trader and his assistant climbed out of the carriage, came over, and grabbed the three kids standing near Keel.

"Wh . . . What are you doing?!"

"No! Stop!"

"Ah, I thought they might remember you."

They had been slaves before, after all.

"Bubba Shield! Don't tell me . . ."

"Yeah, you've already been through this, haven't you, Keel? That's right. You kids are going rebuild your village, and the best way to do that is by becoming my slaves so that we can improve your abilities."

"I . . . I know that, but still . . ."

"Mr. Naofumi! I'm not sure that forcing them is . . ."

Raphtalia voiced her doubts with a worried look on her face.

"Don't worry. It's just a formality."

"No! I never want to be a slave again!"

The little brats were struggling with all their might, but the slave trader's assistant showed no sign of letting go.

"Mr. Iwatani!"

"You think you can rely on charity alone to bring back the village? Are you all just going to wait on Eclair and Melty to rebuild it for you? Do you really think you'll get your village back that way? Seriously?"

The brats groaned in response to my questions. That's right. I'm sure they had already figured it out long ago. The villagers that had been lost weren't coming back. And it was clear that things weren't going to get any better if they relied on Eclair.

"If you become my slaves, you can become strong like Raphtalia here. She played a big role in the battle against the Spirit Tortoise."

"I've heard rumors, but . . . is that really true?"

"Keel has gotten a fair bit stronger, too, hasn't he?" I added.

"Now that he mentions it, you do seem a lot stronger now, even though not much time passed before we were reunited, Keel."

"Really? I mean, right?! Bubba Shield made me his slave and leveled me up."

Keel looked proud of himself.

"Although he did rush into battle recklessly and end up in the hospital. Next time don't be so rash."

"I won't! I got left behind because of my recklessness. I definitely won't let it happen again!"

"So there you have it. To put it another way, you've all been chosen by the Shield Hero, so why resist? Become a slave . . . Become a hero's disciple and join me in my quest to rebuild the village!"

"You changed your wording this time, huh?"

"Am I a hero's disciple, too, Master?"

Maintaining a hierarchy was important. Too many of the people in this world were slackers. I couldn't ignore the possibility that they actually believed that peace would come even if they just sat back quietly and waited.

"It's not like I can't find someone else to help me. But do you really plan on doing nothing? Will you just surrender without a fight and end up back on the slave market again when disaster strikes?"

"Bubba Shield . . . You've sold me! I'm sticking with you!"

Keel came over and stood in front of me. I'm not really one to speak, but this kid was always getting swept up in the heat of the moment.

"I'm going to make it our village again!"

"Good answer! What about the rest of you?"

The other kids from Raphtalia's village exchanged glances with each other.

"Naofumi may sound scary, but he's actually a very caring person."

Melty interjected with what seemed to be her idea of a show of support.

"To be honest . . . we won't be able to take care of you here forever. I think it would be best if you went with Naofumi and learned to take care of yourselves, if possible."

"Princess Melty . . ."

Eclair nodded as if Melty had said something deeply profound.

"I don't see why not. Naofumi has taken it upon himself to come help out, so why don't we all do what we can to work together and rebuild this territory?" added Melty.

"Understood. Friends of Raphtalia, the decision is yours! We'll do everything we can to assist with the reconstruction, too."

After Eclair had finished making her declaration, Raphtalia stepped forward and offered her friends her own take.

"I think . . . Instead of just standing by and watching, I think we should take it upon ourselves to get this done. Right?"

Raphtalia looked over in the direction of the village and then pointed at the flag flying on the mansion grounds.

"That flag that we lost back then . . . It's finally within our reach. I want all of us to take back that place . . . to take back that flag together. So please, work with us to make that happen!"

Raphtalia's friends seemed to be thinking about her words for a few moments, and then . . .

"Okay! I'll do it!"

"You may look different, but you're the same old Raphtalia!"

"Yeah, you said the same thing back when we were still living in the village."

"Yes, I did. Everyone, let's take back that flag!"

"Yeah!"

The slave trader was starting to look a bit uncomfortable. He obviously wasn't okay with this kind of atmosphere.

"Now then, let us perform the slave curse ceremony. Yes sir."

"I'm going to work them like horses. I can't wait!

Muhahaha!" I whispered to the slave trader and he perked up instantly.

"I feel a sudden surge of motivation! Yes sir! Sowing the seeds of hope and then reaping those benefits for yourself! My hat's off to you! Yes sir!"

Was this guy really that simple or did he just revel in the suffering of others?! Whatever . . . I'd now officially received the territory from Eclair, and so we set off for the village.

Chapter Six: Feeding the Herd

Aside from Raphtalia and Rishia, I set tight restrictions on all of the slaves so that the slave curse would punish them right away if they didn't take things seriously. On our first day in the village, I went out with the slaves to start cleaning up the wreckage of the buildings that had been destroyed.

"This house is important to me! It's my home!"

That was Keel screaming. We'd come to the location where his house had been, apparently. But all that was left now was rubble in our way.

"There's nothing wrong with cherishing your home, but the roof has collapsed, and the walls are destroyed beyond repair. I'm sorry, but you have to understand that there will be houses we can repair and others that we can't."

I looked through the debris to see if there were any valuables or items that we could use, but everything I found was either covered in rust or wasn't anything we could use. Luckily the well was still usable. It would take a bit of work, but we could probably use the garden, too.

"I can understand wanting to preserve the memory, but if we're going to rebuild the village, then we need to get rid of anything that's just getting in the way."

"But—"

"Keel! Stop being selfish."

Raphtalia reprimanded Keel. I wasn't going to stop her.

"This used to be your house, right?"

"Yeah!"

"Alright, then the new house that we build here will be yours. Only it will be a communal house that you will manage. More people will be joining us, so I'm counting on you to manage it properly."

"Al . . . alright."

Keel mumbled and nodded.

"That's settled. Now, Filo!"

"Okaaay!"

The instant Keel let his guard down, Filo charged into the skeleton of a house and kicked down the supports, destroying the building.

"Ahhhhhhh!"

I left Keel standing there dazed and moved on to our next task. The building materials and castle soldiers sent by the queen arrived before noon. There was stone, lumber, and . . . plaster?

"Is this the village you are rebuilding, Shield Hero?"

I was sure they had already heard from Eclair and Melty, but the soldiers asked anyway.

"Yeah. I'd like to at least get something with a roof up by sundown. I know it's a lot to ask, but I'm counting on you."

"Leave it to us."

"Thanks. So for now, we'll leave the building to you soldiers. As for Raphtalia, Rishia, and Filo . . ."

"Yes?"

"Yeeees?"

"What is it?"

The three responded when I called their names.

"I'm going to make lunch now. Once you three have finished eating, I want you to take the slaves and go hunt monsters with them."

"Understood."

"Okay!"

"I'll do my best."

"I'll leave it up to you to form parties. I'm guessing the experience probably won't be very good if you all hunt in one big group."

I'd never actually tried measuring it. How did experience points work when everyone fought together? Were they distributed somehow, or were they shared by everyone? I wasn't really sure how it worked.

"Does anyone know how experience works in groups?"

"Umm . . ."

Rishia raised her hand embarrassedly.

"I knew it. You can always count on Rishia at times like these. So?"

"Umm . . . All members of a party receive experience points. The amount differs depending on abilities and level, but the distribution is unbiased. Six people is the limit. Any more than that and the amount of experience begins to drop."

Aha, so that's why Itsuki and his group always left you out!

I didn't actually say that, because all I'd get is a loud "fehhhh!" And I'd had enough of those. So as long as we split up into parties when going out in a big group, there shouldn't be any problem. We'd just form parties of six and that should take care of it.

"If there's still room and they're free, you might try inviting Eclair and the old lady, too."

"Understood. I'll take care of assigning everyone."

I made Raphtalia the group leader and had her create the parties. We currently had a total of ten slaves, so I had her assign four to Rishia and three each to Filo and herself. She put Keel with Rishia since he had already gotten stronger to a certain degree.

"Alright, I'm going to make lunch now, so give me a hand."

"Okay!"

The three of them got busy doing what they could to help with the preparations.

"You're not going to help cook, Raphtalia?" Keel calmly asked Raphtalia, glaring at me as I prepped the food. He had already recovered from his state of shock. That was quicker than I expected. Maybe it was because he was a kid?

"You were always a good cook, Raphtalia!"

"Rafu!"

"Umm . . ."

Raphtalia glanced over at me with a look of uncertainty on her face. What? Was she expecting me to say something? I guess she wanted to show off a bit in front of her friends or something, because she finally said something after hesitating for a moment.

"How about I give you a hand?"

"Oh? That's unusual. You don't have to if you don't want to."

"That's not it. You just work so efficiently that there was never really anything for me to do."

"Oh? In that case, why don't you cut this meat up for me? It might end up tasting better being cut by the katana vassal weapon instead of a normal kitchen knife."

"Understood."

Now that Raphtalia was helping, what should I make? I guess you could never go wrong with grilling up meat.

"Make sure you cut against the grain or the texture will be off. I know you're not Kizuna, but if you have some kind of skill to break down monsters or animals, then it should show you where to cut."

"Okay."

Other than that, I guess I could make a stew, maybe. I'd have to skim off the foam, though, and that always made preparing stews annoying. We didn't have many ingredients, so we were naturally limited in what we could make. Something with vegetables could work, but I didn't want to get too fancy since the slaves would just devour anything I made in an instant anyway. Oh, why not? It felt like a bit of a waste, but since Raphtalia was helping out and all, I figured I'd grill up another dish with cilantro, too.

"That smells good, doesn't it?"

"Yeah, not bad. Should we make a soup, too?"

"Sure."

We could just simmer some of this meat and turn it into a soup.

"Raphtalia."

"Yes?"

"I'm going to throw some Hamburg steaks together, too, so help me mince this meat."

"Un . . . understood."

We worked quickly, cooking up all of the dishes. Raphtalia had mentioned that her parents taught her how to cook, and I could tell she knew what she was doing more than most. But now that I thought about it, I'd hardly ever cooked with her.

"Do you have a special family recipe or anything like that?"

"I guess you could say that. I couldn't make it with the ingredients we have, though."

"Well, maybe I'll have you make it once we get the ingredients you need, then."

Having a female friend cook for me had always been a dream of mine, actually. None of my friends had ever really been the cooking type, though. Now I could look forward to finding out what Raphtalia's family recipe tasted like.

"I . . . I'm afraid of all of the mistakes you'd point out if I tried making it for you."

Huh? That wasn't the response I was expecting to hear from Raphtalia.

"You think I'm some kind of food snob?"

"Aren't you?"

"No way."

It wasn't like I had ever complained about anyone else's cooking. Just what kind of person did Raphtalia think I was? I wanted to live up to her expectations as much as possible, but a food snob? That was unexpected. If any of us was a food snob, it would have to be Filo or Raphtalia. Filo was especially picky about flavor.

"Okay then. I'll make it for you sometime."

"Good. I'm looking forward to it."

"Rafu!"

I loved how Raph-chan hopped up onto Raphtalia's shoulder and started chirping.

"Hey, everyone! Raphtalia and I cooked lunch for you. Hurry up and eat, and then off you go!"

"It's super good this time, too!"

"Yeah! It's so good!"

The slaves all dug in with big smiles on their faces. I went ahead and served the soldiers that were building houses for us, too.

"This . . . This might be the most delicious grilled meat I've ever had!"

"You're kidding, right? This can't be that same turtle meat! They served the same thing at the castle, but it was nowhere near this good!"

My shield's cooking enhancement really was something. There was probably a synergistic effect with the enhancement from Raphtalia's katana that made everything that much better. Maybe rubbing the meat with salt and spices during prep made a difference, too. The Hamburg steaks were gone in the blink of an eye.

The slaves all had their share of my cooking. Considering how they would be when they got back from leveling up . . . Yeah, I'd have to prepare even more food or there wouldn't be enough.

"Okay everyone, I'm going to give each of you a weapon, so get out there and fight!"

I gave the slaves their orders and they began to panic.

I handed each of them one of the old weapons that I had gotten from the castle storeroom. Most of them were short swords meant for beginners. One of the young female slaves was standing there completely pale with her blade in hand, looking just like Raphtalia had at first.

"If you refuse to fight, you'll feel a burning in your chest, so be prepared. Remember, you'll never get your village back that way."

"We get it, Bubba Shield! We're ready to fight, so you just wait!"

At least someone was showing some enthusiasm.

"It's not like I can't find someone else to replace you all. I'm just trying to turn this place into a territory again. But since Raphtalia has always done as I asked without arguing, I decided to reward her by inviting you all to take part. Don't get the wrong idea."

I had gotten used to playing the bad guy since coming to this world. It's not like I was here to do charity work. I would be going back to my own world eventually, anyway, so it's not like I needed to worry about this place. I just wanted to create a place where Raphtalia could live her life in peace.

"He has a sharp tongue, but he's a good person, so don't hold it against him."

Raphtalia added some uncalled-for words of support. I was supposed to be the villain here.

"Okay then . . . Filo, you load the defeated monsters onto that cart and bring them back. We have plenty of uses for them."

"Okaaay!"

They would be our food for the time being.

"Maaaster, what kind of monsters do you want?"

"Ones with plenty of meat, if possible. If you get some of those sheep-looking monsters, then I can make sausages."

"Okaaay! I'll see if I can find some!"

I pointed to Filo's carriage and ordered the slaves inside. They hesitantly climbed aboard, and Filo set off to take them hunting.

"Watch your speed!"

"Okaaay!"

Filo's carriage rattled off into the distance. Of course, she couldn't actually go all that fast while still suffering from the effects of the curse.

"Now then . . . I'll leave the construction up to you guys."

"Huh? Of course!"

I left the construction to the soldiers, set my shield to take care of some compounding, and got started on the preparations for our next meal. It would still be a while before the monster eggs were ready to hatch. I'd have to come up with a way to secure more food before we ran out of Spirit Tortoise meat.

The slaves that had gone out hunting with Raphtalia and the others were back by nightfall. They were all completely worn out. The cart that I had attached to the carriage was loaded up with slain monsters. It looked like they had found some sheep-type monsters, too, just like I'd requested.

"Ugh . . ."

Grooowwwwl. Grumble, grumble. Rummmmble, rumble, rumble . . .

"So hungry . . ."

The growling of their stomachs sounded like thunder. Their bodies were growing rapidly and needed nutrition, and that made them ravenous.

"Glad to see you all made it back. Did they put up a good fight?"

"Yes, they all did their best."

"Fehhh . . . I'm exhausted."

"Well, if they did their best, then that's good enough. Let's eat."

I brought out the stew and steaks that I had prepared in advance using the Spirit Tortoise meat and placed them on the table. I figured it would turn out like this, so I'd made a ridiculous amount of food. It was a ton of food, but it would still probably disappear in a heartbeat.

"Woooow!"

Filled with excitement, the slaves gathered around the table and started eating.

"Maaaster, what about meeee?"

"Yours is right here."

I gave Filo her portion. She got about fifty percent more than the growing slaves.

"Is that all? I want more!"

"If you want more, then go hunt something yourself and eat that."

"Boo . . ."

Filo was sulking. That's too bad. I had already made a ton of food. I couldn't manage any more than this on my own.

"Thank you for the meal!"

What?! They had already finished while Filo and I were talking?! I knew that children were supposed to have fierce appetites, but come on! I hope they were satisfied, at least.

"Alright, brats, tomorrow will be here in no time. Get to bed!"

"Okay!"

We herded the slaves into one of the houses that had been repaired by the soldiers from the castle. The rest of us would stay in the other house that was still being patched up. The windows were broken, so the wind blew right through, but the roof would shield us from rain.

"I'll sleep with the others."

"Yeah, see if you can help them get settled in a bit."

"I will!"

Raphtalia left to go sleep with her old friends. Filo was already half asleep and nodding off. Rishia was busy deciphering the manuscripts that she had received from Kizuna and the others. She had more stamina than you would have guessed.

I got to work compounding in preparation for the next part of my plans. I checked the levels of the slaves while I waited. It looked like they had all reached around level 15, on average. Their stats had increased across the board, too. Judging from my experience with Raphtalia's growth, I'd want them to reach level 30 at the very least, and that included the ones that weren't suited for battle, too.

After some time had passed, I heard a knock on the door.

"Umm . . ."

It was Raphtalia and . . . she had brought several young female slaves with her.

"What is it?"

"Well . . ."

Raphtalia seemed like she wanted to ask me to do something, but she was mumbling. Spit it out! Did she expect me to figure it out on my own or something?

"Did they wet the bed?"

"That's not it. Go on, ask Mr. Naofumi yourself."

"Umm . . . well . . ."

Their stomachs growled, and the slave girls hung their heads in shame.

"Ah, I get it. I should probably make enough to feed the other brats too, right?"

"Thank you."

I headed out to the cooking area outside and started preparing a meal. Jeez. They had gotten hungry again quick. I cut up the monsters they had brought back from hunting and decided to make some simple skewers. Cutting the meat into small chunks was too much trouble, so I just roasted the prepped monsters whole. Once we got things going, we'd need to form a cooking crew as soon as possible, or I'd have no time for myself.

And so the next day arrived.

"Alright, listen up, everyone. I'm sure you enjoyed your midnight snack, but our food supplies are growing scarcer by the day. We need to make up for losses with hunting. In other words, I'll be deciding what to cook based on what you bring back. Got it?"

"Yeah!"

They were almost too submissive. It weirded me out a little bit, but I guess it was fine if they were showing initiative.

"I'll have dinner ready tonight, but the next meal isn't guaranteed. You've been warned!"

"Okay!"

Last night was rough. They kept asking for more no matter

how much I cooked, and they had been genuinely hungry as far as I could tell. I felt like I had been cooking nonstop since we got here. I wasn't their mother after all! Once they had finished growing to a certain degree, I planned to train them to handle a variety of different tasks. I'd just have to hold out until then.

"Thank you for the meal!"

"You're welcome. Now get out there and hunt, and don't come back until evening!"

"Okay!"

Everyone looked more cheerful than they had yesterday as they climbed into Filo's carriage. I wasn't letting Filo go crazy with the speed, so I hoped that the slaves wouldn't get the usual motion sickness common with her carriage rides. It would be good if they reached around level 20, on average, by the time they got back.

Securing food supplies would need to be our immediate focus. There was always *that* . . . But if I used it and it mutated again, who knew what might happen. Even so, it had helped us out of tight spots before, and it looked like the time to rely on it had come once again.

Chapter Seven: Employing the Bioplant

"We're back!"

The whole lot of them had smiles on their faces despite being covered in mud when they got back. They were definitely livelier than they had been yesterday. On the other hand, Rishia looked utterly exhausted. Raphtalia and Filo didn't really show any signs of being worn out. Then again, they were both pretty strong even with the curse's effects in place.

"I see that! Did you all do your best out there hunting again today?"

"Yeah!"

"That goes without saying!"

The adaptability of children really was an amazing thing. It was only the second day and they had already adjusted.

"Alright then. Dinner is ready, as promised."

"Yaaaay!"

They shoveled the food I had prepared into their mouths.

"Now then, Raphtalia."

"Yes?"

"After dinner, I'm going to do something . . . something that might make you mad."

"Umm, and what is that?"

"It's jungle time. It helped us out back in Kizuna's world, too, right?"

Raphtalia seemed to understand what I meant. Her face turned pale.

"Are you going to plant that thing?"

"Yeah. This place is just a barren wasteland, anyway. It's perfect, right?"

"But still . . ."

"It may very well cause problems with the soil down the road, but I did ask the slave trader to choose monsters that could be used to work the land."

"Umm . . . Understood. Desperate times call for desperate measures, I guess."

"I'm glad you understand."

"Considering efficiency, it really is the only choice."

Raphtalia was all about efficiency. But she also kind of worried about keeping up appearances. Now that I thought about it, L'Arc and the others had gotten on to me about her upbringing. She had picked up my habit of haggling over prices. Being told about it about it objectively like that did make me feel a little bad about it.

"I also wanted to take this chance to do a little bit of research. I'm thinking, maybe I can get it to grow some medicinal herbs, too."

"Wait a minute. Don't tell me you plan to modify it even further?!"

"I do. I want to grow something that can make us some money, if at all possible."

That's right. I needed money if my plans were going to succeed. Rebuilding a village with ten or so slaves just wasn't possible. And that wouldn't change much, even if the slave trader did manage to deliver more of the slaves I had asked for.

"Don't worry. I won't be making any crazy modifications that might make it difficult to manage. Producing food supplies is the priority until the slaves are grown up enough to handle problems on their own."

"Sigh . . . Really, please do be careful."

"I know!"

I couldn't afford to do anything that might result in a radical failure, but beyond that, I had to do what I could. I planned to have the slaves help earn money, too—not just fight. And while I was mulling over such things, all the food I cooked vanished.

"Thank you for the meal!"

"You're welcome."

I could hear a clamor of voices as they all talked to each other excitedly. It had only been a few days since we had arrived, but they all seemed to have adjusted to their new life for the most part. And Keel and the other three from the village were already familiar with the area, having grown up here. I was sure this had to be better for their mental health than living the usual life of a slave, at least.

"Alright, everyone. I have something important to say, so listen up."

"Huuuh?"

The slaves were listening with their heads cocked to the side, just like Filo did.

"Everyone come with me."

I walked over to the garden and then checked to make sure they had all followed.

"I have a single seed here. It's a seed from a plant that caused a bit of trouble in a village to the southwest of here."

The castle soldiers seemed to be familiar with the story. They started whispering to each other.

"I made some improvements to that plant, and this seed is the result. You all got hungry last night and ended up eating in the middle of the night, right?"

"Umm, yeah . . ."

Keel nodded.

"You have to understand that I won't be able cook every day like this forever."

"But . . . the Shield Hero's cooking is so good!"

"Yeah! I want to eat your cooking every day!"

"I can't get any work done if I'm always cooking for you all. Of course, if you've worked hard enough to earn it, I'll indulge you all and cook something up."

When it came to development and reconstruction efforts

like this, securing food supplies had to be the top priority. That meant that there was only one thing to do.

"Now then, starting tonight, when you get hungry and I'm not cooking, this is what you are going to do."

I dropped the seed onto the soil and poured some water over it. It sprouted and began to shoot up right before everyone's eyes. The bioplant grew to a height of around three meters tall and began to produce large fruit that resembled tomatoes.

"I've restricted the plant's reproduction to a certain degree, but it should fill this garden before the night has ended. Your job is to manage this plant."

"What . . . are we supposed to do?"

"If it grows beyond the specified area, you trim it. That said, I plan to set aside a good amount of land, so you won't need to cut it for a while. It's up to you to pick the fruit."

"That fruit . . . is it edible?"

"Yeah. As far as I know, they're still producing them in that village to the southwest."

I had seen them being sold as a local specialty in the castle town. I'm fairly certain they were cooking with them, too.

"Feel free to eat some if you get hungry. But if you notice any kind of problem, find an adult and tell them. That's all."

I picked one of the huge tomato-looking fruit and tossed it to Filo. I could tell by her face that she was still hungry, and she gobbled it right up. Several of the slaves followed suit and started eating along with her.

"This is amazing!"

"Yeah!"

"I thought there was no way we were going to rebuild the village at first, but I'm starting to think that with this guy on our side, it might actually be possible!"

Was it just me or were they looking at me like I was some kind of strange being? If things went well managing this fruit, then our food supply issues would be taken care of. On the contrary, if we didn't resolve those issues, it would be impossible to build any kind of useful combat unit in the short three and a half months we had. It was time for me to use all of the knowledge, connections, and tools that I had amassed in this world to see just how much I could accomplish.

It was finally here—the moment of truth!

The next morning came. I ignored the bioplant, which was covering most of the garden, and gave my orders for the morning.

"Oww . . ."

The slaves were complaining of aches and pains all over their bodies . . . growing pains, I was sure. Hmm . . . I checked everyone's levels. Just as I had predicted yesterday, they'd all reached around level 20, more or less. I was excited to see how much more they would grow.

Chapter Eight: Children of the Sea

Several more days passed.

"Ahahaha!"

The slaves were climbing on the bioplant like it was a tree. They'd all reached around level 30, and their growth had begun to plateau a bit. The thing was . . . For whatever reason, almost all of them looked like they were around 14 or 15 years old. They still looked a bit younger than Raphtalia. Was this the age that they became fit for battle?

I thought they might end up being a bit more attractive, but they were all pretty average. Maybe compared to other kids . . . but none of them could hold a candle to Raphtalia. It almost made me wonder if maybe they weren't getting enough to eat.

Keel was probably the only boy among them that you could call attractive. He almost looked a bit girlish, but I guess you could call him handsome. Actually, I suppose it was rude to say this about a boy, but if you imagined a cute girl with boyish looks, that would give you a good idea of his appearance.

That mole-type therianthrope—his name was Imiya or something like that—seemed to have come out of his shell a bit. He and Keel had been running around together and the two were getting along well.

"Hey, Bubba Shield! I'm tired of meat and vegetables. That's all we've had to eat lately!"

"Stop acting spoiled!"

Keel was starting to act overly familiar with me lately. I could come down hard on him, but I didn't feel right scolding him, since he wasn't slacking off.

I guess it was because they felt more comfortable with me now, but more of the kids had started telling me all about their time as slaves. They always finished it up with a thank you. I was glad that morale was high, but still . . .

"We'll go to the ocean and catch some fish, so you can cook them up for us, bubba!"

"I don't remember ever becoming your bubba!"

Now Keel was just being plain cheeky. Maybe it was time for a good chewing out, after all. I could accept "Bubba Shield," but just plain "bubba" wasn't going to fly. But he showed no sign of stopping.

"Ahh . . . if only Sadeena were here, we could be having seafood every day!"

Oh? Raphtalia had mentioned that name before, too. I think she mentioned she was an aquatic therianthrope. She must have really taken care of everyone, because it wasn't just Raphtalia—pretty much all of the kids originally from this village mentioned her from time to time. This was a good chance to find out what kind of character she was.

"Raphtalia. I know you mentioned her before, but just who is this Sadeena?"

"Sadeena was a fisher by trade. She also took first or second place for the strongest fighter in the village."

"Oh? In that case, she must have fought in the wave and . . ."

My voice trailed off as I was about to say "died." It made sense that she would have fought in the wave, and that meant the likelihood that she had died in battle was high.

"If Sadeena had been here, I'm sure we would have been able to fight off the enemies from the wave and the slave hunters, too, bubba."

"Hold on, now. She's that strong?"

"No doubt! I've never seen Sadeena lose a fight. From what I've seen, I'd say she's stronger than that knight lady, too!"

Stronger than Eclair? That would make her a real force to be reckoned with. But if that were true, then it prompted a rather large question.

"Then why was your village destroyed when the wave came?"

"Well . . . Sadeena was far out at sea fishing with the other village fishers at the time."

That made sense. So she wasn't around when the wave hit. Not to mention, when the waves occurred, things got wild all over the place and I'm sure the ocean had been no exception.

I wouldn't say it out loud, but there was a good possibility she had died in the aftermath. Assuming someone that strong had survived, I'm sure they would have returned to the village.

Keel and the others may have enjoyed talking about Sadeena, but it was probably best not to continue this conversation, even though I was the one that started it.

"Come on, bubba! Can't we go down to the ocean?"

"Hmm . . . Do you really want to eat fish that bad?"

Perfect—a chance to change the subject.

"I want to eat fish that you cook, bubba!"

"That's what I want to eat, too!"

"Me too!"

It was like a bunch of Filos had been mass-produced. Thank goodness I hadn't decided to hatch even more filolial eggs.

"Fine. We'll go see what kind of seafood we can catch today. While we're at it, Filo can go swimming and hunt some monsters."

"Okaaay!"

And so I ended up taking the slaves to the ocean. It had gotten warmer lately anyway. So it was good weather for a dip in the ocean. The kids that had grown up here would be familiar with the ocean, so I was pretty sure they would know how to swim.

After walking for a bit, we arrived at the beach.

"Wheee!"

The slaves all took everything but their underwear off and started jumping into the ocean excitedly with fishing spears in hand.

"Rafu!"

Oh? There went Raph-chan, too, running toward the water excitedly. I wondered if I should use the familiar power-up function to raise her aquatic aptitude. I wouldn't have minded seeing her spin her tail like a propeller to swim.

I was thinking about Raph-chan when I noticed we had a little problem.

"Filo! Grab Keel!"

"Huh? Okaaay!"

"Wha?! What are you doing?!"

Filo turned into her filolial form and grabbed Keel just as he was about to jump into the ocean. He was floundering about between Filo's wings, having suddenly been snapped up unexpectedly.

"What's the idea, bubba?!"

"We have a problem. We're going to have to completely rethink how you should be handled."

"What does that mean?!"

The other slaves noticed the commotion and were looking our way. It looked like they had caught on to what was happening. Imiya, who had Raph-chan on his shoulder, approached Keel and asked.

"Keel-kun . . . or should it be Keel-chan?"

"Rafufuuu?"

"Huh? What does that mean? I'm a boy!"

Keel's chest was wrapped in a sarashi cloth, and down below he was wearing . . . a loincloth? Raphtalia walked over and reached her hand out toward Keel's crotch, as if that were something normal to do. She was acting more and more unpredictable lately.

"Keel, do you know the difference between a boy and a girl?"

"Huh?"

"Well, you see . . . boys have . . ."

Raphtalia whispered something into Keel's ear.

"That's ridiculous. If I were god, I sure wouldn't make being a boy or girl that complicated."

"Look at the other boys. No, look at Mr. Naofumi. You see differences, right? His chest is flat, isn't it?"

"What's your point? That thing down there doesn't grow out until you're an adult, and my chest is just a bit swollen. It should heal soon."

Grow out? The kid had quite the imagination. Just what kind of home environment had Keel grown up in before becoming a slave?

I started to envision one of those little girls who talks like a boy. And then an image of Kizuna popped into my head,

raising her hand, saying, "You called?" "Sorry, but no one called for you," I yelled back at the imaginary Kizuna and told her to go away. She disappeared after telling me how mean I was.

Kizuna was no doubt *that* type, but at least she knew that she was a girl. How on earth did Keel not notice during her time as a slave? Maybe it didn't really matter either way? Or maybe the slave trader that sold her kept quiet about it to make her more appealing to a certain kind of twisted clientele?

This country was rotten, after all. There was certain to be plenty of trash with depraved fetishes. Those kinds of perverts would consider someone like Keel a rare find, so they'd probably be willing to pay a hefty fee. That despicable nobleman that we fought had apparently gotten off on abusing children. Then again, all the slaves showed signs of abuse. A sadistic streak was probably something that all of the slave owners shared.

"But . . . but dad used to say that if a boy considered himself a man, then he was a man no matter what anyone else said."

He meant a man of the sea, right? Like a sailor or fisherman? So that's how it was. Daughter wanted to be like daddy and ended up not knowing the difference between a boy and a girl. Actually, the fact that he even said something like that was probably his way of telling her she was a girl.

"I thought Keel was a really cool boy . . . but I guess she was a girl all along."

"I still think she's great. Gender doesn't matter!"

The slave girls were whispering to each other excitedly. I knew girls really went for the whole pretty lady dressed like a man thing, but a girl that wanted to be a man of the sea?

"Come on . . . What's the point in differentiating between boys and girls in the first place?! It doesn't make any sense!"

Keel's gender identity had been shaken to its foundations and she didn't know how to react.

Hmm? Was that Filo jumping in . . . ? Why was she intervening now?

"Well, you see . . . the reason that animals are divided into males and females is so that they can mate. Also . . ."

Filo answered the confused Keel. She went on to eloquently describe the role of man and woman, dressing it all up in rich, luscious language—not as a simple fact of life, but as a sweet, romantic ritual that bordered on the realm of art.

I looked straight at Raphtalia, but she shook her head violently. Was it Rishia, then? I looked over at Rishia, and she screamed, "It wasn't me!" Filo was terrible at explaining things, so the fact that she could go into so much detail meant that someone had to have told her all of this. That left Kizuna's group. It must have been L'Arc, considering what a lecher he was.

"Why do you know so much about this? Did L'Arc tell you?"

"Nuh-uh. I've always known."

Genetic memory? Surely not . . . I bet Filo had done the dirty with some wild male filolial. She must have learned about it then. Or maybe it was when she had been a humming fairy.

"Master's thinking something weeeird!"

Filo protested, a tinge of mortification in her voice. Get over it. Anyway, I'd have to keep an eye out to see if she laid any eggs.

"Boo!"

Her complaining was getting annoying lately.

"Rafu?"

"You don't need to worry about that kind of thing, Raph-chan. I'm not letting any boys run off with you."

"Why are you talking to Raph-chan like you're her father, Mr. Naofumi?"

"Say it to meeee, too!"

Ha! Not likely. You can run off and get hitched with Melty for all I care!

As we were going back and forth, I noticed that everyone still present, including Raphtalia, was turning red with embarrassment. The boys had all jumped into the ocean and still hadn't returned. Were they okay?

"No . . . no way! There's no way I'm going to do anything like that! I would never do that with bubba!"

"Why does it have to be me doing the doing?"

Stop making it sound like I bought and raised you to be a

sex slave! God dammit. Now I was annoyed. This was why I hated little brats that thought about nothing but the opposite sex.

"Enough of this stupid conversation. We have a new rule now. Relationships are forbidden!"

"What?!"

The slaves protested. A rule is a rule, and nothing they said would change that. I needed fighting power, not a solution to declining birth rates. I didn't have time to look after a bunch of new parents and all the little brats they were popping out. Besides, we only had three and a half months! There wasn't even time to pop anything out!

"You can waste your time on that kind of rubbish when your world is peaceful and I'm gone."

"Why?!"

"Why? You know why! Because I hate that kind of stuff! Plus, Raphtalia hates it, too!"

"Raphtalia does?!"

"What?!"

Now even Raphtalia was reacting for some reason. Ah . . . She didn't want me bringing her up. Fine, I get it.

"I'm here to fight the waves, and I plan on taking any of you that are willing to come to fight them with me."

"What?! You mean the waves of destruction?!"

"That's right. I was summoned here to put an end to the

same waves that stole your families from you. If you're willing, I'll take you to fight, too."

I planned on getting more slaves, and I wanted to form several different divisions.

"But first we'll have to face a monster called the Phoenix."

After that had been taken care of, I would form a combat division consisting solely of those that wanted to fight, ideally. Not everyone was meant for battle, after all.

Keel grew quiet for a moment and then finally responded in a sulky manner.

"Well, apparently I'm a girl, so I guess that rules me out, doesn't it?"

"Huh? Not even close. Take a look at the company I keep, why don't you?"

I pointed to Raphtalia, Filo, and Rishia.

"Huh . . . Now that I think about it, they're all girls! That whole thing about hating relationships was a lie, wasn't it?!" Keel snapped.

What was she so upset about?

"Seriously . . . Do you want to participate, or don't you? Which is it?"

"Relationships are forbidden?! How can you say that when you've surrounded yourself with girls?!"

"It wouldn't bother me a bit if Raphtalia were a guy."

"Huh?!"

"What?!"

"What about meeee?"

"A male filolial would be just fine."

"Boo!"

What were they getting upset about? I guess it was time this group of knuckleheads had a lecture.

"Gender equality means that you're treated the same whether you're a boy or a girl. If you can be of use, I'll use you equally, regardless of which you are."

"I get it. Bubba Shield swings both ways. Ultimately, you don't even need to be human," one of the slaves muttered quietly.

Where did they learn this stuff?

"Umm, no . . ."

"Huuuh? What does 'swing both ways' mean?"

So Filo didn't know that one, eh? Maybe the whole genetic memory thing was possible, after all. Wait a second . . . you don't need to be human? Was that supposed to mean Raph-chan and Filo?

"Umm . . . It's something I heard when I was being sold."

"We don't need an explanation! In any case, I can't have any of you starting relationships and ending up unable to fight. So relationships are forbidden!"

Aside from Keel, the slaves all nodded hesitantly, as if they weren't quite convinced.

"Wait, so if I work hard then I can fight, too?"

"Yeah. But thinking about it down the road, after the fighting has ended . . . Actually, you'd probably be a hit with all the creeps that go for that kind of thing, so we'll have you learn to peddle goods."

"What?! Why!?"

"You're one of the better-looking slaves here, and you're not shy. You'd do well peddling stuff, I'm sure."

"I . . . I would? No! I don't wanna!"

"Don't worry. Just be yourself. People are even tougher to deal with than monsters. You'll enjoy it!"

"Coming from you, Bubba Shield, that only makes it scarier!"

Was it something I had done? Having Keel in the vending division seemed like a good idea. If I dressed her like a boy and had her sell accessories or something, I bet the female customers would love it. And then if I paired her with Raphtalia, we could take everyone's money, man or woman.

"By the way, Keel . . ."

"What?"

"The reason you were being rebellious toward me in the beginning is because you had a thing for Raphtalia, right? It's too bad you're a girl. But then again, no one is going to end up pregnant and unable to fight if it's a same-sex relationship, so maybe I should allow those?"

Before the Spirit Tortoise incident, Keel had been a bit on edge around me. She was always glaring at me and going on about Raphtalia this and Raphtalia that.

"Wh . . . what?! You've got it all wrong! Don't be ridiculous!"

Keel started trembling for some reason. She was looking over at . . .

"Mr. Naofumi . . ."

Raphtalia was walking in my direction with a big smile on her face and eyes aflame with murderous intent. Hmm . . . I guess this kind of topic was off limits, after all.

"And that's that. Now get out there and see what you can catch, everyone!"

"Okay!"

After it had been a while, Keel and the others returned.

"Bubba Shield! We caught all of this!"

An ecstatic-looking Keel came over with a net full of fish and shellfish in her hands.

"Yeah, yeah."

I already had the griddle nice and hot. All that was left was to clean the fish and cook them up.

"I'll make some sashimi, since I learned how in Kizuna's world."

Raphtalia started preparing sashimi to go with my cooking. Parasites could be a problem, but everything looked fine, as far as I could tell, using my appraisal skills. And so, just like that I ended up cooking again today. Seriously, enough with the cooking already!

Oh yeah! It was about time to hatch the monster eggs. We had built up a pretty good supply of food. That shouldn't be a problem.

"We're heading back after everyone finishes eating."

"Okay!"

Just past noon, we all left the ocean behind and returned to the village. I wanted to hatch the monster eggs before anything else. I'd already finished binding them to myself yesterday, for the most part. I checked on the eggs, which were lined up in a row in the shed that we were using as a storeroom.

"What are you doing, bubba?"

"We've built up a reasonable stockpile of food, right? Now it's time to get ready to move on to the next stage of my plans."

"Oh."

"The only thing I'm worried about is . . . the filolial."

They were great for pulling carriages, but that appetite . . . Thinking about having two bottomless pits around made me uneasy.

"Meeee?"

Filo had her head cocked to the side while asking.

"Not you. The new filolial egg."

"Filo's going to have a new little brother or sister?"

"Yaaaaay!"

She was so boisterous. She looked like she could be in middle school, but she acted like a child. Then again, I guess she was.

"I guess that *is* how you would classify it . . ."

"Master, do you not want the new filolial to be like me?"

Filo had asked a difficult question. Depending on how I answered, she might think that she was unwanted.

"I want a monster that will pull a carriage and act as a means of transportation. I don't want a bottomless pit."

"Hmm . . . It should be okay, I think."

Filo's answer prompted me to look her way.

"If Master doesn't want it to, I'm pretty sure it won't be like me."

Filo's cowlick was pointing in the direction of the filolial egg, twitching. What was happening? Was she doing something?

"This will be one of my underlings, right?"

Underling!? Well . . . I guess from Filo's perspective, all normal filolials were her underlings.

"Okay then. I'll make it so that it doesn't turn out like me. We can't be certain, if we leave it up to you."

"Can you do that?"

"Yup!"

Filo touched the filolial egg and channeled her magic into it.

"Now it won't turn out like me unless I order it to."

"Oh, umm . . . thanks."

I couldn't help but feel a bit like we had just snipped away at the potential of this soon-to-be-born life, but this place would never be quiet with more than one Filo around, so I guess it had to be done. Depending on how this little experiment went, I might be able to put Filo in charge of raising the filolial.

A few moments later, the eggs began to hatch.

"Peep!"

The first was a filolial chick. It looked kind of purplish. Next were two caterpillars. So these would be able to pull carriages when they got bigger, huh? They were called caterpillands. I tried absorbing a piece of the shell into my shield, but nothing happened. After that came three earthworm-looking monsters called dunes. Were these the ones that would work the land?

I set some basic restrictions for the monsters.

"There you have it. Now, all of you, take these things out and level them up!"

"Okay!"

They put the monsters in a big box and all carried it out to the carriage together, like a bunch of kids that had just gotten their parents to buy them pets. The filolial chick was sitting on top of Filo's head and happily chirping away, despite having just been hatched.

How did I end up in another world playing daddy to a

bunch of kids? I couldn't let it get to me. I just had to keep telling myself that this was all an investment that would pay off when the waves came.

"Oh, another thing . . ."

"What?"

"I'll be forming divisions to take care of cooking and other small tasks soon, so if any of you are interested in learning how to cook, speak up. Preferably, anyone that isn't comfortable fighting and would rather avoid it."

Raphtalia had started helping out with the cooking lately, but it was still just too much.

"I'd like to."

"Me too."

One of the girls and the therianthrope named Imiya got out of the carriage.

"You sure?"

I was pretty sure the girl was one of the slaves that Raphtalia had brought to ask for a midnight snack. As for Imiya, he was a therianthrope covered in fur from head to toe. I could just imagine someone complaining that his fur would get in the food. I couldn't put him in the cooking division, but maybe I could assign him to some other task. He was supposed to be good with his hands. Maybe he had already figured out something else he wanted to do.

"Yeah. I . . . I like cooking. Fighting isn't really . . . isn't for me . . ."

"Okay then. It'll be tough, but do your best."

I looked at Imiya.

"Umm . . . Those small tasks . . . I . . . I want to do those . . ."

"Alright. I'll train you both bit by bit, but you'll still have to level up, too, so don't think you can get out of that."

"I know."

Imiya and the girl nodded and stood by my side.

"We'll be back."

Raphtalia waved to us.

"Okay! Off you go!"

"Don't worry about me, Raphtalia."

"Huh?"

The girl that had joined the cooking division mumbled as she waved back. What was she saying?

"Okay?"

"I'm not worried!"

Huh? Oh, I get it. *He might try to intimidate us, but I'm not scared, so don't worry.* That's what she meant.

"Okay, we'll be back!"

"Here we goooo!"

The carriage rattled off into the distance.

"Now then. You two give me a hand."

"Okay!"

I set about teaching them how to cook and take care of other miscellaneous tasks.

"Bubba Shield, you're good with your hands."

"Oh yeah?"

"Yeah! You're really good at cutting up fish and monsters!"

Being told that didn't feel bad at all.

"My shield has mysterious powers that make things taste better, so I can't really take the credit. When you're cooking, think about the flavor of your . . . parents' cooking, and try to recreate that."

"Okay! I'll teach you how to make something I like, Bubba Shield."

Flavor of your parents' cooking . . . I kind of stepped on a landmine with that one, but she'd replied with a smile on her face. I guess it was fine as long as she was smiling.

All said and done, I ended up being the one being taught something new, but whatever.

"Is this how you're supposed to cut the jewel?"

"Yeah. That's pretty good for your first time."

Considering that Imiya's demi-human type made him naturally good with his hands, I decided to teach him what I knew about compounding medicines and making accessories.

Chapter Nine: Hanging Out the Shield

One week had passed since I'd begun governing the territory . . . or rather, looking after a bunch of brats. The repairs on the houses had been finished for the most part, and it was time to move on to the next stage.

Just like Filo had promised, the new filolial remained a cute little thing, happy just to pull a carriage. As I'd expected, it was nice having a filolial that wasn't a chirpy little blabbermouth. One morning, while the slaves were still asleep, I tried playing a lighthearted game of fetch with the new filolial, like I had done with Filo in the past. But Filo intercepted the stick and ruined the game.

"Master! Filo is best!"

I was trying to build a rapport with the new recruit. Stay out of the way!

"Rafu!"

"Go long, Raph-chan!"

I feinted a throw and Raph-chan cast illusion magic on Filo.

"Ahh! Waaait!"

Filo sprinted off after a phantom stick that would probably go on flying forever.

The caterpillands had gotten bigger, too, and would be

ready to pull their carriages soon. They were herbivores, so we fed them the stalks of the bioplant. This in turn allowed us to get rid of excess bioplant by feeding it to the monsters. They were proving useful in a variety of ways. I could kill two birds with one stone as they say. Plus, the monster trainer must have known what he was doing when he picked them, because they were really docile and easy to handle. The only problem was their speed. They weren't very quick. So traveling around to the nearby towns and villages would be their limit.

The dunes had gotten relatively big, too, and they were already working the land here. They were really docile, too. I'd heard that wild dunes normally burrow into the ground and avoid fighting. Apparently domesticated dunes could be ordered to fight, but they weren't very strong.

Alright, I figured it was time to start peddling goods.

"Well, what do you think?"

I'd prepared two different outfits for Keel. One was a masculine set of armor that suited her preference. The other was a frilly dress meant to throw customers off guard. It was a cheap, secondhand dress, but still . . . Keel had tried the dress on and was blushing slightly while waiting for my assessment.

"Nice! I want you to blush just like that and act like a klutz while you're peddling."

"Bubba! Why do I have to do this?!"

"For money, of course. We can't round up your friends without money."

"Oh yeah . . . But still, this is . . . embarrassing, bubba . . ."

For the first round of Keel's peddling, I'd have Filo pull the carriage and I'd stay inside and observe. My plan was for Keel and Raphtalia to sell the medicine I'd made.

"Okay, Rishia, you're in charge of leveling."

"O . . . okay!"

Teaching the slaves to sell was priority number one. If we didn't do this, making money would be practically impossible. I was sure people would start talking if we hung a Shield Hero sign on a carriage and traveled around the country for three days or so. I'd been making medicines daily so that we could do this, and I was pretty sure we could heal any illness—no matter how serious—as long as I was there.

"And we're off!"

"Wai—bubba! I still get motion si—"

I ignored Keel and took off. We spent the day traveling around to several nearby towns, spending around an hour at each. With Filo running at top speed, that was possible. It had been a long time since I'd last been out hawking goods. Many of the same townspeople from before showed up, acting like they had missed me.

"So the saint was actually the Shield Hero!"

"Oh, uh . . . yeah. I figured I wouldn't get any business if people knew who I really was."

"Sorry for all you had to go through."

"No worries."

They were all just empty apologies, anyway. If I were to now cause a problem instead, there's no doubt they would all be screaming, "So you were the Shield Demon, after all!" I didn't go for the whole "customer is god" thing that Japanese people liked to push. The phrase originally came from something some Japanese folk singer said and wasn't even supposed to mean what people think it does.

"I was given a territory, so I decided to peddle medicines and other goods more extensively to help with the country's reconstruction and prepare for the coming waves. Your business is appreciated. Just look for the shield sign hanging from the carriage."

That's right. There was a sign shaped like a shield hanging on the outside of our carriage right now.

"So you're doing it for the country and our people, I see!"

Making an impression like this would lead to more customers. It might have been a good idea to have Filo's underling pull a carriage in filolial queen form, too. Then again, I didn't want to deal with the racket that would come with it. It might be fine if there was someone else willing to look after the thing, but I'm sure that would never work out.

"You hear that?! Let's give our business to the Shield Hero!"

"Yeah!"

Word of mouth sure was handy at times like these. Even good rumors spread before you knew it. I had no idea how they knew, but customers were showing up to meet us the moment we arrived at the next town.

"Hey bubba, did I do okay?"

After we finished selling our wares, Keel, looking ridiculously embarrassed, asked for my verdict.

"Yeah. Your smile can't sell quite like Raphtalia's can, but several of the customers were grinning because they thought your clumsiness was cute."

"Is that supposed to be a compliment?"

It was the same no matter what world you were in. Seeing that kind of innocence just made people feel good inside. Raphtalia's support role worked well, too. This setup should allow us to make a bundle. Even cheap, poor-quality medicinal herbs would end up being average quality if I used my shield to make the materials. Then, if I used those average-quality materials to make more advanced medicines by hand, the end product would turn out to be above average. We could expect to make a nice profit.

After vending for three days, we'd made pretty respectable earnings. We also bought up medicinal herbs along the way and I used my shield to make medicines out of them. Keel and several of the other slaves had observed our work and seemed to have the basics down, so things were going well. I'd delegate more carriages to peddling soon.

And that's when it happened.

"Well, well . . . If it isn't the Shield Hero!"

The slave trader's carriage rolled up into the village. He'd been visiting a lot lately. I guess I couldn't really complain, though, since I had him searching for the slaves from the village for me. I'd seen him talking to the slaves here, too, though. Would he even try to sell the slaves a slave of their own? I mean, I was giving them a small allowance, but come on . . .

"Did you bring me another slave from the village?"

"Unfortunately, I have brought no such thing. Yes sir."

"Then why are you here?! Go away!"

Should I throw salt over my shoulder? If he tried saying he came to mooch food because he was bored I'd knock him off his carriage.

"Your response to my showing up without a purpose sends tingles of excitement down my spine!"

"I get the feeling you're trying to turn me into your own personal chef lately."

"That was just a joke. Yes sir."

"Are you trying to pick a fight?"

"Not at all. I'm actually here to extend an invitation to the Shield Hero."

"An invitation?"

The slave trader threw his hands up into the air. Everything was theatrical with this guy. Whatever it was, it was sure to be a waste of time.

"Indeed. Since we've had so little luck finding any of the slaves here in Melromarc, I consulted a relative of mine, and I've been told that they are on the market in Zeltoble. Yes sir."

"Ah, I see."

In other words, the slave trader had found out where the slaves were, so he had come here in person to report his findings. What a bothersome guy.

"How long does it take to get there?"

"Let's see . . . Travelling by boat would normally be fastest, but that precious filolial of yours should be able to make it there in around a week and a half, I think."

A week and a half for Filo . . . That was a long way. Even so, it was closer than the Spirit Tortoise country. That reminded me of something. A while back, the other heroes had mentioned that the weapon shop in Zeltoble was really good. That meant they had traveled there. No wonder their levels weren't as high as I expected them to be back then. Their weapons were top-class, though.

"How long by boat?"

"Two weeks."

"Hmm . . ."

I glanced over at the others around the village. Everyone was busy doing his and her part to help with the reconstruction. Raphtalia was teaching some slaves the dos and don'ts of peddling, and Filo was taking a nap. The slaves that wanted to fight had been training with the old lady in the neighboring town during their free time, just like Keel.

Even if I did make the trip, I could use my portal to return to the village at night. With daily reports, things would still be manageable.

"I guess we might as well go, then."

"I thought you might say that!"

"Raphtalia, Filo, and everyone else, too! Gather 'round over here for a minute."

I called everyone, and they came swarming over.

"I'm going to be leaving for Zeltoble in just a bit, so I'll be away from the village during the day. I'll be taking Filo and . . ."

Honestly, if I just went with Filo at first, I could bring anyone else I needed afterward.

"Raphtalia, you're in charge of the village during the daytime."

"Huh? You're leaving me behind?"

"Heh heh heh . . . big sis gets to house-sit!"

"Rafu!"

Before I knew it, I ended up taking Filo *and* Raph-chan with me. Well, I guess I wouldn't have a means of transportation without Filo.

"It's only for a week, and only during the daytime. So relax."

"But still . . ."

"With how busy we've been, we've been split up more and

more lately, right? I'm leaving things up to you because I know I can count on you."

Or was it me that Raphtalia was worried about?

"Understood. If anything comes up, please return immediately."

"If it really bugs you that much, then you can just come with us every now and then."

"You're right. With such a convenient teleportation skill, there's no reason not to make use of it."

I'd be coming back each night, so Raphtalia could either go with us or stay here, depending on the day.

"Alright, we'll be back."

"Safe travels, Mr. Naofumi!"

And so I accepted the slave trader's invitation and we set out for Zeltoble.

Chapter Ten: Zeltoble

Our journey went smoothly, and we arrived at the capital city of Zeltoble.

"Pretty lively place."

We made our way noisily through the city's bustling streets. Even the Melromarc castle town wasn't this lively. Once we arrived, I went back and fetched Raphtalia and Rishia, of course. There was plenty to be uncertain about, and I wanted to be able to fight if needed. It didn't really feel so much like we had traveled to a faraway place, since we were returning to the village at night.

As for Zeltoble, how should I describe it? The country was full of stone coliseum-looking buildings that really stood out.

"What kind of country is Zeltoble, anyway? I don't really know anything about it."

"Well, then, allow me to explain! Yes sir!"

The slave trader began his explanation, full of excitement.

"Zeltoble is known as the country of merchants and mercenaries. Just like it sounds, the country runs on mercantilism and the mercenary business."

"Yeah, I got that impression."

"You know what mercenaries are, I take it. They're people

who earn money by fighting. The country also has strong ties with the guild that oversees all of the adventurer business. As a commercial hub, it single-handedly takes care of everything from distributing weapons and armor to supplying medicines and other consumables that the guild needs. Here money changes hands on a scale that is unheard of in other countries."

Looking out of the carriage as we trotted along down the streets it wasn't hard to believe. The Melromarc castle town was full of life, too, but this place felt like a real smorgasbord. The urban landscape seemed to continue on and on, alternating between bustling business districts and slums.

"The country has no king, by the way. It is administered by a council comprised of the most influential merchants."

"Oh?"

So the country was more of a republic, then? It made sense for a country that touted itself as the country of mercenaries. Maybe it was a merit-based society.

"The country also has a profound dark side, as evidenced by the saying, 'war is fought in the shadow of Zeltoble.' Do be careful, Shield Hero."

"I will."

"My family is based out of Zeltoble. The country has treated our pockets well."

"I thought that might be the case."

That reminded me, I had a nightmare the night before.

A whole crowd of creeps that looked just like the slave trader appeared out of nowhere and started trying to sell me slaves and monsters.

"Zeltoble is famous for the coliseum events that are held all around the country."

"Coliseum?"

He was talking about fighting arenas, right? They were probably pitting mercenaries against each other and betting on who would win.

"It's one of Zeltoble's top attractions. I am confident that attending one of the events would make your whole trip worth it, Shield Hero."

"I'll think about it. So where are we supposed to go now?"

"We need to get off of the main street. Turn down that back alley over there. That should work."

"Got it. Filo."

I guided Filo toward the back alley that the slave trader had pointed out. As soon as we entered the alley, a rope came flying toward Filo from out of nowhere.

"Heh heh heh . . . That sure is an unusual monster you have there, eh?"

A group of brutish-looking guys stepped out in front of us. Did these idiots not know who Filo was? Either way, they reminded me of another group of idiots I knew.

"Hiya!"

"Arghhhh!!!"

Filo kicked the fool that had recklessly tried to capture her with a lasso and sent him flying off into space.

"Huh?! What is this thing?! Stop struggling! Ugh!"

"This monster is a savage! Hurry up and wring its ne—arghhh!"

Ah, Filo had bitten down on the head of one of the idiots. He struggled for a few moments before going limp. I guess he'd passed out.

"M . . . monster!"

"Somebody save me!"

Filo spit the unconscious half-wit out and tore the rope from her neck.

"I prefer them a bit saltier. He didn't taste very healthy!"

". . ."

The thought that Filo might actually turn into a man-eating monster scared me. I had a feeling she was growing up to be a real basket case.

"Filo, people are not for eating."

"Huh?"

She was just a filolial, after all. Maybe it was delayed intellectual development. What a bother. Considering what I needed her for, less intellect would be better.

"Filo. The thing about people is . . . it's the children that taste best. They're nice and tender."

"Rafu! Rafu rafu!"

"Don't tell her that, Mr. Naofumi! And don't you encourage him, Raph-chan!"

I remembered there being a monster from some game or book that said something like that, so I tried repeating it to Filo, but she shook her head with revulsion.

"Nooo!"

"See, that kind of thing works better on Filo."

"Oh, for crying out loud. I can't tell if she actually gets it or not."

"Look, Filo. Don't go putting people in your mouth unless you're trying to scare them. It's for your own good."

"Yup! I just did it because I figured it would make them run away!"

Oh? So she actually understood intimidation and that's why she did it. I guess she was learning, after all. I couldn't have her being too smart, but understanding that much should be fine.

"What was that about being salty?"

"The taste he left in my mouth."

I just had to pray she didn't acquire a taste for humans because of that.

We stopped the carriage in front of a shop owned by an acquaintance of the slave trader, and then we got out and followed the slave trader down the alley. When we came out of the other side, I could see a huge coliseum. It was a stone

building that resembled a domed ballpark, and a brawny man stood guard at its entrance. It must have been a pretty popular place, because there was a long line of people waiting to get in.

"This way."

The slave trader continued around to the back entrance and gave a quick nod to the man standing guard, who then stepped aside and let us through.

"This place is a coliseum on the surface, but underground is a black market where slaves are sold. Yes sir."

"Oh?"

"Of course, the same is true for the vast majority of coliseums in this country. The wares offered vary with each guild. Yes sir."

"What about yours?"

"Needless to say, we deal primarily in slaves. Even so, we don't control the market exclusively."

After continuing on for a few moments, we came to a stairway leading underground. As we walked down the steps, I could hear cheers coming from above. Business must have been good.

"Business seems good on the coliseum side of things. What kind of competitions go on up there?"

"Fights, for the most part, but sometimes there are other events, such as eating contests. Yes sir."

"I'd like to get Filo in on one of those."

I wouldn't have minded seeing just how far that bottomless pit could go.

"Huh? I'm going to enter?"

"It's a possibility."

We could cut our food expenses and even make some extra cash. Then again, I was sure losing would carry significant risks.

"I'm sure that would turn out to be quite interesting. Yes sir."

The slave trader made some kind of strange signal to the brawny man. He knew I was just running with the conversation he started, right?

"So? How much further?"

"We're almost there."

A few moments after he responded, we arrived at the bottom of the stairs. I could see countless cages at the end of a corridor lined with stone walls. There were more cages here than in the slave trader's tent, and they were packed full of slaves with no regard for their race—human, demi-human, or otherwise. I could see a small room beyond the prison area. Inside, another slave trader stood waiting.

"Ohhh! If it isn't Melromarc's—"

"Ohhh! My dear uncle!"

I couldn't believe my eyes when I saw the man that the slave trader was hugging, evidently overjoyed to see him. The slave trader was an excessively obese, odd-looking gentleman who wore a tailcoat and spectacles, and this other merchant had the exact same figure. Even his face was nearly identical. The only difference between them was the design of their spectacles and tailcoats.

"Mr. Naofumi, I think there's something wrong with my eyes."

"What a coincidence. Me too."

"Fehhh . . ."

He had said it was a family business, but these two were practically clones. Shit. My nightmare had become reality. I'd seen something similar in an anime about a girl at a family-run hospital, but this . . . You wouldn't be able to tell them apart at all if they wore the same outfit.

"This is the man that invited you here, Shield Hero. My uncle. Yes sir."

"Well, well, if it isn't the Shield Hero. Pleasure to meet you. That look in your eyes is liable to steal my heart. Yes sir."

"Just stop now!"

This was bad. I was getting goosebumps. I wanted to run away immediately. The thought of having come all that way for nothing pissed me off, though, so I resisted the urge to turn around and leave.

"Now that's a voice fit for a slave driver! How thrilling! Can I interest you in taking my daughter's hand in marriage?"

I imagined a female version of the slave trader.

"Oh god, spare me."

"Spare us both! Did you call Mr. Naofumi here just to make such ridiculous remarks?!"

An angry Raphtalia rested her hand on the handle of her katana. We were searching for her friends and fellow villagers, so you couldn't hold it against her for getting upset. Lash out, Raphtalia! It'll confuse them.

"Ha ha ha! Just a joke!"

"You're bad, uncle."

"Ha ha ha! Not as bad as you are!"

The two were laughing together. I felt sick . . .

"Get back to the subject!"

"You want to talk business, already? I was hoping to develop a bit more camaraderie with the Shield Hero. Yes sir."

"Whether that happens or not depends on how you behave, uncle. Yes sir."

Yes sir! Yes sir! Yes sir! Was there no end to it? I'd seriously had enough. Could I leave yet? I didn't get the slave trader one bit. I had no idea why, but he always agreed with me no matter what I said. It made me think he had a hidden agenda, so I was always on my guard.

"Heh heh heh . . . I fear his ominous aura may bewitch me. Yes sir."

"What, am I supposed to be evil incarnate or something?"

"Oh, no. I'm simply referring to your special knack for

using slaves. It's something that we can sense."

"The Shield Hero keeps his slaves squirming just the right amount and has a charisma that would make them happily leap into the jaws of death for his sake."

"Bubba! I'm hungry!"

"Maaaster! I'm huuuungry!"

"Shield Hero! I'm hungry!"

Why did I hear their cries for food playing in the back in my head? Was that charisma? I couldn't let it get to me . . .

"Enough about that, slave trader. Tell me about those slaves I want."

"Understood. Yes sir. Uncle, what is the status of those slaves I asked you about? Yes sir."

The slave trader asked the other slave trader. The other slave trader . . . Okay, this is getting ridiculous! The Zeltoble slave trader wiped the sweat from his brow.

"About that . . . The situation has become a bit complicated. Yes sir."

"What does that mean?"

"After receiving the request for slaves from Melromarc, I did make an attempt to search, but you're looking specifically for slaves from the village of Lurolona in the Seaetto territory, are you not?"

"That's right."

The territory that I'd been given had originally belonged to

Eclair, and . . . Wait, so Raphtalia's village was called Lurolona? I didn't know that.

"Is that a problem?"

"Very much so. Yes sir."

"Wh . . . why is that?"

The color drained from Raphtalia's face as she asked. I had a bad feeling about this. Or rather, I had a feeling something had happened that was going to cause us a lot of trouble.

"The thing is . . . Slaves from the village of Lurolona in Melromarc's Seaetto territory are currently being traded for exorbitant prices in Zeltoble."

"Why?"

Why in the world would the prices of the very slaves that I wanted to buy be skyrocketing? If this was thanks to some nonsense like fate, then I wanted to find whoever pushed that fate on me and beat them to death.

But no, something as ambiguous as fate had no place in business. There was certain to be a reason for the surge in prices. Was it because the slaves had been victims of the wave? No, that couldn't be it. If that were the case, then the prices would have gone up a while back.

"When did the surge in prices begin?"

"Around one month ago, I would guess. That's when I started hearing Lurolona and the territory being mentioned in several places. Yes sir."

One month ago . . . We were still in Kizuna's world then. Taking into account the difference in the rate at which time passed in this world, that would make it right around the time that the Spirit Tortoise was defeated.

"So it's our fault?"

The Spirit Tortoise had destroyed multiple countries, and the commander-in-chief of the coalition army that defeated that Spirit Tortoise was me, the Shield Hero. The Shield Hero's star slave, Raphtalia, was from Lurolona. It was only natural that the hero who had disappeared into another world in pursuit of the villain, and that hero's slave, would gather attention. Since Raphtalia personally wasn't as well-known as I was, the focus ended up on her village and the fact that she was a demi-human. This was the result. I might have been overthinking things, but it made sense.

"As to be expected of the Shield Hero! Yes sir."

"Shit! I was right?"

"We can only speculate, but I believe the likelihood is quite high."

Damn. To think our heroic deeds had backfired . . .

"If I remember correctly, it all began when a certain merchant offered a lofty reward for the delivery of the slaves. After that, talk of the Shield Hero and his Lurolona slave gradually began to spread. Before long, any slave said to be a Lurolona demi-human—despite being unable to tell whether they truly were or not—began to fetch a high price. Yes sir."

So prices were skyrocketing now even though it had become difficult to tell whether the slaves being sold were actually from Raphtalia's village. I'd seen this before. It wasn't limited to slaves. This was what they referred to as a bubble in stock market terms. You could never know when it would crash.

It was easier to think of it in terms of Japanese yen. Every now and then, the price of yen would begin to rise for some mysterious reason, so everyone would start buying up yen. As a result, the value of the yen would rise even further. There would still be people selling yen, of course, but the majority of people would be buying, and so the price would continue to rise. Right now, the slaves from Raphtalia's village, Lurolona, were that yen.

"Even so, demi-human slaves are everywhere you look. No matter how much of a hot item they are right now, there would just be too many fakes for that trend to continue, right?"

"Indeed. That's why it has become a requirement that the slaves speak not only the official language of Melromarc, but also the unique dialect of the Seaetto territory. Yes sir."

Surely that was something that they could just be taught. Then again, the language that you grew up speaking tended to be more deeply ingrained than most people realized. I had a friend once that was always speaking a certain regional dialect, even though he thought he was speaking standard Japanese. It would be obvious to anyone that knew the difference.

That probably had something to do with the rising prices, too. Since it was only slaves from Lurolona in Melromarc's Seaetto territory, they were kind of like limited-edition products.

"I can't believe this . . ."

Raphtalia seemed to grow dizzy. She stumbled backward a few steps and I reached out and held her in place.

"So what? Is the money that I prepared enough to buy them?"

"To be honest, that's not likely. Yes sir."

"The slaves should be appearing in the underground auctions shortly. Yes sir. I believe it would be best for the Shield Hero to go and observe the situation for himself. Yes sir."

I couldn't imagine a situation so bad that even the slave traders couldn't afford to buy up the slaves. This place sure looked like whoever was running it was filthy rich.

"Fehhh . . ."

Even Rishia's whimper sounded frustrated.

"Well let's have a look, then."

"Right this way. Yes sir."

We put on our cloaks and followed the slave traders out into the Zeltoble night. We made our way through the back alleys, passing a variety of shops before arriving at a tavern. The slave trader approached the counter and spoke to the man standing behind it.

"We'll have a bottle of Goodnight Binary."

The tavern master furrowed his brow and cast a stern glance at us.

"Anything to mix that with?"

"Loose Winner Money. Yes sir."

The tavern master stepped aside so that we could join him behind the counter and then signaled us to follow him. He led us to a door in the back, and we continued through the doorway and down a stairway leading to the basement. Was that some kind of secret password back there? Before long, we ended up in a large hall and were shown to our seats in what appeared to be a special section.

"This is the venue for tonight. Yes sir."

"Ah . . . I see."

So this was the underground arena where they showcased illegal fights? It looked more like a place where you might see the opera or something. Or maybe a concert by some Japanese idol was more likely.

"First, the Shield Hero should familiarize himself with the hand signals used to make a purchase during the auction."

Ugh, what a hassle. The slave trader began to lecture me on the hand signals used to indicate different amounts of money. He started with the cues given to the auctioneer for increasing the current bid by one copper, silver, or gold, and then moved on to the cues for increasing the bid by two, five, and even ten times. The auction began before I could finish learning them all.

The races of the slaves that appeared on the stage varied from human to demi-human to therianthrope. The slaves were divided up into a range of categories—children, adults, the elderly, men, women, etc.—and even minute details, such as lineage, seemed to be treated as part of the product package. On top of that, a detailed introduction included things like place of birth, level, and aptitude for magic.

"Our next slave here has won seven out of ten fights in the coliseum."

A rather well-built slave was standing in the spotlight.

"A coliseum record? So he's a mercenary?"

That wasn't a very impressive fight record. Just a bit above average, maybe.

"Yes sir. He amassed a sizable amount of debt and is participating in the coliseum as a slave in order to repay that debt."

"Ah . . ."

I looked over at Raphtalia. She seemed to be looking over the slaves that were up on the stage.

"Next up is the showpiece of tonight's auction! A demi-human slave from Lurolona!"

The spotlight suddenly moved to the next slave. That was the showpiece? The slave looked like a demi-human child and seemed to be trembling ever so slightly.

"No."

Raphtalia shook her head.

"There was no such child in my village. One of the children did look similar, but that's not her."

"So it's a fake . . ."

No one could tell the difference, anyway. Lurolona slaves were the hot item, so you could just dress it up as that. If you managed to fetch a hefty sum for it, that would be the end of it, even if they did find out otherwise afterward.

"We'll start the bidding at 20 gold pieces!"

Twenty gold?! That high?!

"Twenty-five gold!"

"Thirty gold!"

The price continued to surge. I knew prices were up, but come on! And for a fake?! Even if we did find the real thing, there was no way I would be able to afford it.

"Fehhh . . ."

"Mr . . . Naofumi? I think your face is probably even paler than mine."

"Uhhh . . . yeah . . ."

It got worse. The dud slave currently being bid on was considerably emaciated. We could try waiting until the trend had run its course and prices dropped, but if they were all in this kind of shape then the real Lurolona slaves might very well be dead by then.

But wait, this slave might have received special care thanks to the price surge, and yet it still looked frail. It wasn't unthinkable that one of the real ones might be treated carelessly and end up dead. Not to mention, it was highly likely that they had been abused, considering the condition that Raphtalia, Keel, and the other slaves had been in.

In all honesty, the situation looked really bad. We probably needed to recover the slaves as quickly as possible.

But damn . . . Solving this problem with the money we had just wasn't realistic, and the queen of Melromarc made it clear that providing monetary aid wouldn't be possible at the moment. With the reconstruction efforts after such extensive damage, the funds just weren't there.

"Even if we can tell the real ones apart from the fakes . . . this . . ."

The thought of giving up crossed my mind, but Raphtalia and Raph-chan were both looking at me expectantly. I couldn't say no to those eyes.

"We need to figure out a way to make some quick money and buy up the slaves fast."

Should we buy them one at a time using the money we made from peddling? No, that would take too long. Besides, the amount of money we needed was on a completely different level. We'd also needed to be here at the underground auctions every night to look for the real slaves, and even if we went the route of negotiating with the merchants that purchased them, we would need to prepare enough money to match the purchasing price at the bare minimum.

Maybe I could take advantage of my position as the Shield Hero? No, that wouldn't work. The prices were already skyrocketing. If news spread that someone famous wanted the slaves, prices would surge even higher. Perhaps we should break into the homes of the merchants that bought them and confiscate the slaves? That wouldn't work, either. The slave curse could be set to kill, so that was too dangerous. What about crashing the bubble by spreading nasty rumors about the Lurolona slaves? That would take too long even if it did work.

I could go crying for help to the demi-human country of Siltvelt, or maybe Shieldfreeden, and have them purchase the slaves on my behalf. That would be a last resort, though. I wanted to avoid it if at all possible. They might end up holding the demi-human slaves ransom and force me to go to Siltvelt. I was in the middle of preparing for the next wave. The risk of getting caught up in some kind of mess with Siltvelt was just too high. Even worse, we might get caught up in some kind of big conspiracy that affected Raphtalia and the others, too.

I needed to make a ridiculous amount of money, and I needed to do it fast. Surely there had to be a way. We were in Zeltoble—the country of mercenaries and merchants . . . and underground auctions. Now that I thought about it, the slave trader had been whispering something about making money just a second ago.

"Hey, slave trader."

"What is it? Yes sir."

"How much money can you make fighting in the coliseum?"

We may have been temporarily weakened at the moment, but we were still a lot stronger than your average adventurer, knight, or warrior. I could conceal my identity as a hero and participate in a coliseum fight that allowed betting. Then, if I bet on myself . . . This wasn't horse racing, but it would be like betting on a horse with 100 to 1 odds and winning.

"Payouts range from extravagant to insignificant. Yes sir."

"I'm interested in that extravagant. If we concealed our true identities and fought in a coliseum that allowed betting . . . Let's say we managed to win in the most dangerous one. Could we make enough money to buy the slaves at these inflated prices?"

"Hold on just a moment. Yes sir."

The slave trader began whispering back and forth with his uncle. A few moments later . . .

"It's not impossible. That said, I can't guarantee you will make it out alive. It's quite likely to prove rather dangerous."

"Hmph . . . I'm not worried about that."

I mean, come on. If we were talking about a risk of death, that's something we had faced countless times, and we were still here. I'd fought against the waves, against conspiracy, and against religion. I'd fought against the Spirit Tortoise, and I'd even fought in another world. I had been on the verge of death time and again, and that wasn't going to stop any time soon. If that was the only problem, then I'd face that risk again fighting in the coliseum for the sake of Raphtalia's village.

"..."

Raphtalia looked at me with a mix of expectation and apprehension on her face. Raph-chan was doing the same. Rishia was panicking over what my decision would be, and Filo had her head cocked to the side as if she had no idea what was going on.

"Don't worry, Raphtalia. I'll get your friends back, no matter what."

"Mr. Naofumi . . ."

Raphtalia's expression transformed into one of relief upon hearing my words. I knew this kind of behavior didn't really fit my image, but I had plenty of reason to do this for Raphtalia.

"That said, the prices of the slaves have skyrocketed, and we don't have enough money to buy them right now. I can't say I like the thought of doing this, but we'll just have to buy Raphtalia's friends with money earned by fighting in the coliseum. I'm sorry it has to be dirty money, but it's the only way."

Raphtalia nodded decisively. And so it was settled—we would use the slave trader's connections to take up the gauntlet and fight in the vicious coliseum.

Chapter Eleven: Slave Hunters

Before anything else, we needed to get the money for the wager. When it came to betting, the more money you could wager, the better. Also, if they figured out that I was the Shield Hero, the amount we could make would plummet. That said, I had to get the capital we would need to wager to win it all in one stroke . . .

I considered raising money by offering express transportation to Melromarc using my portal. That was one way to make money in an online game that I had played once. A one-way trip between Melromarc and Zeltoble took two weeks, so there were sure to be people who would jump on the chance to be able to make that same trip instantaneously.

The problem was pricing. Even if people were willing to spend more, you'd probably be lucky to charge somewhere between one and five gold pieces for the fare. Generating positive word of mouth would also be important for getting customers. Smuggling could end up being a problem, but that could be solved by working with whoever was responsible for inspections in Melromarc. Still, making money doing something like that would draw far too much attention. Another issue was only being able to send six people each hour. I wanted to avoid going that route, if possible.

We returned to the slave trader's underground market. I shook my head slowly at a worried-looking Rishia.

"What's up?"

"Fehh . . ."

"Relax, Rishia. I don't plan on making you fight."

"Hmm . . ."

I wasn't sure if it was just poor air circulation or what, but Filo seemed to be less energetic than usual.

"Even if we tried making money by placing some of the stuff we got from Kizuna's world on the black market, doing so in an efficient manner would take time."

We would have to go through the trouble of demonstrating that the items were something worth getting excited about, like we had done with the spirit water. We had the Scroll of Return items, but there were only so many. Even if we talked up the fact that they allowed the user to teleport to the dragon hourglasses, and then set out to produce more, there were just too few to start with. There were the items that could check defeated monsters for drops, but those were still being analyzed. We would need to mass-produce them, and while we had figured out how to do that, it still wasn't clear if they would function properly in this world.

"In that case, I will take care of entering you into the coliseum fights. Yes sir."

"Alright. I don't care if it's dangerous or whatever—just

make sure it's the one we can make the most money off of."

"I look forward to seeing what kind of performance a determined Shield Hero will give. Yes sir!"

"I'm in a bad mood right now. Get out of my sight before I decide to give you a piece of my mind."

"The way your eyes suddenly fill with such sinister intent . . . It sends tingles of excitement down my spine!"

"I guess we should head back to the village for the time being."

The situation had changed. Even if we had a plan now, we still needed to go back to the village first.

"Yes . . . I agree. We should probably explain the situation to Keel and the others."

"That won't be an easy talk . . ."

It wouldn't be fun telling them that we needed to make a ridiculous amount of money to rescue their friends and there was no telling if we'd even be successful. Then again, only four of them were actually from Lurolona, and that was counting Keel. Regardless, the slaves' eyes sparkled with pride for the hard work they were doing to rebuild their village.

"Either way, we need to go back. Later, slave trader."

"I look forward to seeing you again tomorrow. Yes sir."

Truthfully, I'd rather not see him again, but this was for the village. I gave him the obligatory wave while registering the portal location and then we teleported back to the village.

We arrived back in the village, and I was left speechless.

"What . . . the hell?!"

"What's going on?!"

It wasn't just me. Raphtalia, Filo, Rishia, and even Raph-chan were all at a loss for words. The first thing that jumped out at me was the sight of flames pouring out of a building as several soldiers, who had probably been on standby, shouted and ran out of the village with their weapons in hand.

"Hey! What's going on?!"

"Oh! Shield Hero! It's the slave hunters! They're attacking the village!"

I could see a hint of relief in the soldiers' faces when they saw me. Slave hunters?! Slave hunters had shown up at a time like this?! You've got to be shitting me! Like I told the slave trader, I was in a bad mood. And I was going to destroy these bastards.

"No way!"

"Raphtalia!"

Raphtalia gripped her katana and took off running toward the source of the commotion.

"Filo! You go with Raphtalia and annihilate the slave hunters! Rishia, you see to the wounded and protect anyone that can't fight. You soldiers go report to Eclair in the neighboring town!"

"Okaaay!"

"Fehhh!"

"That's already been taken care of!"

That was a relief. They were handling the situation better than I would have expected. I chased after Raphtalia, who had run off into the distance. That's when I noticed that the village was completely surrounded by slave hunters. There were ten slaves in the village. A good number of soldiers were keeping guard over the village, too. There seemed to be quite a few slave hunters, but it was impossible to fully grasp the situation in the dark of the night. That didn't matter . . . We would do what had to be done.

"Struggling is useless!" yelled one of the attackers.

"Hiya!" Raphtalia shouted as she cut down the attacking slave hunter in the blink of an eye.

"Arghhh!"

Blood erupted from the slave hunter's body as he crumpled forward onto the ground with a thud. I was only guessing, but he probably hadn't classed up yet. Or maybe going up against Raphtalia's katana would have been an exercise in futility even if he had already classed up.

"Let's protect the village! Come on!"

I could hear Keel's voice. She was armed, and it looked like she was fighting off the slave hunters successfully, along with the other slaves from the village. I had been a little bit worried, but it seemed like the slaves were holding their own. Perhaps being raised as my slaves had paid off. They had gotten about as strong as Raphtalia had been before she classed up. I wanted to believe that they would have no problem standing up to the likes of slave hunters or bandits in terms of abilities.

"So you want to fight, eh?! Then I won't hold back! Gahhh!"

The slave hunter pointed his sword at Keel and . . . suddenly a hole opened up in the ground below him and he fell in, leaving only his head exposed. Just as I was wondering what had happened, Imiya's head popped up out of the dirt.

"Thanks, Imiya!"

Imiya gave Keel a thumbs-up. So that's what it was . . . Imiya had dug a pit.

"Gweeeeeh!"

Filo Underling #1 was helping defend the slaves and gave the slave hunter a fierce kick. The other monsters seemed to be putting up a good fight, too.

"Now!"

Keel and Imiya had left themselves open to attack and the remaining slave hunters rushed at them.

"Air Strike Shield!"

I blocked their path with a shield.

"Shooting Star Shield!"

Then I cast a force field around us and stepped in between Keel and the slave hunters.

"Bubba!"

"Looks like you guys are putting up a pretty good fight."

"You bet! This time we *will* protect the village!"

Keel's eyes were filled with determination. That's right. She was no longer a poor, helpless slave that had to rely on others to protect her. Now she had the strength to fight back and protect the others in the village against the injustice of the slave hunters.

"We can fight back now thanks to you, bubba!"

"That's good to hear. I see you're helping out, too, Imiya."

"Oh . . . yeah . . ."

Imiya looked proud of himself.

"Hiyaaa!"

At that very moment, Raphtalia flew in like a bat out of hell and mowed down the attacking slave hunters. She was emanating an aura of bloodlust. The slave hunters weren't dead, but their fighting days had come to an end.

"Rafuuu!"

Raph-chan's fur was standing on end as she moved in sync with Raphtalia, assisting her in combat. She kept the enemy disoriented with her illusions while biting one here and batting another with her tail there.

"Alright! Everyone! Now that I'm here, you can all relax. Get out there and show these thieves that attacked your village what you've got!"

"Okay!"

Slaves and monsters alike all whooped together in response.

"Ugh . . . To think that the Shield Hero would show up now! Wasn't he supposed to be gone?!"

One of the slave hunters mumbled to himself as he struggled against Raphtalia, their blades locked. He seemed to have some experience in combat—he used a combination of magic and swordsmanship and he was putting up a good fight. The guy was actually fairly strong.

"It sounds like you were waiting for me to be gone to make your move. Unfortunately for you, heroes have the ability to teleport."

I guess they were foolish enough to think that I wouldn't drop in to check on the village while I was away.

"Raphtalia!"

"What?"

"Can you produce a light bright enough to illuminate the whole village? I want to see how many slave hunters there are. It would also serve as a flare to signal the others in the neighboring town."

"Leave it to me!"

Raphtalia thrust the slave hunter away from her and took several steps back to join me. She sheathed her katana and began to cast a spell.

"Filo!"

"Yup! I'll protect everyone!"

While Raphtalia was casting her magic, Filo launched a flurry of kicks at the slave hunters. Keel and the other combat division slaves followed up, finishing off one slave hunter after another. Even so, it would take someone of Filo's level to make such quick work of the more skilled slave hunters, so the slaves were slowly losing ground.

"Shooting Star Shield! Air Strike Shield! Second Shield! Attack Support!"

I stood in front of everyone and took the brunt of the slave hunters' attacks while casting skills to protect Filo and the other slaves. I grabbed the arm of one of the slave hunters and threw him toward Filo.

"Gah!"

Naturally, Filo finished the slave hunter off with a swift kick.

"Rafu!"

Raph-chan's tail puffed up as she assisted with Raphtalia's incantation.

"As the source of your power, I command you! Let the true way be revealed once more! Flood the area with light!"

"Drifa Light!"

Raphtalia conjured up a ball of light and hurled it up into the sky. The magical light lit up the village like a flare. That was sure to signal the soldiers in the neighboring village, who would then come to our aid.

As the light made its way high up into the sky, I counted how many slave hunters were in the village. One, two, three . . . There sure were a lot of them. Just counting the ones that had been hidden in the darkness, there were a lot of them. I was thinking maybe thirty, but that wasn't even close. There had to be at least fifty just in the area surrounding the village.

There were only five slaves here—including Raphtalia—that were originally from this village. Just how many people did they round up to come capture them? I couldn't believe the lengths that people would go to. Then again, it was safe to assume you could get at least 30 gold pieces per slave if you captured them and sold them off in Zeltoble. I guess the allure of making a quick fortune would attract numbers.

"Hiya!"

Raphtalia leapt forward and slashed at the slave hunters immediately upon finishing her incantation. It was almost scary, the way she was fighting. I guess it was to be expected, seeing as how this place was precious to her—a place worth protecting.

"Brave Blade! Crossing Mists!"

With a katana in each hand, Raphtalia relentlessly cut down one slave hunter after another. She moved gracefully, as if she were dancing on the battlefield. It really was a thing of beauty. Surely I wasn't the only one who thought so.

"Raphtalia . . . You're amazing . . ."

"She looks like she's dancing!"

The villagers were all entranced by the sight of Raphtalia fighting.

"Keep your eyes on the enemy!"

I snapped back to reality upon being reprimanded by Raphtalia and struck back at the attacking slave hunters.

"Ugh . . ."

"What are you fools doing!"

A man who seemed to be the slave hunters' boss appeared. I could see his armor had lost its sheen.

"That's—"

Raphtalia, Keel, and the rest of the slaves from the village were all at a loss for words. What was it? Did they know this guy?

"How long do you idiots plan on fooling around?! You've turned our plan into a failure! You there! How many have you caught?"

"Umm . . . well, we . . ."

The subordinate slave hunter's voice trailed off and the boss let out a loud click of the tongue in angry disapproval. Then more slave hunters that looked like they knew how to handle themselves came pouring in from outside of the village in droves.

"Tsk! To think that the Shield Hero would show up now . . . That wasn't in the plan! Still, he may be a hero, but he's only the Shield Hero. Just wait for him to let his guard down and then snatch up one or two of those brats!"

So this guy was like one of those bosses that always makes ridiculous demands, I guess. But forget about that . . . I was more concerned with the way that Raphtalia and the others had reacted.

"This guy . . . This is the guy . . ."

Keel's face was more distorted with anger now than it was just a moment ago. Raphtalia remained calm, but I could still tell that she was absolutely furious. The fact that her tail was puffed up more than it ever had been before made that clear.

"Raphtalia. Keel. You know this guy?"

I turned to face the slave hunter boss and readied my shield.

"Yes. The Melromarc soldier that came to our village to capture us and sell us into slavery . . . and that killed the village's remaining adults . . . That's this man!"

"Well now! I never would have thought that the little raccoon brat who got away back then would end up with the Shield Hero!"

The slave hunter boss—the former Melromarc soldier—remembering Raphtalia, casually readied his sword. He probably had a pretty good idea how to use that thing, too. Keel and the others wouldn't likely stand much of a chance against him at their current level.

"Mr. Iwatani! Are you okay?!"

Just then, Eclair and the Melromarc soldiers came running up.

"You?!"

"Raphtalia says they're Melromarc soldiers. You know anything about that, Eclair?"

"Yes. They're the soldiers that came here hunting for demi-humans after the territory was destroyed by the wave. I heard that they fled from the powers that be at the time, once they'd found out that you had proven your innocence."

"I see. So basically, they're former soldiers that fled the country before they got their punishment."

The former soldiers turned slave hunters apparently didn't appreciate my wording, because they were all glaring at me now.

So what to do? We had to be careful about Keel and the others that hadn't classed up yet. Thankfully, no one had been caught by the slave hunters yet. But the enemy had come to attack in droves. Even if I had nothing to worry about myself, I couldn't be sure that the others would make it out unscathed. It was only physically possible for me to grab maybe three or four enemies at one time. By my estimates, there were easily fifty or more slave hunters there, so it would be difficult to protect Keel and the others. That said, it seemed like only a select few of them had classed up and knew what they were doing. Those were the ones right here in front of me, so . . . maybe I could manage, after all?

This was also the perfect chance for Raphtalia and Keel. The very villains that had ruined their lives had rolled right up onto their doorstep. Some of the slave hunters had realized they were at a disadvantage and tried to run, but Keel and Raphtalia were not about to let that happen.

"Tsk! You've forgotten your place, shield! They'll be after us now since you had to show up!"

"Like I care? Besides, I can't imagine there having been a single good reason for you lowlifes to run around capturing territory residents just because the governor died."

"Oh, but there was! Or do you not know?"

Huh? He was being serious. Ohhh . . . I get it.

"Are you referring to the dogma of the Church of the Three Heroes cult? Sorry, buddy, but that propaganda won't fly anymore."

"You bastard!"

He sure could yell, but he hadn't tried to attack yet. Maybe he realized that it would be pointless to attack me? No, his eyes gave him away. He was planning something.

"Take this!"

The slave hunters shot flaming arrows at various buildings around the village. What a pain . . .

"Put out those fires immediately!"

Shit! So this is what people meant when they said fighting against the odds. But it wasn't like we were just going to stand by and watch.

"Raphtalia! Keel! Can you handle that guy?"

"Yes . . ."

"We'll protect everyone!"

Raphtalia nodded calmly, and Keel cried out with determination.

"Good. Then you two make those dirt bags pay!"

I quietly uttered an incantation and cast support magic on Raphtalia and Keel.

"Zweite Aura!"

With all of their stats boosted, Raphtalia and Keel charged at the slave hunter boss.

"Filo! You give any slave hunters you find around the village a good kick. Same goes for your underling!"

"Okaaay!"

"Gweh!"

I sent Filo and her Underling Filolial #1 to take care of the slave hunters that were still lingering around the village.

"Mr. Iwatani!"

"Eclair, don't even think about holding back just because you used to serve together. Put an end to these traitors!"

"I plan to!"

Eclair and her soldiers nodded and took a fighting stance.

"It seems like you lowlifes thought this was going to be easy, but today is not your lucky day. You probably expected to crush the villagers, but the only thing getting crushed tonight is you!"

"Come now, it's time to confess your sins . . . and pay the price, you scumbags!"

The rest of the fight was completely one-sided, and we captured a ton of the slave hunters. The boss that Raphtalia had defeated was still alive, although just barely. I thought they had killed him, but apparently they stopped just short of it.

"You're not going to finish him?"

"No . . ."

Raphtalia and the others apparently wanted to hand him over to the authorities and have him punished.

"Now then . . ."

I looked at the hordes of slave hunters tied up and scattered all across the village square. To think they had rounded up and brought so many . . . and the whole lot of them were lowlife trash.

"Damn! They're monsters!" yelled one of the slave hunters.

"You told us we would be able to handle them regardless of their level advantage!"

The slave hunter subordinates were spouting off begrudging complaints at their leaders. That's a lowlife for you—blaming it on his superiors when he fails.

"That's just too bad for you, scumbags. You want the heroes to protect your world? Well, this is part of that."

"Hmph . . ."

"We won . . . Everybody! We won!"

Keel and the rest of the slaves from the village let out a big hurrah in celebration of our victory. Imiya and some kid, who seemed to like monsters, looked like they were getting in on the celebration as well. It didn't matter if they were originally from the village or not—they'd all experienced a similar kind of trauma. Their victory against the vile slave hunters would be good for them.

"Yes, we won. I think that this time, for sure . . . we took back the flag we lost that day," whispered Raphtalia, while gripping her katana firmly and staring off into the distance.

"Flag, huh? You really want a flag that bad?"

"That's not what I meant . . ."

"Raphtalia, this flag . . ."

Eclair interrupted before I could finish, speaking to Raphtalia with a remorseful look on her face.

"I'm sorry. This should have never happened while I was here . . ."

"Don't worry about it, Eclair. But tell me, do you know if there was a flag flying in this village?"

"Huh? Umm, yes, it was a flag presented as a gift to the village by my father."

Aha, so that's the flag that Raphtalia had been talking about.

"Eclair, why don't you fly that flag again as a reward for their victory?" I suggested.

"Mr. Naofumi?" Raphtalia exclaimed in surprise.

"All of the hard work that everyone has put in since coming back has finally paid off. Raphtalia, this is a new beginning for your village, is it not?"

Raphtalia closed her eyes for a moment as if she were reminiscing about the past, and then she opened them again and nodded.

"You're right. I'd like that."

Besides, Keel seemed to be oddly fixated on that flag, too. I'd made her that kid's lunch with the flag on it on a whim once, and she had been completely ecstatic. She held on to the flag like it was a piece of treasure. Now I could see that the flag had special meaning for them.

"Alright then."

I put the conversation with Raphtalia and Eclair on hold and looked over at the slave hunters we'd gathered up.

"What should we do about these scumbags?"

"Ordinarily they would be taken to the castle, where they would then receive a fitting punishment."

"Hmm . . . But with this many of them working together in a coordinated effort . . . ?"

"Of course, it is a grievous crime, in my opinion. Most likely they will have their levels reset and then be held in involuntary servitude."

"Not executed?"

"Normally the principal offenders would be, but . . ."

Eclair looked long and hard at the faces of the former soldiers, who would likely be categorized as the principal offenders.

"These men come from some of Melromarc's more respectable families. Even if they were sentenced to death, it would most likely be a very lengthy process."

"Meaning that if the queen forced it, there would be backlash from the nobility, putting her position at stake?"

Eclair nodded in response. I guess even monarchies had to deal with annoyances like this. Maybe that was why the former soldiers seemed to be taking the whole thing rather lightly. Those scumbags . . . Did they not realize the situation they were in?

"A great deal of emphasis is placed on lineage. If worse comes to worst, the queen could be replaced with someone of the same bloodline favored by the nobility. It's not unthinkable, considering that the country is currently in a weakened state due to the Spirit Tortoise incident."

"Meaning . . . a distant relative?"

That was probably it. It's not like the queen's two daughters would be the only royal family. There would be the head family, and then there would be branches and all of that. The nobility could just pick one of the relatives that aligned with their purposes and have them lead a revolt, seizing the castle and replacing the queen.

"The nobility would probably come up with some kind of pretext like 'our poor soldiers that went missing because the country was a mess finally show up only to be apprehended based on unfounded accusations!'"

"Yeah, they would, even though they're as guilty as can be. What a pain. Should we just kill them off and say that they struggled?"

The mere fact that they were alive would be a hazard with trash like this. I had absolutely no doubt that it would come back to bite us later. In that case, it would make way more sense to just have them take their leave from this world.

"If you used your authority as a hero, that could probably work. However, I would personally prefer that you abide by the country's rules."

"Even if it means a long, drawn-out process that ends up getting them involuntary servitude instead of a death sentence?"

And for something that happened on Eclair's father's territory, their victims would be turning in their graves.

"I get what you're saying. I agree that their actions are unforgivable, but even so . . ."

"You would think that the nobility in charge of the area where the crime happened would get to decide how it was dealt with."

"They would . . . normally. We could indeed decide the punishment of their subordinates."

"Execution, without question."

There was no need to consult the queen.

"Why did so many slave hunters show up here in the first place? Death penalty or not, we need to make them talk—"

"About that . . . I needed to talk to the slaves, so this is the perfect chance. Everyone gather 'round!"

I went on to explain about how Lurolona slaves were being handled in Zeltoble.

"So in short . . . you're saying that they were planning to capture the village slaves and sell them off in Zeltoble while the prices are high?!" Eclair was glaring at the slave hunters with an even more threatening look than before.

"No way . . . Does that mean that we can't get everyone back?" Keel stared at me imploringly, with a look of worry in her eyes.

"Don't worry. I'll do whatever it takes to buy them back. The possibility of more of their kind showing up again is what we have to worry about."

I guess problems like this came along with a sudden rise in prices. We had to figure out a way to put an end to the overvaluation of slaves from this village. I had a whole new set of annoyances to deal with now. In the meantime, I needed to prioritize toughening up the slaves. They still weren't quite ready to class up.

"Bubba! If you're going to compete in the coliseum, then let us compete, too!"

They must have been emboldened by their victory, because Keel and the other slaves who had shown a willingness to fight stepped forward.

"Hmm . . . We could have you compete, but it would be risky . . ."

That was a possibility. But taking them to Zeltoble and having someone figure out they were Lurolona slaves is what really worried me. If they ended up getting abducted in a crowded place like that, finding them would be difficult. Slaves could be tracked using the slave curse, but people weren't stupid. They would probably overwrite the slave curses without hesitation.

I wanted to go all out—get the money and buy up all of the slaves in one fell swoop. This was a matter of urgency, and I had a feeling we were well past being able to raise the money by gradually working our way through the coliseum competitions. But we needed to gather enough money for a massive wager to make this plan work. There was no point if we couldn't bet big.

Of course, it was a given that we wouldn't lose, being a hero and his party. But too many wins would make the bet less lucrative. I had almost zero experience with horse racing or anything like that, but I knew that betting on a clear winner wouldn't make you much money, because everyone else would be betting on it, too. That's why you wanted to bet big and win big before the word spread.

We could sell something of value . . . If only we had a bunch of gold or something. As the thought crossed my mind, I looked at the slave hunters and suddenly it hit me.

"I just came up with a good idea."

I had a big, mischievous grin on my face. Raphtalia must have noticed and had a good idea of what was coming, because she rolled her eyes.

"Mr. Naofumi, you're going to try something crazy, aren't you?"

"Yeah. I'm going to go fetch a certain someone. I'll be back in about an hour, so wait here."

I used my portal to teleport back to Zeltoble on my own. And then . . .

"Oh? Shield Hero, I thought you returned to the village? Yes sir."

"I did, but something came up. I want you to come with me."

Around an hour later, after the cool down expired on my portal skill, I returned to the village again with the slave trader and his flunky.

"Mr. Naofumi? Umm . . . where did you . . ."

Raphtalia was looking at the slave trader with her head cocked to the side in confusion. The other villagers were also watching, curious as to what was about to happen. Eclair and the soldiers were looking at the slave trader with their brows furrowed.

"Eclair. The responsibility for these scumbags technically hasn't been given to the authorities yet, right?"

"That's true, but . . . What are you planning to do, Mr. Iwatani?"

"Just be quiet and watch. I came up with the perfect way to take care of this."

"Be careful, Eclair. This is where Mr. Naofumi usually says something completely outrageous."

Hey, what happened to Raphtalia believing in me? Then again, I was well aware of the fact that I tended to do crazy things at times like these. She had winced when she heard about how I sold the spirit water. Kizuna had been really proud of the whole thing, though, so she'd just acted normal and didn't say anything.

"You know what will happen to you if you even think about touching us, right?"

The slave hunter boss was trying to intimidate me. The scumbag probably thought he would get off easy, and he certainly didn't think he was in danger of dying or anything. Surely we wouldn't do anything that would endanger the queen's position, right?

"Relax. I'm going to let you all live, just like you want."

The underlings all showed visible signs of relief when they heard that. The boss, on the other hand, seemed perplexed. I guess he wasn't as dumb as he looked.

"Slave trader, can you make these scumbags my slaves?"

"I can. Yes sir."

"Surely you don't intend on turning them into slaves and forcing them to help develop the territory or protect it from other slave hunters, do you?" Eclair suddenly chimed in.

Did Eclair really think I would do something so lax? Then again, it wasn't a bad idea. I could use the slave curse to set harsh restrictions that would kill them if they disobeyed orders. But there was a fatal flaw in that plan.

"And just let them wait for a chance to have someone they know remove the curse? I'm not that dumb."

Several of the slave hunters must have been thinking about doing exactly that, because they had been grinning slyly, but now they were looking confused.

"The reason I'm making them my slaves is to force them into my party and to make the next part of my plan easier."

"Wh . . . what are you going to do?" Rishia asked, looking at me nervously.

Rishia was here? She had just kind of faded into the background for a while there.

"I'm going to take them to Zeltoble. And then I'm going to sell them. As slaves, of course."

"Wha—"

Eclair was at a loss for words. Raphtalia sighed in dismay. That's right. What we needed right now was a huge sum of money so that we could go all in and win big at the coliseum. Every little bit counted.

Of course, if we sold the slave hunters off as slaves, there would likely be some Melromarc nobility ready to rescue them by buying them back. There was even a risk of them getting away before that, if we weren't careful. The slave hunters probably knew that, because they still didn't look too worried. They probably figured that they wouldn't fetch a very good price anyway. But I wasn't going to let them off that easy.

"Slave trader. Do you happen to have any relatives in Siltvelt?"

"Of course. Yes sir."

"Good. In that case, I want to sell these scumbags to those relatives. Let's see . . . Tell them that they're being offered by the Shield Hero and that they're the slave hunters that captured the demi-human slaves originally from the Seaetto territory."

The slave hunters' faces suddenly grew pale. The slave trader, on the other hand, was looking at me with the biggest smile on his face that I had seen so far. First there was the fact that they were being offered by the Shield Hero, which would raise their value, since the country worshipped the Shield Hero. Then there was the fact that they were notorious criminals that had slaughtered or enslaved countless demi-humans from the Seaetto territory, which was supposed to be a symbol of friendship between Melromarc and Siltvelt.

How would the Siltvelt demi-humans view such people? It would be infuriating. The living embodiment of evil to them, I'm sure. If such a person showed up on the slave market and was purchased . . . what would happen to them? It went without saying that they would be beaten and abused as a form of stress relief, just like Raphtalia and the other slaves from her village had been by the nobility in this country. This is what it meant to pay for something with your life.

"That . . . that's not even funny! Selling us to Siltvelt?! That's not something a hero would do!"

The slave hunter boss started raving.

"It's not as bad as a country's soldiers killing and selling off their own citizens. I'm sure you scumbags have a pretty good idea of the hell that these slaves have been through."

"This is different! There's no reason we should have to go through that!"

"So what . . . It's okay to force it on them, but it's not cool when it's forced on you?"

I was at a loss for words. There's always a chance that soldiers will die in war, yet the thought of being tortured and dying a painful death as a slave frightened these guys. Just how pathetic were they?

"Here's a quote that I was relatively fond of back in my world, just for you scumbags: 'Don't shoot at people unless you're ready to be shot.'"

It was something that some hard-boiled crime fiction detective had said. If you weren't ready to suffer yourself, you had no place making anyone else suffer.

"Ridiculous! It only makes sense that demi-humans would suffer and die! You can't compare civilized human beings like us to lowly demi-humans like—hrrmg!"

The guy was annoying me, so I gagged him to shut him up. The faces of these scumbags distorted with fear was a pretty glorious sight. It wasn't quite as good as the time Trash and Bitch were forced to prostrate themselves before me, but still . . . These scumbags deserved at least this much. It was their fault that these demi-humans here ever became slaves in the first place. Now it was their turn to become slaves.

"Eclair, you're a straight arrow, so you probably can't condone this, but these scumbags need to be punished appropriately. And I'm going to use the money that I make from selling them to get the Lurolona villagers back."

"Ugh . . ."

Eclair groaned ruefully but showed no signs of taking any further action. After all, she knew that if we turned them over to the authorities they might end up getting off easy.

"Another thing, Eclair. This will set an example. Slave hunters will know what to expect if they try to attack the village again."

The attacks would never stop if there was no real

punishment worth speaking of. There were likely those that would come even with the risk of execution. But what if it meant getting caught, enslaved, and being abused? If we showed them that there were punishments worse than death in this world, then any slave hunter still considering coming to the village were sure to give up. Not to mention, the village was being protected by the Shield Hero.

"Mr. Naofumi . . ." Raphtalia began.

"I'm doing this no matter how absurd you think it is, Raphtalia. I'm going to do whatever it takes to rescue your friends."

Maybe she wouldn't like living in a place that was built using dirty money. Sure, I wanted to save the day with honest money like the gallant hero of some novel, if possible, but I didn't have the leeway to choose my means. The lives of the Lurolona slaves might very well have been in danger while we were here wasting time with this mess. Raphtalia believed in me and this was for her, too. Standing around waiting wasn't an option, even if Raphtalia didn't like the alternative.

"Bubba . . ."

Keel called out to me with uncertainty in her voice.

"Do you think less of me now? Either way, I'm the boss here. I appreciate your willingness to come forward and volunteer to fight in the coliseum, but right now you need to forget about that and focus on becoming stronger. Leave the dirty work to me."

I turned my back to the slaves and took a step forward. That's right. They didn't need to get their hands dirty. They could leave that to me.

"This isn't the time for you to be taking risks. You're going to protect the village, right?"

"Yeah . . ."

In any case, I could probably make a good amount of money if I sold off this many slave hunters. It had been an unexpected hassle, but it worked out in our favor in the end.

I stood there, staring silently at the portal cool down time hovering in my field of vision.

Chapter Twelve: The Department Store

Each hour, I transported another batch of the enslaved slave hunters to the slave trader's place in Zeltoble, and by the time I finished it was around noon the following day. I'd taken a nap or two, but it had been light sleep, so I didn't feel like I had slept at all.

"I will get in touch with my relative in Siltvelt. Yes sir!"

I'd taken the slave trader back with the first batch of slave hunters and he'd contacted his relative in Siltvelt right away.

"I've been told that the reaction is favorable. Yes sir. Reservations from local nobility for the slaves being offered by the Shield Hero have flooded in, and apparently they are already holding an advance auction."

"Ohhh . . ."

"In which case, we can pay you for the slaves before the trading is actually completed."

A money order, in other words. Then again, we had the technology to send and receive communications, so I guess it wasn't quite the same.

"This went so well that I almost want to pat myself on the back."

"The slaves you've provided should be transported to

Siltvelt by some time tonight. Yes sir."

It felt like throwing meat at a bunch of drooling wild dogs that hadn't eaten for days. I knew Melromarc was full of trash, but apparently Siltvelt was just as shady. Then again, I'm not sure what that made me since I was taking advantage of that shadiness.

Raphtalia seemed a bit disappointed. She was sighing while I was talking with the slave trader, but the slave hunters were getting a fitting punishment. And I had even secretly cleared it with the queen. Melty had showed up that morning, appalled by the fact that the queen had given the plan her unofficial blessing. Apparently she was using it as a bargaining chip for negotiations, since traitors of Melromarc were being sent to Siltvelt, which of course made Siltvelt happy.

We returned to the slave trader's underground slave market and went over everything one more time.

"In any case, it looks like we have enough money now to bet in the coliseum."

It was time to get together with Raphtalia, Filo, Rishia, and Raph-chan and think about how to proceed, just like we had done yesterday.

"Despite how we got it . . . I guess you're right."

"If we want to really hit it big in one go, then we have to be prepared to accept the risks. We need to make sure we understand the rules and other details of the coliseum that we'll be fighting in, too, right?"

If we were going to compete in the most dangerous of the coliseums, where the outcome was literally a matter of life or death, the consequences of leaving anything to chance were just too great. And there was no way I could compete on my own and expect to win. I was the Shield Hero, after all. All I could do was defend.

I'd approached the old Hengen Muso lady about participating, too, by the way. But she had built a reputation for herself in the coliseums before and had been banned from competing. That old lady's past was riddled with mysteries.

"As a general rule, they're elimination tournaments. Assuming the Shield Hero will be participating, I recommend competing as a team. Yes sir."

"Obviously."

"In that case, you can enter as a team of three or a team of five."

Three people . . . I guess that would be me, Raphtalia, and Filo. I wasn't planning on having Rishia participate in the first place, so that was pretty much the only way to go. I could have Raph-chan sub in for Filo depending on the situation, though.

If we went with five people, I could take Raph-chan and . . . maybe bring Keel or someone else. Even so . . . I wanted to avoid going with five people if possible. Raph-chan wasn't all that strong, and while Keel and the others had gotten stronger, they still lacked experience. I couldn't face Raphtalia if something went wrong and they ended up with the kind of injury that would leave a mark.

"Having your subordinates participate in a one-on-one coliseum might be good, too. Yes sir."

"That's the thing . . . How competitive is the one-on-one coliseum?"

Raphtalia's katana was a vassal weapon from another world. I was sure she could win easily, even if it was the coliseum. Umm . . . was it just me? This was starting to feel a lot like the story from a popular old fighting manga where they ended up competing in a coliseum-style fighting tournament.

"The overall stakes and prize money are generally higher for the team competitions. Yes sir."

"Team competition it is, then. Winning little by little is too much trouble."

If I could participate, then teaming up with Raphtalia and Filo would be the safest bet . . . as long as the matches didn't have any strange rules, that is.

"In that case . . . I'll have you entered into an underground coliseum tournament that will be held soon. Yes sir."

"Are there any special requirements to enter or anything else we need to worry about?"

"We'll give the entry a little push to make sure it goes through. Yes sir."

How dependable. Other than that, we just needed to make

sure we didn't do anything that wasn't allowed.

"What about the rules? If they're too complicated or the house takes the winnings or something, then I'm calling this off."

"Three-on-three, no level classes, no race restrictions. That's it. Yes sir."

"Surprisingly simple."

Simple was nice. Oh, and then there was the issue of how the winner was decided. I'm sure the slave trader had purposefully omitted this part. He handed me a pamphlet that appeared to be the coliseum rule book. It was written in the languages of all the different countries, including the official language of Melromarc. It said that a victory would be declared when an opponent died, lost consciousness, or admitted defeat. And then, below that . . .

"The key point is there at the end. Yes sir."

"Participants are to provide their own weapons?"

"Yes sir! The sponsor of the next coliseum fight is the weapons merchant guild. Yes sir."

So it was an underground coliseum backed by the weapons merchant guild . . . I could only imagine what kind of powerful weapons would show up at such a competition. Of course, we were using the legendary shield and a vassal weapon from another world, so we couldn't really complain, regardless.

"If you like, perhaps you might consider observing the

underground coliseum tournament that is currently being held. It may prove to be informative, I think. Yes sir. The tournament is being held at the same time as the slave auction. What would you like to do?"

Well, that did make sense. Seeing what went on would make it easier to come up with a strategy.

"In that case . . . Raphtalia, can you go to the auction tonight and keep an eye out for any Lurolona slaves?"

I could have gotten Keel and the others to help, but showing them that kind of thing probably wasn't a good idea, since they had been traumatized and all. Then again, the same could be said about Raphtalia . . .

"Yes. That's fine."

"We really should make a complete list of everyone that was in the village. Can you do that, Raphtalia?"

I gave Raphtalia a pen and something to write on. It would be more efficient if we took full advantage of the slave trader's connections, to search for the slaves, instead of just relying on Raphtalia's eyes.

"Oh, umm . . . yes!"

Raphtalia started making a list on the piece of paper like I had asked. After all, not all of the slaves would be appearing in the auctions. I'm sure there were some slaves being held elsewhere, too. If we made it clear whom we were looking for beforehand, it would be possible to move straight to direct negotiations later.

"Fehhh . . ."

"Alright then. Since we'll be competing in a dangerous coliseum fight, we should give some thought to how Raphtalia should approach offense."

"Oh, umm . . . okay."

Right now, the katanas Raphtalia had consisted of those she had gotten from monster materials and those that she had copied in Kizuna's world, which still worked here. That meant there were a lot of gaps in what she could use, and her weapons hadn't been adequately powered up, either.

Thankfully she could use the weapon she had gotten from the dragon emperor materials, but her stats still weren't high enough to make much use of the katana she'd gotten from the four holy beast materials. That's why she'd been making do with the dragon emperor katana for the time being.

The weapons made from the dragon emperor materials were exceptional pieces of equipment—Glass and the others favored them, as well. You could probably get by with relying solely on one of those weapons, but it was also better not to underestimate the importance of basic stat improvements and uncovering new skills. Not to mention, the katana still hadn't been fully powered up, apparently.

"Slave trader. Are you familiar with any well-known weapon shops in Zeltoble?"

"I can have you taken to one, if you like. Yes sir."

"Hmm . . . Yeah, let's do that."

It was a really busy city. So getting lost was a real possibility.

"I'll have someone take you right away, then."

A brawny man raised his hand, volunteering himself.

"Alright then. Let's go."

The slave trader's assistant took us to the biggest shop in Zeltoble. It was a huge building that looked like a department store.

"Oh? If it isn't the Shield Hero!"

I noticed a familiar face tending the shop on the first floor.

"You're mistaken."

That's right. The accessory dealer that I met a while back was beckoning me over. I acted like I didn't know him.

"This is my shop. I would absolutely love for you to take a look around."

I couldn't help but feel like he was telling me, "You'll take this shop over, one day." If I kept ignoring him he was likely to just interpret that as acceptance. I sighed and made eye contact.

"You've got a big shop here, eh."

"I sure do. Can I help you find something, Shield Hero?"

"I came to look at weapons and armor."

"That would be the second floor. Before that, can I interest you in any of the accessories here on the first floor?"

I looked around. There was an inordinate number of

glittering accessories on display throughout the shop. Honestly, I felt like I was about to go blind.

"Not interested. I make my own."

"I knew it! Tell me, have you been using what I taught you? There may come a time when you need to make something magnificent, and you won't be able to do that if you let yourself get rusty."

"From time to time. It's saved my life more than once."

That was the truth. I had made the cap for my shield and Raphtalia's sheath just recently. The only problem was that I hadn't been able to make any accessories that worked as well as the ones in Kizuna's world. The haikuikku-like effect that triggered when Raphtalia unsheathed her katana didn't work as well here, either. It only made her about as fast as Filo when she used the skill. Apparently the materials that I used to make the sheath didn't exist in this world, so I had been mulling over whether I should try making her one with different specifications.

Other than that, I had been making accessories for the slaves using materials from monsters. Working with monster bones was my latest obsession. They were hard, and they gave higher stats than you would have expected. What was really nice was that imbuing them didn't degrade the quality much. The downside was that the imbued effects weren't that great.

"Here. It's just a rough piece, but have a look."

I showed him an accessory that I had been working on, albeit not very seriously.

"Oh! A bone accessory!"

"Is that not a thing?"

"Oh, you do see them from time to time, but . . . Hmm, yes. It's a bit cheap, but it's imbued with effects that a practical adventurer would appreciate."

"It may be cheap material, but it's still good for working on design, right?"

"By the way, I hear that you now have a territory of your own."

"If you want to set up shop there then why don't you come by?"

"I'm going to hold you to that!"

The accessory dealer's eyes twinkled devilishly as he shouted. That just made me want to make things difficult for him. That's the kind of person I was.

"You better not get in the way of development. Also, expect to be charged a fee for doing business there."

"Of course! Heh heh heh . . ."

It seemed like the majority of the merchants I knew were a real depraved bunch. If he really did come to the territory, I'd have to keep close tabs on him.

"How is the accessory business treating you these days?"

"Business is good! We did just have quite the catastrophe,

after all. Even the civilians seem to have realized that it's up to them to protect themselves."

The circumstances seemed to be treating his pockets well.

"Also, I've gotten in on the miraculous Cal Mira accessory business that you got started, as well."

Oh yeah . . . He was talking about the advice I'd whispered to that fraudulent merchant back then. I'd seen those accessories show up every now and then, and it always surprised me.

"Anyways, I'm going to go look at the weapons."

"I look forward to our next meeting!"

"Yeah, yeah."

"Go easy on them at the underground coliseum tournament. Of course, I fully expect you will win, so I won't be taking part this time."

"—!"

Shivers ran down my spine. To think he'd already heard in such a short amount of time . . . Just how connected was this guy?!

"I'll be rooting for you."

"Thanks."

Dealing with corrupt merchants always wore me out.

"Fehhh . . . That merchant is quite famous, you know."

"I thought that might be the case."

"They say he'll put you out of business if you get on his bad side."

"Don't worry. He likes me."

On the contrary, I was more afraid he'd try to force me to take over his shop. Rishia and I continued chatting as we climbed the stairs up to the second floor.

"Woooow, this is grreeeat! So shiiiiny!"

It looked like a showroom, with all kinds of weapons on display. Filo couldn't take her eyes off all the shiny objects. She may have looked like a human, but she was a bird monster, after all.

Let's see . . . A variety of siderite weapons, like swords and spears, were lined up in a row. Ahh, they were showroom products meant to attract attention and could only be handled and looked at in the showroom. Yeah, these were definitely the weapons that the other heroes had copied. Oh? There was some Spirit Tortoise gear, too. The materials were being sold to fund reconstruction efforts, after all. I'd heard about it while peddling goods, and apparently working with the materials was difficult.

It was all pretty much the same stuff that you could buy in Melromarc, but everything was priced super high. I was a bit surprised to see that a shop this big was full of weapons that didn't seem to have much processing done to them. I guess it was different when they were made in other countries.

Hmm . . . I looked at the shields, too, but they were pretty much the same as what the old guy had in his shop. There did seem to be a few that I hadn't seen before, so I figured I'd try picking them up.

"Excuse me. Is it okay if I hold this shield?"

"Go right ahead."

After making sure it was okay with an employee, I went about picking up any shields I hadn't seen at the old guy's shop and activated weapon copy. Spike Shield, Frisbee Shield, Jewel Shield, Platinum Shield . . . I just copied them all.

"Raphtalia, did you find any katanas?"

"Umm, yes. They're over here."

Oh? I guess that was the country of merchants for you. There seemed to be a lot of imports from countries in the east. Raphtalia gripped the handles of all of the katanas on sale at the shop. Of course, there was no telling what the people at the shop would say if we told them we were copying all of their weapons, so we just kept quiet. It kind of felt like shoplifting, though.

"Hmm?"

I noticed a weapon on display in the shop that was labeled "not for sale." It was one single-edged sword, and I could tell with one glance that it had been made from the Spirit Tortoise materials. I tried using my appraisal ability to analyze it.

Spirit Tortoise Sword: quality: —

It was no use. My appraisal skill wasn't high enough to fully analyze the sword. It was probably on the same level as the White Tiger Katana.

"By the way, Raphtalia . . ."

"What is it?"

"Will a normal sword work?"

"Umm, no. Unfortunately not."

So it wouldn't let her copy a normal sword, after all. This one was a job for Ren, the Sword Hero. That made me wonder . . . Could Ren use katanas? Now that I thought about it, Raphtalia's fighting capabilities were similar to Ren's since they both used a type of blade. I'd tell him about the sword whenever we finally found him and took him into custody.

In any case, it was obvious that this Spirit Tortoise Sword was a real masterpiece, and the display made it clear you weren't supposed to touch it. It was probably going to be sold at an upcoming auction. Amazing. I guess there really were true masters of their craft out there, after all. I'd have to tell the old guy at the weapon shop all about it later.

"Maaaaster!"

Filo called out to me from the claws corner.

"What is it?"

"There are all kiiinds of claws!"

"Looks that way."

The thing was, Filo used different sizes of claws depending

on whether she was in her human form or filolial form. Judging from recent experiences, it would probably be fine to just go with a size that would work in her human form.

"It doesn't look like there are any worth replacing your current claws."

The Inult Claws had gotten lost, so I'd given Filo the Karma Dog Claws that I'd kept for backups. She'd gone ahead and given Melty the Filo Pajamas, so she didn't have those, either. Of course, Filo didn't need them anymore since it had really just been the performance-enhancing effects that triggered when she was with me that made them useful, and not their defenses.

Anyway, I didn't see anything on par with the Karma Dog Claws in the claws corner. There was a set of magic silver claws that looked like they might have pretty high attack power, but not enough to make it worth replacing her current claws.

As for Rishia, the Pekkul Rapier was more than enough for her. Just as I'd expected, we were at a point where any weapon upgrades would need to be custom jobs. There was still armor . . . Replacing Raphtalia's armor might not have been a bad idea, but . . .

"What is it?"

"Do you want to buy some expensive armor?"

"Shouldn't you be the one doing that, Mr. Naofumi?"

"You do have a point . . ."

I was currently using some old magic silver armor that I'd gotten from the queen. The castle blacksmith had taken it upon himself to touch it up a bit to make it look like my beloved Barbarian Armor—the armor the old guy had made for me. It was only a backup, but apparently he really wanted me to keep this look. It had relatively good stats for standard-issue armor. Even if I did replace it, it wouldn't have been much of an upgrade.

Rishia . . . Yeah, she didn't need armor. It wasn't like she was going to fight in the coliseum, after all. I had one last kigurumi, but I still wasn't sure if I should have her wear it. She seemed okay wearing the old breastplate, so maybe she had finally gained some self-confidence at last.

"Rafuuu?"

Raph-chan? I would have loved to have her wear an iron pot or a tea kettle and a hood, but they didn't seem to have anything like that for sale here. We came to look at weapons and armor, but it started to feel like this had been a waste of time.

"It doesn't seem like there's anything worth buying here, so we're leaving."

"Leaving alreeeaddyy??"

I looked out over the streets of Zeltoble from the window. If we went around visiting all of the shops in Zeltoble, we might have been able to find some hidden treasure. It was certainly conceivable that kind of thing might end up on sale in a place as crowded as this. The atmosphere of this city reminded me of something . . . It was the marketplace from an online game that I used to play. Still, I didn't think that pointlessly wandering around the city was a good idea. Maybe we needed to get some inside information.

"Let's head back to the slave trader's place for now."

"Yes, let's."

"Umm, okay."

"This was fuuuun!"

"Rafuuu!"

And so we finished our little peek at the weapons and armor shop and headed back to the slave trader's underground slave market.

Chapter Thirteen: The Underground Coliseum

Night fell, and the slave trader had me taken to the venue where the underground coliseum tournament was being held. I was the only one going. I'd sent Raphtalia and Raph-chan to the slave auction, and Rishia was off elsewhere gathering information. And I'd assigned Filo to be Rishia's bodyguard.

I'd taken a peak at the coliseum the slave trader managed earlier that afternoon, and it felt kind of like going to a baseball stadium. But this one seemed to put more emphasis on drinking and just having a good time. The spectator seating was sectioned off like an outdoor food court area despite being underground, and the coliseum itself was one of those fighting rings with the tall fence like you might see in a good, old RPG. There were slot machines and poker tables, too, so it almost felt more like an underground casino than an underground coliseum. Still, the coliseum was obviously the highlight, so the arena was what stuck out most.

I wasn't sure what the current match was, but they were going at it. Let's see . . . The odds were posted. It looked like betting ticket sales had already closed and the spectators were just watching the match. The match was between . . . Oh? Ohhh?!

"A panda . . ."

A panda therianthrope was fighting in the coliseum tournament. The opponent was . . . an elephant therianthrope, it looked like. What a crazy fight.

"Ha! That oversized body is all you have going for you, just like usual!" the panda yelled out.

"Hmph! At least I'm not the one just rolling around and running away!" retorted the elephant.

I wasn't sure, but it seemed like the elephant might have had a slight advantage. I could feel the ground shaking quite a bit even from pretty far away. Was it using magic or something? I could vaguely feel the flow of magic coming from that direction.

The panda therianthrope must have been using magic, too, because the area around it turned into a bamboo forest. It looked like it would be slow, but it was jumping gracefully from one bamboo stalk to another, moving all around. The elephant therianthrope went about mowing down the bamboo, clearly irritated.

I looked over at the spectators passionately cheering them on.

"Go for it! That's it!"

"Get him, big sis Larsazusa!"

"There's your chance, Elmelo! No! You missed it!"

They looked like armed adventurers . . . mercenaries, maybe?

There were several groups like that here. Of course, they were outnumbered by spectators that looked more like nobility or merchants. That's the type that was sitting near to where I was. The bar area seemed pretty lively, too. So we'd be fighting in a place like this, huh? It was a spectacle through and through. Then again, the open coliseum had been, too.

As I was just sitting there thinking to myself, I noticed some guy that looked like he might be the barkeep glaring at me. It looked like not drinking would draw attention, I guess.

"Give me a pint of whatever you've got."

Nothing happened when I drank, anyway. I'd never been drunk in my life. I grabbed the pint and went back to watching the match. A few moments later, I heard a commotion coming from behind me.

"Gulp . . . gulp! Aahhh! Come on, finish your drink already!"

Someone sounded like they were in good spirits.

"Gulp . . . I'm not finished yet!"

I could hear onlookers oohing and aahing excitedly. Whatever it was, it seemed just about as lively as the match itself. I turned around to look and there was a group of people gathered around in a circle clapping and calling out, "Chug it! Chug it!"

"Nnn . . . Not bad, eh?! Ugh . . ."

And then a loud slam echoed out, followed by applause.

"Aww! The competition is weak, as usual! Is there no one

here that can give a gal a run for her money?"

The voice I heard had a slightly provocative tone to it.

"There's no way anyone could beat Nadia!" someone's voice rang out.

"Yeah! Exactly!"

"Boy oh boy, that was quite the performance!"

"There you have it! I'll be taking this money, boys. Oh, and the drinks are on you!" Nadia replied to the crowd's cheers.

They finished the exchange and the crowd dispersed, carrying away the loser with them. What a petty game. I'd never understand what people found appealing about drinking contests. I had gone back to watching the match, still thinking about such absurdity, when I heard a voice that sounded like the woman from the drinking contest.

"Oh? Here's a new face. First time here? You don't look like you're having much fun now, do you?"

I glanced in her direction without moving. Standing there was a beautiful woman that had a Japanese air about her. She had long black hair, and her skin and facial features were on par with Raphtalia. She was in her mid-twenties, maybe. Her hair and skin reminded me of Glass, but there was something different about her, too. Glass's facial features and expression gave off an air of seriousness and grace, but not this woman. She looked more like . . . the cheerful, big sister type.

A human? No . . . Her arms and legs were black. Almost

like they were wrapped in rubber. She was pretty much half-naked with the clothes she had on. Her chest was wrapped in sarashi cloth under a vest, and around her waist was a . . . I guess you'd call it a fauld? Depending on how you looked at it, you might call it a loincloth. She had a harpoon strapped to her back.

I remained silent and looked away from her. She didn't seem like someone I needed to waste my time with.

"Oh? Were you watching the match?"

She helped herself to the seat next to me and tried talking to me again, but she must have noticed the leave-me-alone vibes I was sending her way, because after that she didn't show any further sign of forcing the conversation. But then an audacious grin appeared on her face, and she rested her chin in her hands and began speaking slowly.

"Today's match goes to little Sasa. Little El hasn't noticed yet, though."

"Huh?"

The fighters were named Larsazusa and Elmelo. Sasa must have been some kind of nickname.

"Oh, could you not tell? Little Larsazusa is going to win today."

From what I had seen, the elephant therianthrope—Elmelo—had been going all out rampaging around, and the panda therianthrope had been forced to go on the offensive.

Honestly, taking strength and everything else into account, too, I couldn't see how the elephant could lose, even if the odds were in favor of the elephant. But then . . .

"Hiyaaaa! Bamboo Claw!"

The panda thrust its claws into the ground while casting a spell and . . . the ground started shaking, and a massive stalk of bamboo shot up straight through the elephant and smashed into the ceiling of the coliseum.

"Gah!"

After a moment, the stalk of bamboo shattered and dissipated into the surrounding air. There was a loud crash and the whole venue shook. The elephant had fallen over onto the floor and lay there absolutely motionless as a pool of blood spread out from under it. Was it dead?

As the thought crossed my mind, a stretcher was brought out and a doctor began treating the elephant as attendants carried him away. Then the referee came over and raised the panda's hand into the air.

"We have a winner! Larsazusa!"

The spectators cheered loudly, their oohs and aahs echoing throughout the venue. Considering the odds, anyone that bet on the panda would probably be really happy with the outcome. They seemed to be pretty competitive odds, too.

"Nice call."

They began cleaning up the arena immediately and the panda went back to the waiting room.

"What can I say?"

I'd sensed that the panda recited some kind of magical incantation during the fight, but I'm sure the elephant had been on guard, too. In all actuality, the elephant had gotten off several whammies of its own.

"You didn't bet on the fight then, did you?"

"Nah, I just came to do a bit of recon—see what this underground coliseum is all about."

This woman . . . She seemed to know the coliseum pretty well. I got the feeling that it wouldn't be a bad idea to talk with her a bit.

"Oh? So you're interested in fighting in the coliseum, then?"

"I guess you could say that. Betting is a secondary goal."

I wouldn't worry about betting until our odds were set to make a big win.

"In that case, you should have come a bit earlier . . . The main event has been over for a while now."

"Oh, really?"

"Yeah. See that monster they're cooking over there?"

I looked over in the direction that she was pointing. They were right in the middle of chopping up and cooking some monster that looked like a dinosaur. The dishes were being served to the nobility, who were eating it like it was fine dining. Was that part of the spectacle, too?

"They're cooking up the monster that was killed in defeat at tonight's main event."

"Those kinds of things fight in the coliseum?"

"Yep. That's the specialty here—dangerous matches with no guarantee of survival."

I guessed people wanting to see that kind of sensation is the whole reason entertainment like the coliseum existed, after all.

As I thought about such things, I looked over at the monster. From what I could see . . . Hmm, I wonder. What was the cause of death? It didn't look like it had been killed with a blade or anything like that. It might just have been hard to tell—it had already been chopped up by the cooks—but judging from the head and the whites of its eyes and skin, it seemed like the cause of death had been some kind of magic. Powerful fire magic, maybe? That didn't seem quite right, either.

"So what kind of coliseum match are you looking to fight in? I'll tell you everything you need to know, darling."

The woman continued on, cheerfully. She got on my nerves a little bit.

"Hey! Keep the drinks coming over here, will you?"

She was ordering me drinks without even asking! There was a whole row of drinks lined up in front of my seat now.

"You're paying."

"Am I, then? So what do you want to know?"

"Let's see . . . Things to watch out for here. I'm especially interested in the next big competition."

"I see. I'll tell you all about it then, darling. The next competition is a team-fight tournament. The rules are generally three-on-three, no level limit, and you can bring your own weapons."

"I already know that much. What I want to know are the nitty-gritty details of what to watch out for and things to be careful of. Then again, it's not like I can really believe what you say."

I was asking a complete stranger in a place like this. It was just for reference and nothing more. The woman was refilling my cup, again without asking. She seemed to be implying that I'd need to drink up if I wanted her to talk. Fine. I chugged a drink.

"Ohh . . . Let's see, then . . . You'll probably want to watch out for participants that send in wild and vicious monsters that have no monster seal."

". . ."

What would be the point in sending wild monsters into the coliseum? And without a monster seal, there had to be some kind of catch. We'd have to be careful. I looked back over at the monster being cooked. She was probably referring to that thing.

I wondered what participants would consider a threat. I'd heard that the maximum level for people in this world was 100. Anyone fighting in the coliseum would be high-level, I assumed. Well, the open coliseum . . . The coliseum that the slave trader managed was split into classes by level, but this was one had no classes or restrictions.

Wild monsters—that's what would provide an element of threat to a bunch of max-level fighters. I suddenly remembered watching Fitoria defeat the Tyrant Dragon Rex a while back. Honestly, just how powerful had that beast of a monster been? It's not like we hadn't been able to put up a fight, but from what I could tell, "tough battle" wouldn't have even begun to describe it, if Fitoria hadn't shown up. If there were ordinary adventurers out there that could defeat that thing, then there would be no need for evacuations.

"I get it. Wild monsters have no level limit, and that means there are monsters over level 100 that they can send in."

It would probably be easier to think of it in game terms. If you had three level 100 fighters and they were faced with a level 200 monster, what would happen? We weren't talking about a rough fight, here. But if they weren't careful, none of them would survive. There were monster hunter games where you had to fight in a small coliseum, and those were the really tough ones.

Of course, I couldn't imagine there being anything on the level of the Spirit Tortoise. What would be the required level to fight that thing, anyway? I'd been able to stand up to it as a hero around level 75, but that was only because my hero adjustments essentially made me about four times stronger at the time.

Not to mention, the reason Raphtalia and Filo were able to put up a good fight was because they had my growth adjustments and had gotten all kinds of special stat boosts during their class-ups. Still, they wouldn't have been able to defeat it without me. That thing was on the same level as a castle siege or a raid boss. We had Ost's help, too.

If I had to make a quick estimate of the level required for a normal adventurer to confront the Spirit Tortoise head-on and defeat only the outside body . . . I wasn't really sure what kind of abilities normal adventurers had, but I'd say level 250 would have been the minimum.

Of course, that was if they fought it alone. It would probably drop a bit if there were several adventurers. Even so, the level would still need to be high. At least 200, I'd say. And if we were talking about a bunch of adventurers that weren't much stronger than Rishia in her non-awakened state, then they'd lose no matter how many of them there were.

Even if the monster were only around level 120, a single adventurer—no, even with three adventurers—knowing whether they could win or not would still be unclear. All said and done, you really couldn't underestimate differences in levels and basic stats. You might think that level 100 would be similar for a monster and a human, but just looking at Raphtalia and Filo made it clear that wasn't the case. And if you were faced with three of those monsters, then what? It was the kind of risk you could only find at the no-holds-barred underground coliseum tournaments.

"Bingo! Nobility from some country or another will send in recreationally caught wild monsters for the enjoyment of seeing whether or not they can be defeated."

The woman went on drinking cheerfully. It was hard to believe she had just been taking part in a drinking contest from the way she was knocking them back now.

"It was only one this time, but the next competition will be team battles. That means there will be three of those things."

Hearing that made me realize just how scary these rules could be. So it was best not to assume that the opponent would be limited to humans or demi-humans. I would have to let Raphtalia and Filo know about this, too.

She refilled my cup again. I guess she had more to tell me.

"Other than that . . . Depending on the situation, there are times when they will change the terrain to make it more advantageous to the opponent."

"Meaning?"

"When an opponent that can fly is sent in, sometimes they will prepare an iron cage around the arena so that the fight isn't too one-sided."

So the organizers would shift the odds in favor of one side or the other to keep the match interesting.

"That has to suck when that works against you."

"Also, there is support from spectators. Spectators can pay to provide assistance to the opponent they bet on."

In other words, spectators could shell out large amounts of money to help shift the outcome of the match in their favor and win big. What a pain in the ass. There was no such thing as foul play here. No fair matches. I guess competitive odds are what you got in exchange for that.

"The next competition is sponsored by the weapons merchant guild, so you can expect expensive weapons to be thrown at the fighters."

So there are dangerous wild monsters and there is also the risk of opponents being able to swap the weapons they brought for even better ones.

"But hey, spectators attacking the fighters directly is strictly prohibited, so you don't have to worry about that."

"What about indirect support magic?"

"It's possible if someone pays the right amount."

It was probably best not to entertain naïve ideas like all you needed to do during a match was focus on the opponent in front of you. Thinking it over, I chugged another drink that she had poured for me. But seriously, how much did she plan to make me drink? I could hear it all swishing around in my stomach.

"That will be in the rule book for the match you participate in, so make sure to look that over and you should be fine."

I looked at the section where the rules were listed.

The following support will be permitted during this match—

There it was.

"You can drink, can't you? This is starting to get fun!"

She seemed to be enjoying herself as she watched me chug drink after drink.

"Yeah, alright," I said.

"Anyway, that pretty much covers what you need to watch out for."

"Oh yeah?"

There was nothing left for me to do here. I stood up, ready to leave.

"Oh? Leaving already, are you? Let's have a few more drinks!"

"No more for me. But you gave me some good info. I'll pay for the drinks as a sign of my gratitude."

It was obvious that she was planning to have me, the newbie, pick up the tab in exchange for some information. Then again, I was stingy. Normally there was no way I'd do something like picking up a tab, but it was a fact that the information had been helpful. Considering what lay ahead, I could just think of the money spent as part of an investment.

"That wasn't what I was after, you know."

"Whatever you say. One final question."

"What might that be?"

The next match had started, and it looked like they were being given the support that she had been talking about.

"How did you know who would win in that last match?"

I'd thought that I couldn't tell because I wasn't familiar with the rules, but that still didn't fully explain it. As far as I could tell, the fighters in the last match hadn't received any assistance.

"Intuition, maybe?"

"Seriously? Intuition?"

Then again, I knew that intuition couldn't be underestimated. Watching Filo made the power of wild instincts painfully clear, for example.

"If you think of anything else, just come see me again, darling. I'm here every night, and I'll be happy to tell you what you want to know."

Her response was curiously lighthearted. So she really hadn't had any kind of ulterior motive when approaching me?

"Then again, I can't really recommend participating in the underground coliseum, either."

Her parting words left me strangely uneasy . . .

Chapter Fourteen: Ring Name

Anyway, keeping in mind what that drunkard woman had told me, we completed our entry into the underground coliseum tournament.

We had several days left before the event. Right now, I was at the slave trader's place with Filo, waiting on Raphtalia to get back. Rishia was still in the middle of gathering information and looking over some documents.

The slave trader forced our entry through for us, so to the organizers we were still just some no-name mercenaries for the time being. Although, I had a feeling the accessory dealer must have been involved, too, or our entry probably wouldn't have gone so smoothly. I guess this was the Zeltoble underground, where anything goes, so it was probably safe to assume that this level of foul play was practically expected.

Anyway, things would be slightly different than they had been for the matches I'd seen while talking to the drunkard woman. Instead of the competition being held only at night, matches would take place day and night for several days on end . . . or so I was told. It was because this competition was one of the biggest and there were a ton of fighters participating.

We would be fighting once per day. Personally, I thought

they should just sift out all the weaklings in preliminaries, but the merchants wanted to move their money with each fight, since it was a lengthy tournament. This was all according to the slave trader's explanation. He did say the number of times we fought each day was supposed to increase in the latter half of the tournament, at least. It made no sense from a Japanese person's perspective.

Anyway, it would make things more difficult if they figured out who we were from the very start, so Raphtalia, Filo, and I planned to wear masks and other equipment that would hide our faces and conceal what our races were.

"By the way, higher-ranking fighters will be rewarded with money and other various goods. Yes sir."

"That may be so, but . . ."

The grand prize was indeed impressive . . . 150 gold pieces was a pretty nice chunk of change. But the amount of money changing hands in this tournament was far greater. I had ordered the slave trader to place our bet on ourselves just before the advance betting ticket sales ended. We had to make sure we won big. The whole point of participating was to be a dark horse and come out on top.

Fighters would also receive a fight purse for each match they won. Of course, that would just be chickenfeed to us.

"Understood. I'll make it a straight bet for the overall tournament. Yes sir."

"So there are bets for each fight, too?"

"Some people do make money that way. Yes sir."

That would actually be the better approach to betting. Deciding your bets all at once, in the very beginning, wouldn't be nearly as enjoyable. My bet was simply based on what I knew ahead of time.

"All that's left is to gather more funds, I guess."

We would be using the money we got from selling off the slave hunters, but that still might not be enough. We would need to pay attention to our odds in the first place.

"The open coliseum . . . You were saying they have eating competitions in Zeltoble, too, right? Should I have Filo compete in those?"

"Huh? Am I going to do something?"

Filo was a pig, so maybe we could use her as a competitive eater to win some money.

"There is a prize, but it's not more than perhaps 20 silver pieces for the overall winner. Yes sir."

"Not bad, but not great, either. Plus, we probably don't want to have people recognizing her since I'm going to have her compete in the coliseum, too."

"In that case, you might consider having her compete in the filolial races. Yes sir."

"Filolial races? We're pretty much talking horse racing, right?"

I had a feeling that would be more realistic. It seemed like people were always winning a lot at the horse races, so that might not have been a bad idea. Maybe we could aim for a big win like we were in the underground coliseum.

"The problem is that you have to compete in regional races several times before you can compete in the high-stakes races. Also, there's still a month or so before it's the season for the high-stakes races. Yes sir."

"Ugh . . . I could consider having Filo compete if we could bet big in one go, but otherwise . . ."

"Due to how the betting works at a fundamental level, that probably won't be possible. Yes sir."

Let's say I entered Filo in a tiny regional race as a no-name filolial and placed a straight bet on her. I wanted to bet big to win big, but as soon as I put the money down for the bet, the odds would swing in her favor a proportional amount. If there were no other attractive bets, or if there just weren't many people betting in the first place, then the whole plan would be pointless.

This was true for most competitions, but according to the slave trader, winning bets wouldn't be paid out until all of the betting money had been gathered from the betters. Regardless of how much we bet, if the overall pot wasn't huge, then our winnings wouldn't amount to much, either. On top of that, we'd be screwed if people figured out who we were, so we couldn't really afford to make money by participating in the legit side of things.

"Sigh . . . Oh well. I guess for now, other than watching the slave auctions to see if any Lurolona slaves show up, we might as well head back to the village to do some peddling or training."

"That would seem reasonable. Yes sir. By the way, Shield Hero . . ."

"What?"

The slave trader stopped filling out the tournament entry papers to ask a question.

"What should I put down for your ring name?"

"Hmm . . ."

Putting down something obvious like "The Shield Hero's Party" would make concealing our identities pointless. The same would probably go for using my own name. The fact that the accessory dealer already knew we were participating in the first place made it feel like what we were doing was pretty reckless anyway, though. This was probably just one of those things. I needed to pick some random name that wouldn't give me away.

"'Rock Valley's Party' should do."

"Where did that come from? Yes sir."

"It's my last name in English. It was my nickname in another world."

Now that I thought about it, a lot of skill names and stuff were just English words . . . But I guess that was just because my shield was translating them for me. Raphtalia and Filo were actually using the Melromarc language when they were casting spells and stuff, after all. But it was easy to forget that.

It was unlikely anyone would make the connection with my last name, Iwatani, right? To do that, they would have to be someone from another world, like Ren, Itsuki, or Motoyasu. Still, it was scary to think that I had no idea what words really meant in this world. The slave trader looked confused, so I might have gotten the pronunciation wrong or something. Like maybe it would be translated differently if I pronounced it Lock Barley or something.

Just then, Raphtalia and Raph-chan walked in sighing, back from the underground auction.

"How did it go?"

"We saw one."

"I see . . ."

So she had found a Lurolona slave.

"How high did the price go?"

Raphtalia cast her gaze downward when she replied.

"The bidding stopped at . . . 95 gold."

Who knew just how high the prices would jump. I really wished this ridiculous bubble would burst already, but we had no choice but to deal with the situation as it was.

"I guess all we can do for now is head back to the village and train until the coliseum tournament starts."

"Agreed. Let's win this . . . no matter what!"

Raphtalia was looking at me with her eyes full of strong determination. That's right. We'd been left with no choice but to fight to get her village back.

"Raphtalia, I'm thinking we should probably address each other using aliases during the matches. What do you think?"

"Umm, okay. What should they be?"

"Hmm . . . I'm going to go with Rock for my alias."

I doubted anyone would associate that with the Shield Hero, but what about Raphtalia and Filo?

"Rafu?"

I wanted something with a twist. Raphtalia would probably get mad at me if I called her something like Raph-chan No. 2, though.

"You're thinking about something rude, aren't you?"

"Hmm . . . Alright then. Raphtalia will be Shigaraki, and Filo will be Yakitori."

"Nooo!"

Filo had the nerve to complain. What was wrong with "Yakitori"? Did she not like grilled chicken? It would be easy to remember.

"Mr. Naofumi, that's a bit mean even for you, don't you think? Look. Filo doesn't look very happy now, does she?"

Bah! I guess I had to pick something else if Raphtalia was going to complain.

"Fine. Raphtalia will be . . ."

"Hold on. So my name was something rude, too?"

I guess she didn't get the tanuki reference and had only been complaining about Filo's alias.

"Who knows? Filo will be . . . Humming should work."

She had been a monster called a humming fairy in Kizuna's world, after all. No one in this world would know that.

"Mr. Naofumi? Are you listening to me?"

"Filo, you can call me master like usual during the matches. Just call Raphtalia big sis."

"Okaaay!"

Master was just a general title and wouldn't give away my name.

"Mr. Naofumi!"

Right now, we needed to buy up the slaves from Raphtalia's village as quickly as possible, so there was no turning back for me, no matter what.

We returned to the village, and it ended up being the day before the coliseum tournament, by the time all of us had gotten fully prepared. Filo spent her time playing with the slaves, and she must have recognized the village as something she wanted to protect, because she was looking forward to fighting now.

Raphtalia apparently finished powering up the katana that she got from the dragon emperor materials to a sufficient level.

And now we were on standby in the waiting room at the underground coliseum in Zeltoble. We would be fighting daily from here on out. Until we won the tournament, that is.

The Zeltoble coliseum was inherently secretive, so the careers of the fighters were packed full of fabrications. As a result, I'd heard the odds tended to favor the more well-known fighters. That meant that neither the nobility nor anyone else would be paying any attention to someone like a newcomer hoping to win big. I guess no matter what world you were in, there would still be those extravagant types who didn't mind losing money, since they didn't work for it anyway.

"This is our first match. Let's try not to bring ourselves too much attention."

According to the slave trader, the opening ceremony had been held earlier today around noon, and the tournament bracket had been announced. He said the teams that were lucky enough to be seeded wouldn't be fighting until the latter half of the tournament. We were fighting in the very first round, so I already couldn't help but feel like things were a bit unfair. Then again, this was nothing compared to being framed and left penniless mere days after being summoned to another world, and then being stigmatized on top of that.

The time for our match was drawing near. It was evening

now. The tournament started sometime around noon, I think, so it had been going for a while now. Our opponent for this match was some mafia-sounding team called . . . the Topak Family. The odds had already been fixed, but if we came on full-force, practically screaming, "Actually, we have the Shield Hero!" then the opposing team would probably be flooded with support. They might end up with really nice weapons and equipment and huge amounts of support magic being cast on them nonstop, and that would really suck for us. Even worse, it was possible the organizers would force some kind of weird handicap on us.

I wanted to keep as low a profile as possible while still making people think our party was amazing. In that case, maybe we should finish them off with a single blow and not even leave anyone time to give them support. Or we could pretend to struggle and make it look like we just barely managed to win. Either way, we would have to see how strong they were first.

"For now, you lead the attack, Filo. Raphtalia, you provide support from behind. If you can show the spectators an illusion, then do that."

"So it's up to meeee?"

"Yeah."

"What is the point of deceiving the spectators?"

"Make it so that we don't stand out too much. For example, if you can make it look like we're struggling, then do that."

"I think it should be possible, but . . . Don't you think that's a bad idea?"

Hmm . . . It wasn't against the rules, but then again, it could be problematic if the organizers stepped in. It was a risk we had to take.

"Even so, Raphtalia, at least make it look like I'm attacking the enemy. I don't want anyone figuring out that I'm the Shield Hero."

"Then what about your skills?"

"I'll just have to avoid using them as much as possible. They'll probably just think yours are special techniques you developed on your own."

Up until now, I had been using my skills nonstop left and right, so I was a little bit worried. Regardless, it would be best to avoid being noticed if we wanted to advance through the tournament without having to face any unnecessary obstacles.

"Looks like it's almost time. Come on, Raphtalia and Filo—cover your faces at the very least. Don't forget to use our aliases."

Filo put on a domino mask and tied a bandana around her head. Raphtalia was wearing a kabuto helmet to cover her face and ears so that people couldn't tell what race she was. She had hidden her tail, too, of course. I was using an iron mask to cover my face, too.

A gong sound echoed throughout the air, and we headed

out of the waiting room and toward the arena. Cheers filled the air. The venue was packed—there were far more spectators now than when I'd come to observe before. To think that there would be this many people at an underground coliseum . . . Oh, and nearly everyone in the audience was wearing masks, like maybe they were nobility that had come here in secret. It was a pretty unsettling sight, really. I bet all kinds of countries would have been in trouble if you killed off all these creeps.

As I was standing there thinking about such things, three muscle-bound mercenaries that looked like they knew how to fight came strolling out of the entrance on the opposite side.

"And now, a faceoff between Rock Valley's Party and the Topak Family! Are you rrreeeaaddyyy?!"

The announcer was practically screaming as he stirred up the audience.

"Ha! This guy brought along a girl and some kid. Who let this bunch out of the show tent?"

"Hold up, the audience will love it if we do something brutal to that girl and kid right in front of this guy, don't you think?"

"Yeah, you're right. Alright, let's start by beating this guy to a pulp and then that's what we'll do."

What a vulgar bunch. Didn't they know it was always the small fries that licked their chops like that before a fight? Actually . . . I wasn't sure who was worse—these guys or the bandits we always ran into while peddling.

"You good?"

"Yup!"

It was probably best to assume we wouldn't be receiving any support from the spectators. Then again, it was only our first match and wouldn't be drawing much attention, so there was no need to worry about that . . . right?

The spectators were cheering a bit, but I could tell from their eyes that they were just hoping to see the kind of tragedy these creeps had mentioned. On the contrary, if the unquestionably weak-looking team with the girl and a child ended up winning, that might build some excitement, too. If we gained a certain amount of popularity, then we might be able to get some support, too.

"Let the battle . . . BEEEEGGIIIINNNN!!"

Another gong sound echoed out and the match began—and in the same instant, a blunt weapon that looked like a morning star was tossed down right next to where the Topak Family mercenaries were standing. From the look of it, it seemed like a pretty impressive weapon. Someone must have thrown it in, hoping the other team would use it to make a mockery of me.

"Zweite . . . Aura"

In a whisper, I cast support magic on Filo. Then I picked her up from behind and lifted her up onto my shoulders. She must have realized what I planned on doing, because she climbed onto my shoulders and held her claws up out in front of her.

There was a reason for putting her on my shoulders. I had a convenient little skill called "abilities increase while carrying (medium)." As long as someone was on my shoulders, they would receive an overall increase in abilities for a period of time. Filo was currently in her human form, so she wasn't very heavy and wouldn't slow me down.

"Master, what should I dooo?"

"Hmm . . . It's probably best not to show all of our cards yet, I guess."

Being too strong would make us stick out. We should probably just stick to a low-key strategy for this match. According to the slave trader, our opponents were relatively unknown, so there was no need for theatrics. Yeah, I'd even come up with a signature phrase to go with it.

"Alright! Make it hard, and make it quick!"

"Okaaay!"

Filo started focusing her attention like she did when preparing to use haikuikku.

"Huh? What's that pose?! Is she getting ready to play a game?"

"This is going to be a piece of cake! Hahahahaha!" the opponents shouted. "It's going to feel good celebrating tonight! And we even get to have some fun with a girl!"

The Topak Family mercenaries all grabbed their weapons and started running our way. One of them swung the morning star—the thing seemed like one of those special named weapons—and I blocked it with my shield. It struck with a heavy thud and flames burst from the tip of the morning star, engulfing me in hellfire. So it had a special effect, huh? I guess it was a nice weapon, after all. I deflected the flames with my cloak, but there was a pillar of fire rising up from under my feet. Although, with my high defenses, the flames were kind of just bouncing off.

"It's hot!"

The heat was getting to Filo. Her arms and legs had extended just a bit outside of the area I had protected. The pillar of fire itself was still down there, although it wasn't burning me. I flapped my cape and the remaining pillar of fire dissipated for a moment, but then it reappeared. So it even had a residual effect . . . That weapon was even better than I thought.

"Hahahaha! This thing is awesome!"

The mercenary was maintaining a bit of distance from me, as I stood there in the pillar of fire. He started whirling the morning star around like he was going to come after me, and then he swung it at me from the side. Paying attention to the path of the morning star, I reached my left hand out and grabbed it by the chain, bringing it to a sudden halt.

"What?!"

"Ah! Raising a hand to Chief? How dare you! Take this!"

"Hiyaaa!"

I held on tight and the Topak Family mercenaries all crowded around me, swinging at me with the weapons they had been given. Oh! How nice of them to gather up in a tidy little group for us!

"Humming, you ready?"

"Yup! All set!"

"Alright then!"

After jerking the chain and pulling the mercenaries closer, I grabbed Filo and . . . hurled her at them as hard as I could.

"Goooo!"

Filo activated haikuikku just as I threw her and then followed up with Spiral Strike, plowing into the Topak Family mercenaries.

"Uwaaaaa!!!"

Filo's landing was showy, yet graceful. It was kind of like she had used a finishing move. She did look pretty cool. Her wings added to the elegance, too. Gasps were coming from the audience. Moments later, the Topak Family mercenaries fell to the ground, completely covered in lacerations.

That was Filo's haikuikku-Spiral Strike combo, performed from my shoulders and bolstered by my Zweite Aura support magic. Even if our stats were only one-third of what they usually were, would they be able to withstand an attack like that?

"Huh? Is that all you've got? You must be a bunch of low-levels. This is what happens when you underestimate the coliseum."

I flashed a cruel smile and made sure to speak loudly while trampling on the faces of our fallen enemies. The spectators had been speechless, but they must have liked that, because they erupted into cheers. I was still holding on to the bundle-of-fun morning star that created fire pillars.

That's right... The only reason it ended so soon was because the opposing team lacked training. That's the impression I was going for. Being high-level might have been a prerequisite, but what high-level meant would depend on the tournament. With no classes, the definition was unclear.

"Im . . . impossible . . ."

One of the enemies let out a groan.

"Shut him up."

"Okaaay! Smash!"

"Ugh!"

Filo trampled on each of the Topak Family mercenaries, knocking them out cold. The match itself had gone smoother than I thought it would.

"We... we have a winner! Rock Valley's Paaarrrtttyyyyyyyy!"

The announcer must have realized that the opponent's team was done for, because he declared our victory. Just like I expected, being forced to either kill the opponent or render them unconscious sure was a hassle. I would have preferred knocking them out of bounds or something, but there was nothing like that in this tournament.

"Phew . . ."

Raphtalia finished casting magic from her position in the rear and whispered to me.

"I made it look like you finished them off, just like you asked, Mr. Naofumi."

"Nice work. Thanks."

That should clear up any suspicions of me being the Shield Hero, up to a point. I waved my hand as a declaration of our victory and then nonchalantly picked up the morning star that the Topak Family mercenary had dropped and headed back to the waiting room.

"Umm . . . Mr. Naofumi? What are planning to do with that weapon?"

"Huh? I figured it was ours to keep."

No one had said anything, and this was a coliseum where people fought to the death. There was no rule against stealing an opponent's weapon. The merchant-looking guy that had provided the support for the other team did seem a bit bitter, but he obviously wasn't hurting for weapons.

"Make good use of that weapon!"

He may have looked bitter, but that's what he yelled out at me. He was probably thinking that if we used the weapon and won, it would be lucrative for his shop or the merchant guild he belonged to. But I could only use my shield, and Raphtalia couldn't use anything other than her katana, either. That left

Filo, but Filo was fond of her claws. I figured I'd ask her anyway.

"Filo. You want to use this weapon?"

"Umm . . ."

She didn't seem to like the idea. Besides, even if Filo went swinging the thing around violently, there was no guarantee she could actually make good use of the weapon.

"Alight, Filo, how about this . . . From now on, when a match starts, you fling this weapon at our opponents."

"Okaaay!"

With Filo's superhuman strength, if she flung the weapon at the opponent it would probably intimidate them a bit, at least. After that, who cares? Then we could just use it at the village or maybe sell it off. As long as we used any weapons we grabbed at least once in a match, it would be free advertising for the merchant guild that we took it from, and they might even decide to provide us support later on. Oh! That was a good idea, even if I do say so myself.

Anyways, there wasn't much point in sticking around at the venue. The teams that would be fighting in the next match were already standing by, so we could either watch their match or just leave as soon as possible and get some rest. Being our first match, the fight purse was pretty insignificant. Filo must have thought that the morning star I gave her was a new toy, because she was having fun swinging it around in the air.

"Jingle-jaaaangleee!"

It was an adorable sight, but then again, that was a weapon she had in her hand.

"Be careful. That thing is dangerous. Make sure the ball doesn't hit anything, at least."

"Okaaay!"

In the end, Filo took the morning star with her back to the village and played with it like a toy together with the slaves. It was a fun weapon that made pillars of fire wherever it hit. The little brats even wanted to use the weapon to make a campfire. It wore me out just making sure they didn't set any buildings on fire.

Our second match was the following day.

"Our next opponent is . . ."

I guess there was no point in checking our opponent's team name or anything, really. Our objective was to win every match and come out on top, after all.

As I stood there thinking, the gong rang, and then we made our way into the arena, and . . . when we saw our opponents, we all immediately went on the defensive. There were three griffins inside of a cage.

"Kweeeeh!"

They were all riled up and ready to go. So these were those dangerous wild monsters, huh? We'd never fought a griffin before . . . griffin elite. The griffins' monster name appeared in my field of vision. I guess they were some superior type of griffin, then. I had no idea what level a normal adventurer would need to be to defeat one, but apparently it was a relatively interesting fight card, because there were more spectators than yesterday.

We just had to get stuck with a troublesome opponent, didn't we? This was exactly the kind of match that drunkard woman had warned me about.

"Grr . . ."

Filo started acting menacingly. That reminded me, filolials and griffins apparently didn't like each other. I seemed to remember reading something about griffins regarding horses as enemies in some fantasy book once. I see . . . It must have had something to do with both taking pride in being used as a means of transportation and fighting over who was the best. Filolials didn't get along with dragons, either. It sure seemed like were a lot of monsters filolials didn't like. Oh well . . . At least it had gotten Filo motivated.

"Humming, are you going to be able to hold back?"

"Grr . . ."

Yeah, that wasn't going to happen. She was probably going to go all out.

"Alright, Humming. When the match starts, you fling that morning star I gave you at them. Whatever you do, don't change into your filolial form."

There were sure to be nobility and others among the spectators that would realize we were the Shield Hero and crew if they saw Filo, the bird god. Never mind the fact that a monster that could turn into a human would surely draw way too much attention. I wanted to defeat the enemy before that happened and without standing out, if at all possible.

I guess there was no choice. We'd have to give up on the "moderately strong dark horse rises to the top, out of nowhere" scenario. Still, I wanted to keep the fact that I was a hero hidden, if possible. There was just too much of a difference in the burden that would come with being a hero versus some powerful yet nameless fighters.

"Okaaay!"

What else?

"Ra . . . Shigaraki, can you handle those things?"

"I'll try."

"Let the battle . . . BEEEEGGIIIINNNN!!"

When the gong rang, the door of the cage that the griffins were in opened.

"Kweeeh!"

The griffins rushed out of the cage, glaring at us, and approached at a ridiculous speed. They were moving so swiftly that it seemed as if they might pounce upon us at any moment. Several of the masked nobility in the audience were whispering and watching us, their eyes brimming with curiosity. More than likely, these things had probably brutally murdered their opponents in a previous match or something. There was even still blood on the griffins' claws.

"I'm going to end this in one blow."

"Yeah, it would be a hassle if they ended up getting assistance."

Raphtalia placed her hand on the handle of her katana.

"Zweite Aura"

Whispering once again, I cast support magic on Raphtalia, who then lunged forward into a sprint. She may have been suffering from the effects of a curse, but with her level adjustments, she could still be quick. The more I focused, the slower everything around me seemed to move. That was probably true for the griffin elites too, though.

"Take thiiissss!"

Filo flung the morning star at the griffin elites with all of her strength.

"Kweeh?!"

That must have caught them off guard, because the griffin elites started flapping their wings in an attempt to get out of the way. The morning star smashed straight into one of them and a pillar of fire shot up, engulfing it in flames.

"Hiyaaa!"

Raphtalia drew her katana and started moving even faster.

"Instant Blade! Mist! Thrusting Technique! Lethal Formation One! Lethal Formation Two!"

She delivered a strike to the alpha griffin elite that had been standing at the front and then quickly cut down the other slightly smaller ones behind. Sure, it might not have been Kizuna's Blood Flower Strike, but she still cut through them pretty damn fast. Raphtalia spun her katana around, flinging the blood from the blade, and then returned it to its sheath.

"I'm sorry. I'm still a bit slow, unfortunately."

The alpha griffin elite was practically split in two at the chest, and the other two griffins behind had splattered blood all over the place before falling flat on the ground. Was that a bit too much?

Well, I guess the nice thing about Raphtalia's skills is that they didn't appear so blatantly unusual, like my attacks did. Of course, they had skill-like elements to them, too, but at first sight, it just looked like she had swung her blade around really fast. I'm sure people would realize you were a hero immediately if you started making shields appear in mid-air. Or maybe they would think it was magic? Hmm . . . I still wasn't sure where that line was drawn.

Both the spectators and the announcer were speechless.

"We . . . we have a winner! Rock Valley's Paaarrrtttyyyyyyyy!"

The announcer screamed out, and after a brief delay, the spectators burst into cheers. We had finished the fight so quickly that they didn't seem to know how to react.

"As expected, I still can't fight at my normal level. I had to use a skill just to be able to defeat an opponent like that in one blow."

"Yeah."

"Jingle-jaaaangleee!"

Filo picked up her beloved morning star and came back over to us. I gave a perfunctory wave as we headed back to the waiting room.

"I wanted to avoid standing out, but it looks like that's going to be difficult."

"Yes. I'm sorry."

"Don't worry about it. You only did what I told you to do."

We would just have to accept it. Perhaps it was being careless, but I didn't want to force her to hold back, either.

"You want to go back to the village, Filo?"

"Yup! By the way, where is Rishia?"

"I've got her gathering info about the coliseum."

Rishia was with Raph-chan gathering information on the more powerful teams. I wasn't sure how much she'd actually be able to figure out, but she was knowledgeable about all kinds of things. I figured it might prove to be helpful one way or another.

"Bye-bye! I'll be good, so don't worry about meeee!"

That morning star was quickly becoming her new favorite toy, and lately she had been swinging it around everywhere she went . . . What part of that was being good? I was pretty sure good little girls didn't go around creating pillars of fire. That was literally playing with fire and just asking for something bad to happen.

"Yeah, yeah. Don't play with that thing too much."

"Okaaay!"

I used my portal to send Filo back to the village. She disappeared instantaneously, right before my eyes.

"Okay, Raphtalia. I'm counting on you again, tonight."

"Understood. The time to be depressed has come, once again."

"Yeah."

We didn't have the money, so we couldn't buy the remaining Lurolona slaves. It was painful just watching them being bought off, but if we didn't keep an eye on who they were being bought by, then we wouldn't be able to purchase them when we finally did have the money.

"But it's not like there's no point. Just keep at it."

"I know. Alright, then you keep at it, too, Mr. Naofumi."

"Will do!"

I was going to go watch the remaining coliseum matches, like Rishia had been doing. I'm sure if Raph-chan had been in the audience rooting for me, it would've made me happy.

Chapter Fifteen: Surprise Attacks and Conspiracies

It's not like I was planning on making a habit of it or anything, but I headed back to the tavern where I'd met the drunkard woman. Things were relatively lively there, but the matches were still going on, so the customers seemed to be mostly paying attention to the coliseum. Judging from the atmosphere, mercenaries and other participants with upcoming matches had gotten together there and were exchanging information.

"Oh?"

I grabbed a random seat and ordered a drink, and the same drunkard woman from before cheerfully made her way over to where I'd sat down. Damn! I'd been seen!

"You seem to be advancing in the tournament quite nicely. I saw your matches, you know."

"You figured out it was me, huh?"

I'd gone to the trouble of wearing an iron mask so that no one would recognize me. But she had obviously figured it out.

"I could tell by your build and how you move."

That made me think . . . When someone puts on a mask or something like that in an anime or manga, suddenly even their own family doesn't recognize them. They'd probably be made in an instant in real life. I guess you could say the fact that they didn't notice meant they must not have been very close. Had my plan been pointless?

"By the way, I never introduced myself, now did I? I'm Nadia."

". . ."

If I told her my real name, it might give my identity away. What should I do? Whatever. I would just use my ring name.

"I'm Rock."

"That's right, isn't it, little Rock? Tell me, little Rock, have you gotten used to things at the tournament?"

"We haven't been struggling as much as I thought we would."

Fighting without revealing how powerful we really were was surprisingly difficult. In the end, we'd pretty much, halfway, given ourselves away. Itsuki liked to do things that way, apparently, but I just didn't get it. We were only concealing our strength because it would cause problems for us if people found out. If there was no need to stay hidden, I'd happily send Filo on a rampage without hesitation.

"Everyone is paying attention to you, you know? You did finish those griffins off really quickly, after all."

"So that *was* a standout fight card, after all . . ."

Nadia gave an affirmative response in her usual overly familiar style and then ordered a ridiculous number of drinks, just like last time, before continuing the conversation. Just how much did this woman love her alcohol, anyway?!

"Aahhh!"

Several mercenaries began to approach us, but the drunkard woman, a.k.a. Nadia, waved them away with a casual flick of her hand. She'd said that our fight had gotten us some attention, so maybe they just wanted to ask me some questions.

"Well then, little Rock . . . How about I give you part two of things to watch out for at the tournament, then?"

"Huh?"

You mean there was more?

"Well, it's really more common sense—it's not so much a problem that you'll encounter at every tournament, but it's something that participants should always be on the lookout for."

"Oh, I see."

"It's an especially prevalent problem for the official coliseums, and you can even get disqualified for it in some cases, you know."

"Spit it out already, why don't you?"

Nadia responded by pouring a drink in a stein and passing it over to me. So she wanted me to drink it? Fine . . . whatever. I chugged whatever it was that she had filled the stein with. It was some kind of fruit wine. It even still had some of the fruit left in it. It had infused well, giving the wine a really fruity flavor. I had a feeling I'd drank something like it before.

"Aahh . . . So? Tell me already."

I placed the empty stein back on the table.

"Hmm . . . Well . . ."

She had really played it up, whatever it was, but she didn't seem like she was going to talk any time soon.

"Little Rock, you really hold your liquor well, don't you?"

"It's the same as water to me. I've never been drunk in my life."

This Nadia woman's eyes grew wide. She seemed genuinely surprised. What was that reaction supposed to mean?

"Well, then . . . I guess I should tell you, shouldn't I? But it'll be easier just to show you, so how about we get out of here and enjoy a little stroll in the night air."

"What about the matches?"

"The next few matches are all teams that won't be advancing much further in the tournament. I already checked them out yesterday, so don't worry about them."

Hmm . . . Nadia's intuition had been right about who would win the other night. She might have been right about these, too. Plus, those mercenaries from earlier seemed strangely interested in us and kept glancing over in our direction. I had to admit, it was getting on my nerves. It probably wasn't a bad idea to just leave the information gathering to the inconspicuous Rishia and head back early, myself. I didn't think my identity had been revealed, but still . . .

Nadia stood up and I followed her out, leaving the coliseum behind.

The nighttime streets of Zeltoble were brimming with activity—the phrase "a city that never sleeps" fit perfectly. There seemed to be quite a few shops catering to debauchery lining the streets, as well. Judging from the shop signs there were places for humans, demi-humans, and other races, too. Taverns were all over the place, and you could hear the uproar of voices coming from within. That said, Nadia said she wanted to enjoy the night breeze and headed down a small back alley that ran alongside an irrigation canal.

Zeltoble was situated alongside a waterway that led to the ocean, so it was possible to travel there by boat. Perhaps that was why the smell of the night air reminded me of the sea. The intricate canals running alongside the back alleys made it feel kind of like you were in Venice. It actually seemed like a pretty nice area for a leisurely stroll.

"Now then, little Rock, continuing our earlier conversation . . ."

"Yeah?"

"It may be that it happens relatively more often when people start paying attention to you, but regardless of that . . . did you not notice a certain phenomenon occurring, starting around the first round?"

"Huh?"

I tried to recall the first-round standings that Rishia had compiled for us. I hadn't really paid much attention, since I was only interested in our own results, but had there been anything odd about them?

Hmm . . . Now that I thought about it, our match had been moved up ahead of schedule. It did make me wonder why the previous match could have ended so quickly. They had been making more adjustments to the schedule just earlier, too. I thought about how all of that matched up with today's standings.

"The number of wins by default is peculiarly high."

I guess there would be fighters that signed up to participate and then just didn't show up for the tournament, right? Or maybe it was because no one worried about staying on schedule? That would suck if you ended up being the one affected by it. I mean, come on . . . Just how poor was their time management?

I considered several of the more peaceful possibilities, but the answer had already appeared in the back of my mind.

"Exactly. You know why that is?"

". . ."

Her suggestive phrasing sent beads of cold sweat running down my back. At that very moment, I heard the sound of a weapon being drawn, and a group of aggressive-looking men appeared in the alley and surrounded us. Damn . . . Had I fallen for a trap?

Under the circumstances, I had to consider myself on my own. Could I get away if I just defended against their attacks and ran to a crowded area? But wait! Surely I could drive them back if I used a shield with a counterattack, right?

This woman! To think she set me up! Just who the hell does she think she—

"Oh? You boys think this is all it will take to stop a girl like me, do you?"

"Can it, woman! You two are sitting ducks out here, and roast duck just happens to be our favorite! How could we pass up an opportunity like this?"

This guy acting like the boss of the belligerent bunch . . . Yeah, he'd been at the tavern. I guessed they were mercenaries. They looked like they had been in a few fights before.

"Nadia! And you, too, Rock Valley! Do us a favor and . . . die!"

The boss shouted out his rallying cry and the surrounding men all lunged at us. I held my shield out to defend against their attacks, but . . .

"Now, now . . . I've got nothing against children being a bit feisty, but you boys are just plain naughty, aren't you?"

Nadia spoke quietly as she took the harpoon from her back and began to cast a spell.

"As the source of your power, I command you! Let the true way be revealed once more! Lightning! Strike down and penetrate those before me!"

"All Drifa Chain Lightning!"

Several blindingly bright bolts of highly condensed lightning shot from the tip of Nadia's harpoon, piercing right through the group of belligerents!

"Gahhhhhh!"

"Arrrghhh!"

She was fast! She moved like she had been in quite a few battles. And the flashes of crackling lightning moved as if they had a mind of their own, jumping from one belligerent to another and striking the whole bunch down.

"This piddling bunch is all that came? That's no fun, now is it?"

The men stood there twitching with their heads thrown backward for several long moments. Finally, they fell to the ground, their eyes rolled back. The way they looked . . . I'd seen this before! That monster that they had been serving up at the coliseum back when I first met Nadia had the very same look!

"I'm not . . . finished!"

"Oh?"

One of the men that hadn't been wounded as badly as the others stood up and rushed at Nadia. Was I being completely ignored? Well, I had no obligation to help Nadia, and as far as I could tell from the way she moved, it didn't look like she needed my help, either. Nadia quickly spun her harpoon around and thrust it hard at the man's chest while taking a firm step forward.

"Gah!"

It connected with a loud thud and the man went flying, disappearing into the darkness of the alley. Shortly afterward, the sound of his body smashing into a wall echoed out . . . followed by silence.

"I guess that's it, isn't it?"

As if to signify an easy victory, Nadia twirled her harpoon around before returning it to its place on her back.

"I guess that explains it, wouldn't you say?"

"Pretty much."

The reason for the wins by default was fighters were ambushing their opponents. The opponents would be rendered unable to fight . . . Some of them would probably end up incapacitated or even dead. There were probably cases of it backfiring on the attackers, but that meant that ambushes like this were common. There was a lot of money at stake in this tournament, not to mention the whole thing was shady to begin with, after all.

Ah, so that was why you could place early bets on who would advance in the tournament—there would be cases when participants were eliminated without even making it to their matches. Did people actually trust the tournament betting system? I was surprised anyone would be brave enough to place a bet at this competition.

"Your approach to the matches isn't bad, little Rock, but

making a display of strength that convinces opponents to just give up, because they can't win, is another possibility, you know."

"You mean, because otherwise, I'll have to deal with pests like this coming after me?"

"Well, it's not like eeeeeveryone will give up, since there is money involved, you know."

But this woman . . . she was unexpectedly formidable. I guess she wasn't just a drunkard, after all.

"They fight dirty and they'll use every trick in the book, so watch your back. Hanging around spacing out in a place like that tavern is just asking for trouble. Even if it's a girl like me giving you trouble."

"Putting it like that must mean that you're willing to fight dirty, too, if it means winning."

"That's right. I already made one attempt on your life, you know."

What? What had she done? Had she used her magic to try to shock me along with those other guys? That's too bad, because hitting me with a stray bullet wasn't going to make me flinch. Or maybe she had poisoned my drink? I had a skill that detected poisons, though, so there's no way I wouldn't have noticed. Realistically speaking, with all of the skills I had from my shield, it would be near impossible to assassinate me. And yet here she was saying she had done something to me.

I was puzzling over the issue when Nadia suddenly took my

hand and placed it on her chest for some reason. She was rather well endowed. She probably had Raphtalia beat, by the looks of it. Now that I thought about it, this might have been the first time I'd touched a female's chest.

"Boobies!" she suddenly exclaimed.

Was this woman some kind of half-wit? I was just starting to enjoy the moment and she had to go and ruin it. I jerked my hand away from her.

"Oh . . . ?"

"So what? What did you do to me?"

"Oh, that . . . Let me make up for it by confessing my love for you!"

"Stop screwing around or I'm leaving."

"You're too serious, little Rock!"

The drunkard woman cackled cheerfully when she responded. I wished she would stop playing games and just answer already . . .

"I mixed rucolu fruit into your drink, earlier."

"Ohhh . . . that was it? Is that all?"

"It's used to assassinate people, you know? Especially at taverns . . ."

Well, I guess it was supposed to be something you diluted with water before drinking. For various reasons, people had begun offering it to me at villages I visited while peddling, almost like a proof of identity. I see . . . So the shield wouldn't react if it was something that I wouldn't consider a poison.

But seriously, I hadn't even considered that rucolu fruit might be used that way. The thing seemed like it would actually be great for assassinations—arsenic wouldn't even compare. My body apparently didn't react adversely to it, but still . . .

Nadia quickly wrapped her arms around me and kissed me lightly on the cheek.

"What do you think you're doing?!"

Was she trying to come on to me? Give me a break! Nadia began walking away slowly. After she had taken several steps, she stopped and looked back over her shoulder at me. She grinned when she spoke, but I wasn't sure if the look in her eyes was cheerful, worried, or excited for what was to come.

"I really hope that we don't meet in the coliseum, if at all possible."

And then Nadia disappeared into the back alleys of Zeltoble, followed by the tapping of her footsteps.

"I really hope you give up before that, if at all possible . . ."

Those were her parting words. What was that supposed to mean? She had tried to poison me, and yet she still told me all about—and even showed me, in action—the risks of the underground coliseum, and then she disappears before I can figure out if she's flirting with me or worried about me. Then, to top it all off, she tells me to give up? I'm sorry, but giving up wasn't an option for me.

I left the back alley and headed back toward the slave market to meet up with Raphtalia and the others.

"Did you see any of the villagers?"

Raphtalia came out to meet me.

"There weren't any today."

"I see. That's good."

Rishia finally returned, accompanied by one of the slave trader's assistants who had been acting as her bodyguard.

"Fehhhh . . . That was scary!"

"Rafu!"

"I hear it can be dangerous for you, if people think you're involved. There are people out there who will do anything to win, apparently."

"Fehhh!"

Keeping our safety in mind, I used my portal skill and we returned to the village after that. I don't know if it was our scent or what, but Filo came running up immediately.

"Master! Welcome baaaack!"

"Thanks. It's late already. Are the brats asleep?"

"Yup. I sang them a lullaby and they started saying they couldn't eat any more."

What a stereotypical dream . . .

"What about you, Raphtalia, did you have any problems? I found out that coliseum tournament participants apparently get targeted for attacks."

"Huh? Oh, so that's what that was? I did cut a few people down to protect myself . . ."

So she had already taken care of it. She had beaten them at their own game. I guess our match tomorrow would be a win by default. Even so, *cut them down*? I was a bit worried about the path Raphtalia was headed down.

"Did you polish them off?"

"That makes it sound so violent . . . I only injured them. They should be able to move again after two or three days."

I had to wonder about that. After all, Raphtalia had grown up to be pretty tough.

"What about you, Mr. Naofumi?"

"Me? Umm . . . Someone I met at the tavern warned me to watch out for ambushes if I wanted to advance in the tournament. I didn't really get any good info other than that. How did things go with you, Rishia?"

"Huh? Me?! Umm, I managed to get a look at some documents related to matches in the underground coliseum."

"Oh . . ."

We could probably use that info to check which opponents to watch out for, like high-profile fighters that were always winning.

"There are all kinds of fighters, it seems, but there is one in particular competing in this tournament that we need to watch out for. If we end up facing this fighter, it's almost certain to be a difficult battle."

"Difficult doesn't mean impossible, right?"

"Umm, right . . ."

Rishia had seen the kinds of battles we had faced with her own eyes. The underground coliseum tournaments might show you just how formidable people could be, but surely that was child's play compared to something as dreadful as the Spirit Tortoise. Not to mention, having seen Kizuna, Glass, and their crew in action made even the strongest people seem weak. That's the kind of company we had been doing battle alongside, so I sure wasn't afraid.

"So? Who is the fighter?"

"Umm . . . The one we need to watch out for is a person who fights alone—even in team battle tournaments—and almost always wins, or at least places near the top. There was one other similar fighter, but that one isn't participating in this tournament."

Taking on a team battle tournament by yourself . . . Just what kind of hero was this? Maybe one of the seven star heroes was secretly participating in the underground coliseums? It was possible. Honestly, I wouldn't have been surprised if one of the other three holy heroes that had gone missing showed up in the tournament.

"So? Who is it?"

"Umm . . . The person goes by the ring name Nadia, apparently."

Say what? It was that drunkard woman, in other words? You've got to be shitting me. Then again . . . I had only seen one of her attacks, but judging from her skill with magic and the way she moved, it kind of made sense. It had only been by coincidence, but to think I had become acquainted with someone like that.

"Is something wrong?"

"Nah, it's nothing."

Either way, if we ended up fighting her, we would have to be careful.

Chapter Sixteen: Nadia

After all was said and done, the coliseum schedule was changed so that we would fight twice per day, due to a relative decrease in the total number of matches. We had gone on to win for several days in a row now. The day after the ambush had been a win by default, as expected. It even made me consider the idea that going out and waiting around to be ambushed might be a surprisingly good strategy.

Under normal circumstances, our competitors and their backers would be using all kinds of dirty tricks to interfere with our advancement. But I had the accessory dealer and the family of slave traders backing me. Their support also came with their extensive connections throughout the Zeltoble underground.

Speaking of the accessory dealer, I'd dangled the topic of the materials we'd gotten from Kizuna's world in front of him and he'd pounced on it. That guy could smell a profit from a mile away. I wanted to use him to my advantage and figure out a way to mass produce the items that emulated the drop functionality of the holy weapons and their ability to summon people to the waves.

The slave traders and the accessory dealer . . . Thanks to these two entities, the usual underhanded, roundabout efforts to get in our way had been nipped in the bud. Also, the slave trader had apparently heard some kind of strange rumor going around about everyone backing off of us, because we had ties to Nadia.

We had gotten a lot more recognition and ended up being considered one of the more notable teams. We did tend to end our matches pretty much as soon as they started, after all. The guy that threw in the morning star, that had become Filo's new toy, started rooting for us at all of our matches. He'd thrown in a different weapon just recently, too, and Filo had been flinging that one at our opponents as well.

That pretty much summed up how we had been advancing in the tournament. Most of the competitors had already been eliminated, and with only a few fight cards left, we were now in the semifinals.

"Who's our opponent for tomorrow's match?"

"This is the featured fight card for tomorrow. Yes sir."

The slave trader wiped the sweat off his forehead as he handed me a piece of paper. It had our opponent for the next day's match written on it. The name on the paper was . . . Nadia. It looked like she had been placed in the bracket as a seed. I guess the time to fight that woman had finally come.

"Is that the participant that Rishia mentioned?"

"Yeah, it is."

"Huh? The person we fight tomorrow?"

Filo was staring intently at the paper in my hand, like she was really interested.

"She uses lightning magic, but she's not a magic user, so to speak. She's a formidable opponent that can handle herself in close combat, too. She's been fighting her way through team battle tournaments all by herself."

"I wonder just how strong she is."

Then again . . . The way we had been fighting up until now was pretty atypical, too. Defeating the enemy as soon as the announcer screamed "begin" was the norm for us. That was pretty much how all of our matches went. It was only natural that we would end up becoming famous.

"If we can make it through this one, all that will be left is the championship match. The money to buy the village slaves back is almost within our reach!"

"Yes! But . . . lightning?"

"Fehhh . . ."

"You've done a lot to make this happen too, Rishia. You and Raph-chan better be rooting for us."

"Rafu!"

Raph-chan jumped up on Rishia's shoulder and howled. There was no avoiding it. In the end, winning this match and advancing to the next round was our only option.

The next day, we were getting prepared for our fight in

the waiting room at the coliseum. Outside it had been erupting into cheers all day. Our next opponent was an infamous freak of nature that had fought her way up through the team battle tournament all alone. Still, surely she couldn't be stronger than Kyo or the Spirit Tortoise, right? Even so, there was no denying that letting our guard down for even a moment could prove to be fatal.

If we won today, tomorrow we would be fighting in the main event—the championship match. They publicized the event ahead of time. The schedule was ridiculous.

"Maaaster! Can we gooo yet?"

"I guess it is about time. Alright, let's head out, then."

"Yes, and then if we win tomorrow, we can finally rescue the village children."

We had to be careful when facing our opponent today. There might be some kind of catch. I could think of several possibilities.

Here's one . . . What if there was some kind of unspoken rule about who would win that was decided from the start? We hadn't really had to deal with any interference so far, since we had a pretty powerful bunch backing us. But you never knew what kind of obstacles might show up during the middle of a match. Like . . . what if some kind of ceremonial-level support magic was cast on Nadia during the fight? It wasn't unthinkable.

"Let's not take any chances today. Let's finish this . . . and let's make it quick!"

"Agreed!"

"I'll do my beeest!"

We dashed out into the arena, which was surrounded by hordes of nobility, who had come in search of stimulation. They burst out into a roar of cheers. Nadia was already waiting in the arena.

"Oh my, you ignored my advice and showed up anyway, now didn't you?"

"Sorry, but there's a reason that I have to win this match and move on to the finals."

Before the match began, Nadia approached and extended her hand out as if to shake.

"I guess there's no choice then, is there? I don't plan on holding back, though, so you better show me what you've got."

"I don't plan on losing, even if it is you."

We shook hands, and Nadia gave me a friendly hug and whispered in my ear.

"Might that reason be to buy the Lurolona slaves . . . I wonder."

Huh?! This woman knew all about my plan! I couldn't imagine how the information had been leaked, but that meant that she knew what we were after.

"This is the perfect chance if you're looking to make a lot of money quick, isn't it? I'm afraid I'm not going to let you win, though, darling."

She seemed to be under the impression that I was planning on buying the slaves so that I could resell them and make a profit. There was no point in correcting her. In the end, we still needed the money to get Raphtalia's fellow villagers back.

"You took the words right out of my mouth."

After I responded, Nadia gave me a quick nod and put some distance between us.

"And now, a faceoff between Roooooock Vaaallllleeeey's Party . . . and . . . Naaaaadiiiiaaaaaaa! Are you ready?!"

The announcer was shouting like crazy. Every time it made me wonder if that screaming messed up his vocal cords.

"I expect a fair fight, you two! Let the semifinal battle . . . BEEEEGGIIIINNNN!!"

Gooooonnnggggg!

A huge gong sound echoed throughout the coliseum, taking the whole thing one more step over the top.

"Alright then, darling, here I come!"

Nadia held her harpoon up high out in front of her, about to cast her magic.

"We won't let yooouuu!"

"That's right!"

Raphtalia and Filo moved in to strike first, just like we had discussed beforehand. The two of them moved simultaneously, closing in on Nadia rapidly. Raphtalia lifted her katana up over her head and swung it down hard, while Filo struck from the side with both of her claws in an attempt to get inside Nadia's guard.

"Careful now!"

Nadia took several steps backward and . . . she dodged that?! She evaded Raphtalia's and Filo's attacks by a hair's width, as if she had seen right through them.

"We're not finished!"

"Take thiiiis!"

Raphtalia followed through with her katana, continuing the swing upward while thrusting forward. Filo crouched down, slipping in another strike.

"Your swordsmanship sure is straightforward, isn't it? Sorry, but swings like that won't work on a girl like me!"

Nadia brushed Raphtalia's katana off to the side with her harpoon and then used it to vault up into the air, dodging Filo's attack before spinning around and leaping over her back.

"Wha . . ."

"Oooohhh!"

Raphtalia was at a loss for words, but Filo seemed genuinely impressed. The way Nadia responded to their attacks made it obvious that she was a highly skilled mercenary. There was a good reason she had become famous! She'd seen through all of our attacks so far. That was the only explanation for the way she moved.

"Wow! Woooow! Master! I'm gonna do that thiiing!"

"Go for it!"

Filo quickly jumped up on my shoulders and began preparing to use haikuikku. In the meantime, Raphtalia continued to attack Nadia.

"Hiyaaaaa!"

But Nadia continued to dodge every attack at the last moment, as if she could easily predict the path of Raphtalia's katana.

"I can tell you're not used to using a katana. Your lines are all too straight, like you're fighting with a sword, you know? That poor katana is capable of so much more."

Just how strong was this woman? Damn! Did that mean our stats were too low to defeat her head-on? I guess I had no choice, then. With Filo still on my shoulders, I quietly began reciting the incantation for my support magic, Zwiete Aura.

"As the source of your power, the Shield Hero commands you! Let the legends be revealed once more! Support her completely!"

"Zweite Aura!"

I would cast my support magic on Raphtalia to increase her stats and then wait for an opening to cast it on Filo, too, so that we could end this right away . . . or so I thought. I finished reciting the incantation and the instant the magic took its effect on Raphtalia . . . Nadia glanced my way and . . . cast a spell.

"As the source of your power, I command you! Let the

legends be revealed once more! Dispel the power that supports her!"

"Anti-Zweite Aura!"

"What?!"

I realized that the Zweite Aura support magic I'd cast on Raphtalia had been erased. That's right . . . I conjured the magic myself and successfully cast it on Raphtalia, and yet it had been shattered into pieces.

Hold on now! I'd heard that even drifa-level magic could be obstructed, but to block zweite-level magic with such a short incantation . . . Just how skilled was this woman?!

Nadia had rendered my Zweite Aura ineffective. It took a few seconds before I fully understood what had happened, and Raphtalia had also made her attack under the assumption that her stats would be increased, so she ended up missing by a long shot.

"Wha . . ."

"You're wide open!"

With her harpoon in hand, Nadia crouched low and thrust at Raphtalia. The attack was powerful and heavy, just like the one she had delivered to the mercenaries back when we got ambushed.

"Ugh! Ahhhh!"

The attack connected, and Raphtalia went flying and smashed into the arena wall, which let out a loud cracking sound.

"Ra—Shigaraki!"

That was close. If a monster skilled enough to nullify support magic figured out who we really were, there was no telling what kind of attacks she would come at us with.

"I . . . I'm okay."

Raphtalia wobbled to her feet. She had her hand on her shoulder, where the harpoon had connected.

"Ugh . . ."

Nadia went right into casting another spell, as if to say she wouldn't let an opening go to waste.

"Should I throw jingle-jangle?"

"Let's not do that. It would be no joke if that weapon ended up getting used against us right now."

We were already struggling against a single harpoon. We could end up forcing ourselves into a corner if we let her steal that morning star from us. Right now, we had to focus on making sure Raphtalia could continue fighting. I pulled some healing medicine out of my pocket and ran over to Raphtalia. I rubbed it on her wound while casting healing magic. Surely healing magic cast at point-blank range couldn't be obstructed, right?

"Thank you, Mr. Nao . . . Mr. Rock."

"No worries. Anyways, that woman is a monster!"

Our stats may have been lower than normal, but we were undoubtedly still far stronger than your average adventurer. And yet she had easily dodged all of Raphtalia's and Filo's attacks. She must have been ridiculously strong. I had expected the fight to end with Raphtalia's and Filo's opening attacks.

I checked my status screen and several sections were blurred out. I'd suspected this might be the case, but apparently the arena area was under the effect of some kind of magic. I wasn't sure if it was Nadia's doing, something paid for by the spectators, or if the organizers were secretly interfering, but I guess I was going to have to get out in front and restrain Nadia myself.

"Is it my tuuurn?"

Filo's question signaled that she had finished preparing for her haikuikku-Spiral Strike combo.

"I guess so. It looks like we can't afford to hold back with this one."

I'd hoped to make it through this thing without revealing our secret, but this wasn't the kind of opponent that would let us off that easy.

"Shigaraki, I'm going to use my shields to restrain the opponent. Once I do, you attack along with Humming. Got it?"

"Un . . . understood."

Thanks to the healing magic, Raphtalia was still able to fight. We had to make it through this or it was all for nothing. There was no other choice. I walked toward Nadia slowly.

"Oh? You're changing your formation, I see. Is it finally

time for you to make an appearance, little Rock?"

"I guess so. They say you're supposed to save the main performance for last, but I'm going to make an exception and personally put on a show just for you."

Up until now, Filo and Raphtalia had finished off all our opponents before I ever had to do anything, but that wasn't going to work here, so I had no choice but to join the fight.

"In that case, I've got my magic ready to go, so . . . How about I give you a little performance, too?"

"Here I come!"

I took off running with Filo still on my shoulders. My stats had been reduced by the curse, but I was still pretty quick. It felt like the rest of the world was moving in slow motion as I sprinted toward Nadia. Nadia was considerably quick, too, as she pointed her harpoon at me and cast her spell. I had no idea just how powerful her magic could be, but I'd show her I could withstand anything she could dish out!

"You better not be thinking about taking this straight on, darling. You won't survive!"

"As the source of your power, I command you! Let the true way be revealed once more! Thunder and lightning! Eradicate those before me!"

"Drifa Thunder Burst!"

As I ran toward Nadia, she cast her magic and . . . an ultra-thick bolt of lightning came hurling right at me. The roar of the thunder and the flash of the lightning were so intense that I thought I might end up deaf and blind—that's how highly condensed the magical power of her attack was.

There was a ceremonial magic spell called Judgement that brought lightning down from the sky. It was the same one that the high priest of the Church of the Three Heroes used on me in his surprise attack. All by herself, Nadia had just hurled a magical attack at me that was pretty much on the same level as Judgement. This monster of a woman blew my mind. She was so powerful it made me want to lecture her about not showing up to help when we were out fighting enemies like the Spirit Tortoise.

I hugged Filo close and protected her with my shield and cape as I kept running. The magic that Nadia had cast smashed into me with a loud crackle. Speed was everything when it came to lightning. Only an instant after I first laid my eyes on it, it was right there in front of my face. It was a formidable attack, and "burnt black" wouldn't even begin to describe the damage it would have done to anyone other than me.

"Eat this! Our true joint attack!"

I could feel myself being electrocuted by the bolt of lightning, which I deflected with my shield, before hurling Filo with all my might.

"Un . . . unbelievableeeeee! Rock Valley just took Nadia's finishing move head-on and launched a counterattack of his ownnnnnnn!"

The announcer was practically screaming at the top of his lungs, and the spectators erupted into cheers. Who cares about that! Right now, I needed to focus on defeating the enemy in front of me.

"Take thiiiiiissss!"

Filo channeled all the magic power she had stored and launched her haikuikku-Spiral Twist combo straight at Nadia.

"Oh my! Impressive! That was my finishing move, too, you know?"

Nadia shouted excitedly when she saw Filo flying at her at a speed even faster than her own lightning had been. I couldn't tell if she was flustered or just happy. Surely there was no way she could outmaneuver Filo's attack, right?

"From what I saw in your other matches, she can maintain that increased speed in her movements for three seconds. That means she'll deliver a powerful attack during that time, right?"

"Yah!"

"In that case . . ."

She'd predicted that I would counterattack by throwing Filo? No, that wasn't it. She must have realized that we would use the time she was casting her magic as our chance to launch an attack. Nadia hugged her harpoon close and began casting another spell. Yeah . . . She was practically announcing that she was going to reuse the thunderclouds that had appeared when she made her previous attack.

Her incantation was fast—too fast! I'd never seen anyone use magic like that!

"As the source of your power, I command you! Let the true way be revealed once more! Lightning! Become the force that protects and supports me!"

"Drifa Lightning Speed!"

Magic . . . Such a profound art. There was a thunderous roar, and lightning rained down onto Nadia herself, but the lightning enveloped and electrified her body as if it were some kind of support magic. Rather than facing Filo's charge head-on, Nadia made a large, yet swift, evasive maneuver.

This was bad. I was guessing Filo's attack would continue on in a straight line. She could probably alter the path slightly, but haikuikku would wear off before she actually managed to connect with Nadia. It wasn't likely that Spiral Strike on its own would be enough for a decisive blow.

"Kyaahhhh!!"

Filo made some kind of noise that sounded like a shriek as she hurled toward Nadia. Crackling charges of lightning were jumping from the electrified Nadia to Filo, just like static electricity. Ouch . . . Filo was spinning around in what was basically a special, lethal move, but even so, I'm sure getting electrocuted would still be painful.

"Here I goooo!"

Filo still hadn't given up. In that case, there was only one thing for me to do.

"Air Strike Shield! Second Shield! Dritte Shield!"

I made sure Nadia couldn't dodge, by placing my shields behind her, at her feet, and beside her, leaving her with no escape. The shields would protect Filo from being electrocuted, while also restricting Nadia's movement, to make sure Filo's attack landed.

"Oh! That's an interesting little trick you have there, isn't it? You surprised little ol' me!"

"I have a few of those up my sleeve."

The only way she could go was to her other side or up. If possible, I wanted to keep her from moving sideways to help make sure Filo's attack connected. As if to grant me my wish, Nadia crouched ever so slightly in preparation to jump to the side.

"Not happening! Shield Prison!"

I added my finishing touch by placing my Shield Prison to her side and sealing off her escape route! How did she like that! That was my shield interference combo that had cornered even L'Arc! My job may have been to protect, but I could still pull a trick like this off, too!

All that was left was for Filo's Spiral Strike to connect, and then Raphtalia could attack.

"Oh my! You sure are impressive! But . . ."

Nadia thrust her harpoon into the ground hard and used it to swiftly propel herself up into a back flip over the shield that I had produced behind her.

"Waaahhhh!"

Filo charged smack dab into my shield, and along with a loud crunching sound, all of her speed and power vanished into thin air. Damn! But I still had Chain Shield!

"Cha—"

Before I could finish calling out the skill name, it felt almost like the air suddenly began to cling to us. It felt like air resistance . . . Just trying to move my arm felt cumbersome. What was happening?

As the question crossed my mind, I looked around and saw bubbles coming up out of the arena floor, as if we were at the bottom of the ocean or something. I could still breathe, so just what was this?!

"Oh? I guess our exchanges were too fast for their liking. It looks like they've used magic to alter the playing field and slow things down."

What?! Hindering us at a time like this?! This coliseum allowed spectators to provide support by making a monetary offering. I guess this was just an extension of that.

"The thing is . . . This is cooperative magic known as The Great Deep, and it artificially creates an underwater environment, which just happens to be where I fight best! I guess I really can't lose this one now, can I?"

"No way . . ."

Raphtalia had leapt in front of me, with her katana readied

to strike in a follow-up attack, but she blurted out in surprise.

"Damn it! Chain—"

"Too bad! You're one step too late."

The situation felt like some kind of farce comedy, as Nadia used my shields to shield herself, while thrusting Filo away with her harpoon. She then used it to hold Raphtalia off after parrying her strike.

Just how many fights had this woman been in?! I'd played my shield skill trump card to block her escape route, and she still dealt with the situation in a flash. Interference from the audience and our stats might have had something to do with it, too. But I had a feeling she was probably our most formidable opponent yet, when it came to pure skill.

"Ughhh . . . That was ouchieeee . . . But!"

Filo had smashed into my shield. Not to mention, she'd also been electrocuted by the lighting surrounding Nadia. But she pulled herself together and went to attack again. She was starting to look pretty beat-up.

"We're not done! Chain Shield!"

I wasn't going to just stand back and watch. But damn, I guess it was because of the artificial underwater environment. Nadia's lightning was fanning out over a wide area now. It would have been one thing if we could nullify it, but apparently that wasn't possible. So Nadia was hitting all of us with her attacks—with that formidable lightning! It was no problem for me, but that wasn't the case for Raphtalia and Filo. Still, if I could just subdue this woman then Raphtalia and Filo could attack unilaterally!

"Got you!"

Chains now linked my shields, which then closed in on Nadia. I used the shields to bind her body tightly, restraining her movement.

"Oh, little Rock! You naughty boy, you!"

"Oh, shut it!"

Despite being restrained, Nadia pointed a hand at Filo and quickly cast a spell.

"Zweite Thunder Bolt!"

"Again, not happening! E Float Shield! Change Shield!"

Her attacks were still fanning out and proving to be a real pain in the ass, but I had to do what I could. I cast E Float Shield and willed it to move to where it could protect Filo. Then I used Change Shield to change it to Iron Shield, since that was a metallic shield that seemed like it would be conductive and thus absorb electrical-type attacks.

"Oh my!"

Nadia's thunder bolt smashed into the shield, electrifying the shield but nothing else.

"Don't forget about me!"

Raphtalia had backed off so that I could trap Nadia with Chain Shield, and now she lunged forward with her katana held high over her head.

"You're lively as usual, aren't you? But you're still full of openings!"

"Huh? Ahh!"

Paying no attention to the restraints I had placed on her, Nadia grabbed her harpoon with her free arm and used it to trip Raphtalia. Raphtalia attempted to regain her balance, but Nadia used that momentum against her as well and gave Raphtalia a light shove. It knocked her onto her bottom right in front of my eyes. Damn it. This underwater stage was nothing but trouble for us.

"I guess that means you're next, little Rock."

Even worse, the Chain Shield time limit had been reached and the effect wore off. It was just me versus Nadia now.

"Give it your best shot!"

I may have been cursed, but my defense rating was still the same as usual. There was hardly any magical attack that would leave me with more than a scratch.

"Drifa Thunder Guard!"

Nadia called the crackling lightning down onto herself. It seemed to be counteroffensive magic that would protect the user. That would work well in a situation like this, but it would take a lot more than that to hurt me.

"Oh? Did you come prepared to deal with my attacks, then?"

"You could say that."

It's not like I'd devised a special countermeasure. I was just confident that I could withstand her attacks with my defense rating.

"By the way, little Rock, are you not going to raise a hand against me?"

Nadia seemed to be suspicious of the fact that I was fighting against her barehanded. Sorry, but I couldn't use a weapon even if I wanted to.

I wasn't sure if it was more support for Nadia, but I felt magic flowing around the arena. We had been artificially placed underwater, and now thunderclouds began to appear overhead. Seeing clouds, while underwater, was the kind of peculiar sight that you could only experience in another world.

Just how much support were they going to give Nadia?!

"Ughhh . . . I can feel the sparklieeesssss . . ."

Even worse, the electrical output of Nadia's Thunder Guard was so high that Raphtalia and Filo couldn't even attempt to attack. Even if I used Change Shield to switch my Float Shield to a shield that would give the electricity somewhere to go again, there was just so much lightning surrounding us that it wouldn't even matter!

"Ugh . . . Even for little ol' me, this is a bit . . . much . . ."

I looked over at Nadia. She was still smiling, but I could see a sense of urgency in her expression. I wasn't sure if it was because she was taking damage from her own lightning or if

Raphtalia's and Filo's attacks had taken their toll.

"You're not making this easy, you know."

Nadia stabbed at my back forcefully with her harpoon, but it simply made a loud thud and showed no sign of penetrating. The fact that she couldn't use defense rating attacks, like the old Hengen Muso lady, was my only consolation. Otherwise, even I would have been in some serious trouble.

"Here I go!"

"Me toooo!"

It wasn't like Raphtalia and Filo had just been hanging out doing nothing, while staring at the wall of lightning—they had been preparing to use skills. They couldn't really get close, so they would need to use either a ranged magical attack or a skill.

"Wind Blade! Vacuum!"

Raphtalia took a quick-draw stance before unsheathing her katana and hurling a blade of wind at Nadia.

"Drifa Wind Shot!"

Filo seemed to have fired off a highly condensed ball of wind. They were up against a dense wall of lightning, after all. It was obvious they had put some thought into choosing their attacks. Raphtalia's skill made a loud cracking sound as it smashed through the wall, and Filo's magic followed right behind.

"Yeah! Nice work! Attack Support!"

A dart appeared in my left hand and I stabbed Nadia with it. The stabbing itself had basically no effect, but the effect of the Attack Support skill would increase the damage of the following attack twofold. Would she be able to withstand that?

"Oh?"

Nadia raised her harpoon high overhead as if to strike down the oncoming attack, but apparently casting two spells at once was too much even for her. Raphtalia's and Filo's attacks were nothing to make light of, either.

"I guess I have no choice, do I?"

Nadia took her harpoon and . . . broke it in half?! When she did, the power inside of it . . . some kind of magical power came flooding out. I felt an explosion of magic power originating from the harpoon.

I'd seen something like this in a game. There was an attack that had been some kind of finishing move and could only be used once because it required you to sacrifice your weapon. The trade-off for the power was that your weapon would be destroyed, and you could never use it again. To think a weapon like that existed in this world!

"That could be dangerous if you let it hit you in the wrong spot, just so you know."

Nadia threw the broken harpoon at Raphtalia's and Filo's attacks, and it smashed right into them. In the same instant, a blinding light flashed and the harpoon exploded.

"Kyaaaahhh!"

"Ahhh!"

Raphtalia and Filo were thrown backward by the force of the explosion. A protective membrane that must have been some form of support magic appeared around Nadia, and the explosion blew right by her like a strong breeze. I was standing by her side, and it was the same for me.

This support from outside the match was a real pain in the ass! Damn them! All of their support had been going straight to Nadia for a while now, too!

"You sure are tough, woman!"

"You think so?"

"We're not done!"

"Yup! Take thiiis!"

Raphtalia and Filo sprung forward out of the cloud of dust, ready to strike.

"Oh! I like your spunk!"

Nadia use the remaining half of the harpoon—the piece that had been broken off by the lightning magic—to intercept Raphtalia's katana.

"Argh . . ."

Raphtalia struggled against Nadia's harpoon while being electrocuted, and Filo used that as her chance to attack. Nadia twisted around in an attempt to dodge the attack, but Filo's claws dug into her skin.

"Oh my . . . Impressive!"

Nadia's harpoon had taken on the form of a lightning bolt.

But she changed it for just an instant, which was long enough for her to swipe at Filo and send her flying away.

"Kyahhh! Awww . . . I almost had heeerrrr!"

"That leaves one more now, doesn't it?"

Raphtalia was still struggling with Nadia, who then used the remaining half of the broken harpoon to . . . deliver a swift jab to Raphtalia's chest. The way she pulled off these ridiculous attacks, so casually, made it seem like it was all some kind of big joke or something.

"Huh? Uhh . . . ?! Ahhhhhh!"

A small explosion sent Raphtalia flying right in front of my eyes, as if she had been hit by a grenade. But Raphtalia broke her fall skillfully and sprung to her feet with her katana held out in front of her.

"I guess expecting to finish you off with that would be overly optimistic, now wouldn't it? I already used the bigger explosion earlier, unfortunately. Taking that one point-blank might have been dangerous, even for a girl like me."

To top it all off, Nadia had the nerve to use my cloak, of all things, to shield herself from the force of the explosion.

"Ugh . . . You're so strong . . ."

Seriously! For a single person to be this strong, surely they would have to be some kind of monster, right?

And then, finally, someone threw a couple of robes into the arena as support for Raphtalia and Filo.

"What is this? I see! Fi—Humming! Put this on! It will nullify the lightning!"

"Woooow! Neeeaaat!"

Raphtalia and Filo threw on the robes that had been tossed into the arena.

"Little Rock, you can't just keep hanging all over me like this, you know? Don't you think you should approach our relationship a bit more strategically?"

"Shut up! I don't have time for that kind of thing!"

Luckily, she no longer had a weapon, as far as I could tell. This was a chance I wasn't going to pass up.

"Aww, that's too bad. In that case, I guess I'll make the first move."

Once again, Nadia seized the chance to begin casting magic while Raphtalia and Filo were busy putting on the robes. Damn! Was there nothing I could do to stop her? The woman never really made much of an attempt to attack me, but even if she had, my counterattacks were pretty limited.

The Demon Dragon Shield had a counterattack effect called "C demon bullet," but it didn't seem like it would have much of an effect on Nadia. I don't know if it was because it was categorized as a counterattack, but her Thunder Guard didn't trigger it at all. I guess being able to counterattack counterattacks would just make things too easy.

At last, it looked like Nadia had finally decided to focus her attacks on me, perhaps because I was restricting her movement. I was sure it would just be some ranged magic attack. In that case, I would just surround us with shields and have them all fire off counterattacks at once.

Nadia began brazenly chanting her incantation.

"Air Strike Shield! Second Shield! Dritte Shield! Shield Prison! Change Shield!"

"As the source of your power, I command you! Let the true way be revealed once more! Lightning! Paralyze those before me!"

"Drifa Paralyzing Thunder!"

Wha?! She had cast a status effect-type spell that wouldn't register as aggressive! I had completely miscalculated her intentions! I'd changed my shields expecting to produce a counterattack, but they showed absolutely no response.

"Ugh . . ."

The powerful paralysis magic loosened my grip on Nadia slightly.

"Oh! Impressive! That would have paralyzed a normal opponent and rendered them completely immobile, you know."

While she was talking, Nadia took advantage of the tiny opening I had shown to escape from my grasp and put some distance between us.

"I've had to grow tough to survive."

Thankfully I had increased my resistance to status effects. I'd figured I would never know what to expect in the underground coliseum, but . . . man, this fight was tough. Regardless of any differences in our stats, this Nadia woman was a ridiculously capable fighter. If we hadn't been affected by the curse, winning wouldn't have been a problem, but it still would've taken more than just brute force, most likely. She wasn't the type of opponent that you could beat with lower or even equal stats.

Even so, it didn't make sense that we were having this hard a time. There had to be something else going on. It made me wonder if . . . maybe some kind of spell had been cast on us to lower our stats, and some kind of support had been given to Nadia to raise hers? Whenever I tried to check my status screen, something just felt off.

Should I just use the Shield of Wrath and incinerate everything in sight? The thought suddenly crossed my mind. But I wanted to avoid relying on that shield, even for reasons other than reduced stats. Luckily, Raphtalia and Filo could still fight. Not to mention, robes that would nullify the lightning had been thrown into the arena to help them out. If I could get hold of and restrain Nadia again, surely things would go better this time.

And just then, a second harpoon was tossed into the arena toward Nadia. Damn it! Did their support have to have such perfect timing?!

"It's been a while since I faced an opponent that pushed

me this far, you know. I guess it's time for little ol' me to . . . get serious."

Nadia switched her stance to a shallow squat and the surrounding spectators burst into cheers. They were expecting something interesting to happen.

"There it is! Nadia has finally decided to take off the gloves and turn into her animal form! Everyone! Feast your eyes on Nadia's no-holds-barred coommmmbbaaaatttttt!"

Animal form?! If I remember correctly, therianthropes were basically demi-humans whose animal element was more prominent. Just recently, the slave trader had also told me that there were types of demi-humans that could change into their animal form at will. And their stats would skyrocket upon changing. In other words, all this time, Nadia hadn't been fighting seriously. This was bad . . .

Magic power began gathering around Nadia, forming something that resembled fog and making it difficult to see her. A black silhouette was probably a good description. Along with a bubbling sound, Nadia's body began to swell up. I considered trying to stop the transformation, but it was happening too fast. It probably would have been over by the time I got anywhere close to her.

Moments later, Nadia's transformation was complete. Her new form featured a vivid contrast of white on black. Her face had become streamlined, and she had the kind of forked tail that would help a fish move around in the water. Although, it looked far more powerful than what a fish would need. Her skin was glossy—you might have mistaken it for rubber at first glance. She had a dorsal fin on her back that looked like a shark fin, but she didn't look scary like a shark would.

Well, I had seen this kind of animal used in foreign horror films, but not nearly as often as they used sharks. On the contrary, it was usually an animal that ended up forging friendships with young boys or something like that.

"Huh?"

Raphtalia uttered something that made it clear she was dumbfounded, but this wasn't the time for that. We needed to pay close attention and be ready to respond.

This animal was one of the more popular attractions at aquariums in Japan. Of course, since Nadia was a therianthrope, she had two arms and two legs, unlike the actual animal. Yeah . . . The animal I was familiar with that most resembled Nadia's new form belonged to the infraorder Cetacea, parvorder Odontoceti, family Delphinidae, genus Orcinus . . . In other words, it was a killer whale.

I had seen a variety of different therianthropes since coming to this world, but this was my first transforming killer whale. She looked like a real heavyweight that wouldn't be able to move very quickly . . . but I was sure that probably wasn't the case. She was about the same size as Filo in her filolial form. To be blunt, she was huge.

"Alright then . . . Here I come!"

Considering how powerful she was and the fact that she used lightning, I was imagining a therianthrope that was part raiju, nue, or some other magical creature. Or maybe a dragon? A tiger or something could have fit the image, too. But she ended up being an aquatic therianthrope.

More important than that was the fact that she had been holding back until now. It was safe to assume that all of her stats had increased. That was evident from the way she was moving around the artificial underwater environment so effortlessly, with just a tiny wave of her tail. Yeah, I was sure we would regret it if we let her appearance fool us. She was probably building up speed to prepare an attack.

Her strategy initially appeared to depend primarily on magic, but perhaps that was because she didn't use brute force, until she had changed into her animal form. It was probably pretty rare for her to transform, so attacking in this form was something she saved for times when her opponent had some kind of equipment that enabled them to deal with her magic.

"Umm . . . uhh . . ."

Raphtalia was just standing there in a daze, staring at Nadia as she swam around.

"Stop just standing there! You want to die?!"

This wasn't an opponent that we could finish off in one blow, you know!

"Ra—Shigaraki! Let's do this!"

I tried to get her on board, but Raphtalia was in a complete stupor and had let her guard down entirely for some reason.

"Big sis!"

Filo tried getting her attention, too, but it was useless.

"Here I come!"

Nadia readied her harpoon, accelerated even more, and shot straight at us to deliver her attack. I jumped out in front to protect Raphtalia and put out multiple shields in front of us. Just as I was about to cast Shooting Star Shield . . .

"Sadeena?"

Chapter Seventeen: Farce

Huh? Raphtalia . . . was talking to Nadia? Nadia was closing in at a ridiculous speed, but when Raphtalia spoke to her, she came to a sudden halt directly in front of us.

"Oh?"

The audience broke out into a commotion upon seeing Nadia stop.

Hold on . . . Sadeena was supposed to be the fisher from Raphtalia's village, right? The incredibly strong fisher that was . . . a therianthrope . . . They'd said an aquatic therianthrope, right? All of the details were matching up! Did that mean Nadia was actually Sadeena?! No way, a coincidence that huge—

"It really is you, isn't it, Sadeena? What are you doing here in a place like this?!"

Raphtalia loosened her equipment to reveal her ears and tail.

"Hmm . . . I'm surprised at how big you've gotten, but you must be little Raphtalia, right?"

"Yes, it's me, Sadeena."

A coincidence that huge . . . was possible, apparently. This was a good thing, right? One of Raphtalia's fellow villagers was standing right here in front of our eyes, after all. Nadia, or rather

Sadeena, stared at me hard for a moment and then cocked her head to the side, like she was trying to figure something out. Then she smiled cheerfully for some reason.

"This sure is a surprise, isn't it? Do me a favor and pretend like we're fighting so we can talk for a bit, will you?"

"Sure."

"So why are you here fighting in this tournament?"

Sadeena changed her target and came after me with her harpoon, pretending like we were struggling with each other. Raphtalia and Filo rushed in swinging, as if to engage in close combat, and then acted like they had been parried and thrown back.

"We needed to get our hands on some money quickly so that we could purchase the village children. We're currently rebuilding the territory where the village used to be."

Raphtalia spoke quietly as she explained the situation to Sadeena. The way everyone was looking at us was really starting to bother me. Up until just a few moments ago it had been all-out warfare, and now we were just kind of poking back and forth at each other.

"I guess it would probably take a while to explain how that happened, wouldn't it? You've really become something, little Raphtalia . . ."

She seemed to be getting sentimental . . . Everyone was watching us!

"Hurry up and make some more of that lightning from earlier. Raphtalia and Filo, you two do some kind of showy attack that looks like a finishing move. I'll use some flashy skills, too."

"Understood."

"Okaaay!"

Sadeena cast one of her more impressive-looking lightning attacks over a wide area. It spread out all the way to the arena walls with a thundering roar. I did my best to look like I was struggling and put out my shields to protect against her all-show-and-no-go attack. Then we waited for Raphtalia and Filo to attack. The two of them fired off their own flashy skills back to back.

The truth was, it was all just being staged, using illusion magic. In the meantime, we continued our conversation.

"Why couldn't you have fought in your animal form from the start?"

If she had used that form from the beginning, Raphtalia probably would have recognized her right away . . . Apparently Raphtalia didn't know about Sadeena's human form, either. If she had, we wouldn't have ended up in a mess like this.

"Oh? Take a look at yourself, little Rock. I could ask you the same basic thing, you know? Using my human form is like wearing a disguise for me."

I could understand what she was trying to say. We were

wearing kabuto helmets and other equipment to conceal our faces. For Sadeena, her human form wasn't her everyday form, in other words. I was tempted to make a snide remark about how that must have felt. I'd have to ask her about it later.

"Well, what should we do about this, then?"

I returned my thoughts to the problem at hand. If Sadeena wasn't our enemy, that meant we should be able to settle this battle by talking things over.

"We have a ton of money bet on ourselves. You figure out a way to lose on purpose."

"As much as I'd like to, I'm afraid I can't do that. I need the money, too, and I've already used quite a bit of it, actually."

"Alcohol?"

"Oh shush. I've been buying up the village children, with a little help from a merchant who has a thing for me."

Sadeena explained the whole situation briefly and . . . Well, basically, the skyrocketing prices of the Lurolona slaves was partially her fault. Sadeena said she'd bought several of the villagers and was harboring them somewhere in Zeltoble. It was the shady merchant, the one working for her, who had originally offered the reward for the Lurolona slaves to help find them more quickly. But that backfired and ended up causing the prices of the Lurolona slaves to soar. And so, in order to scrape up the funds to purchase the overpriced slaves herself, Sadeena had enlisted the help of another shady weapons merchant to get her into the underground coliseum, among other things.

Why didn't she search for the slaves in Melromarc and buy them there to begin with? Jeez . . . That's what I wanted to say, anyway, but then I realized that the stigma of being a therianthrope would have made that difficult, prior to the Church of the Three Heroes being dismantled. In that case, it would have been quicker to place the order in Zeltoble, where it would be a lot easier to make money, too.

So according to Sadeena, her job at the tournament was to the make it to the finals and then throw the championship match. It had been decided that her opponent in that match would be a dark horse, and her loss would ensure a big win. Apparently she had gone into debt purchasing the slaves, too . . . So in all actuality, the Lurolona slaves that she was harboring were essentially hostages!

"What should we do then, I wonder. If we're not careful, I could have a price placed on my head and the slaves could end up being sold off, you know?"

"What kind of debt are we talking about?"

Sadeena told me the total amount of debt she'd incurred. Damn . . . It was a lot. Still, it was about even with what we were set to win on the championship. If the people who had lent her the money could wait until we got the payout . . . things might just work out.

Sadeena must have figured out what I was thinking,

because she put a good amount of distance between us and then nodded. Alright! In that case, it was time to put on a farce.

"Chain Shield!"

Chains extended out as the Chain Shield skill linked the shields that had been scattered across the arena, and they all started spinning. The shields restrained Sadeena immediately, making it look like she had left herself open. If Sadeena had been serious, I'm sure she would have broken the chains or just dodged.

"Shigaraki! Humming! Use your finishing move!"

I yelled at them as loud as I could. They must have understood, because they both nodded and began preparing, building up magic power. Sadeena started trying to break free of her restrictions but made it look like she was having a hard time. A large crashing noise rang out.

"Hahaha! Those are no ordinary chains, you know? You're not going to get out of those unless I let you!"

I threw in some contrived commentary to buy time for Raphtalia and Filo to finish their preparations. The audience was brimming with climactic tension. We would keep going until they had reached maximum satisfaction with the performance. Sadeena was grinning. This wasn't the time to smile! What if they realized what was going on?!

"You're in for a big surprise if you think these restraints will work on a girl like me!"

"Muhahaha! Go ahead and struggle all you want!"

We threw in a bit of back and forth like that, and then, finally, Raphtalia and Filo finished preparing their magic. At the very same instant, Sadeena used brute force to break free from the chains that had been restricting her, tearing them to pieces. I responded with a shriek.

"Whaaat?!"

If this had been for real, I probably would have just clicked my tongue in annoyance. Even I had to admit, the whole performance was pretty lame. But the audience seemed to really be getting into it, and they erupted into loud cheers.

"But it's already too late! Let's do this!"

"Let's!"

"Okaaay!"

A huge tornado appeared. Did Filo really understand the concept of putting on a performance? I was a bit worried at first, but she'd produced a cyclone so massive that none of the Zweite Tornado spells she had cast before even came close. At first glance, it appeared to be a super, powered-up version of the magic she had been using so far. Raphtalia fired off a fake skill to go along with Filo's magic.

"Illusion Blade!"

Immediately after she shouted the name, countless katanas appeared and began swirling around with the tornado. The whole thing was headed toward Sadeena. The katanas hit her dead-on, almost as if they were being sucked in toward her.

"Uuugggghhhhhh!"

She was putting on a real performance over there. *I escaped from the chains, but the katanas landed a direct hit!* That's what she was acting out. And that scream sounded like it hurt! I almost thought she might really be in pain, but I couldn't imagine Raphtalia actually hurting one of her fellow villagers. The tornado and katana onslaught continued for twenty or thirty seconds and then . . . stopped.

". . ."

Sadeena was just standing there with a well-performed look of shock on her face. Several moments later, she fell backward onto the floor with a loud thud. Apparently that's not what the spectators were expecting to see, because the whole coliseum fell silent.

"There's no way I can win this one. I give up!"

Pretending that she had exhausted both spirit and technique, and lacked the physical strength to continue on, Sadeena admitted her defeat.

Chapter Eighteen: Exhibition Match

After a short pause, the audience burst into cheers.

"We win."

It had turned out to be a pretty blatant farce, but we still had a lot to do after this. First, we would have to go work something out with the merchant that Sadeena was working for. Otherwise, there was a good chance that Raphtalia's fellow villagers might end up being sold off as compensation for Sadeena's debt, before we even got our hands on the prize money.

Either way . . . the next fight was sure to be a throwaway match. I didn't even want to consider the possibility that our opponent could be as strong as Sadeena.

"Sheesh . . . You sure surprised me with that one."

Sadeena offered us her insincere felicitations. Then again, the plan had been for her to throw a match from the very start, so surely an upset like this wouldn't be a problem. At least that's what I thought, but apparently the people running the tournament weren't happy with how things turned out. A messenger ran up to the announcer and passed him something, which the announcer then read out.

"Ahem . . . The organizing committee would like to express their heartfelt appreciation for the excitement shown by our guests today. Furthermore, they would now like to conduct a quick survey in an attempt to provide our guests with an even more enjoyable experience."

Even the announcer had a suspicious look in his eyes while reading the message. I had a good idea what was going on, but there was no point in complaining. The spectators broke out into a commotion. They hadn't called it a disqualification or anything like that, since the underground coliseum basically had no rules to start out with. But they could still take action under the guise of providing additional entertainment. That was my guess. They probably couldn't do anything to us directly, due to the involvement of the slave trader and the accessory dealer. So they had decided to deal with us right here like this.

"The members of the tournament organizing committee will now be making an appearance."

After the announcer finished speaking, up near the top of the coliseum, near the seating area reserved for distinguished guests, several pudgy merchants appeared. The one that looked vile enough to be their representative raised both of his arms into the air, as if waiting for applause.

"Members of the audience! We, the organizing committee of this tournament, come before you now in an attempt to provide you with an even more enjoyable experience today."

He spoke slowly in a loud voice to ensure that everyone in the audience could hear him. The match was already over, so what was he planning on doing?

But actually, I'd felt this kind of atmosphere before. I could sense that something really bad for us was about to happen. The whole thing about the tournament champion having been decided from the start annoyed me to begin with, and now they were trying to mess with us on top of that. It reminded me of the shit I'd had to put up with from the Church of the Three Heroes and friends.

They hung up some kind of banner behind the distinguished guest seating.

"How would you all like to see our fighters here compete once more in an exhibition match?! What say you!"

"Whaaat?!"

I tried to express my disapproval. Raphtalia, Filo, and Sadeena obviously felt the same, but they had been left speechless with shock.

"Oh my . . ."

Damn! So they could just deal with an unexpected result by obstructing the contestants and making it look like part of the entertainment. In stark contrast to our expressions of disapproval, the audience clapped in excitement. This was bad. If we tried to refuse, they would just declare it a loss by default or something.

"And noooooowwww! Their opponent!"

The merchant snapped his fingers and three figures

appeared at the fighters' entrance of the arena. Huh? What was up with them? Was the way they were walking supposed to look . . . natural? Some weirdo dressed like a clown came walking out along with two masked, life-sized puppets . . . or whatever they were. They looked like mannequins that had been dressed up. I had no idea what they actually were because of the masks.

"Little Rock, this could get a liiiittle bit dangerous, just so you know."

"Why is that?"

"That fighter has gotten popular lately for going around and wreaking havoc at all of the tournaments in this area. She's incredibly strong. I was under the impression she wouldn't be participating in this tournament, though . . ."

Had they brought someone in that wasn't even participating? Maybe they bribed her? I seem to remember Rishia saying something about watching out for this one. Regardless, surely we should be able to win with someone as strong as Sadeena on our side, right?

"That's right! It's Murrrdeeerrrr Pierrot!!!"

So it was some messed up clown? Talk about a creepy ring name. Of course, whatever her name really was, that was just how it had been translated so that I would understand. An earsplitting roar of applause came from the audience.

"An exhibition match featuring Rock Valley's Party and Nadia versus Murder Pierrot! The survey results will be tallied in three minutes! Bets will be accepted for ten minutes following the beginning of the match! What say you?!"

The spectators all began noisily talking it over with each other, but the way they were looking at us . . . Their eyes were filled with bloodthirsty curiosity. Well, there you go. I guess we could give up on the possibility of the survey results being in opposition of the match.

"Furthermore! All bets made on the Rock Valley's Party versus Nadia match will be refunded immediately! Everyone! Why not use that extra cash to bet big now and perhaps win big?! So tell me, yay or nay?! Those in favor, raise your hand!"

More than half of the spectators in the venue raised their hand in response to the merchant. Bah . . . They played right into his hands.

"But seriously, how can they get away with pulling something like this off?!"

"Little Rock, take a good look at what's written on the banner behind the merchants . . ."

"Why? What does it say?"

It was written in several different languages, but it took me a while to find the only one I knew, which was Melromarc's written language.

"It says that, as a special exception, all bets placed on Nadia will remain in effect at the predetermined odds, should Murder Pierrot win. Anyone that originally bet on me will be in favor of the match, since that means they haven't lost anything yet. Did anyone bet on you prior to the match, little Rock?"

Ugh . . . I wanted to win big, so I'd gone out of my way to make sure my bet was placed anonymously. Aside from us, the slave trader, and the accessory dealer, there may not have been anyone else.

"Hold on! Can they really do that?! Surely they can't just decide on a rule that ridiculous, even if it is the underground coliseum!"

"That's why they took a vote, and the vote ruled in favor of it."

The organizers were rotten, but this audience was no better! They all just improvised to get whatever they wanted, no matter how ridiculous it might have been!

Then again, if I thought of it from a merchant's point of view, I did kind of understand. The organizers had sent Sadeena in as an assassin, but she ended up being defeated unexpectedly. They would have to make up for that loss somehow. But relying on their authority to interfere with the opponent would be difficult. In that case, the only real option would be to force their play by winning the support of the audience.

The announcer was averting his gaze. He wouldn't be able to make things any more disadvantageous for us than they already were now. If they went too far, the spectators would become suspicious. In all actuality, some of them already seemed to be confused by the survey. It was a heavy-handed move, and if they took it any further than this, their true intentions would be exposed. That meant that winning this match would essentially be the same as winning the championship!

"Alright! Might as well use this time to cast some healing magic."

I figured we should treat our wounds and recover our strength as much as possible, before the match started. I tried to cast healing magic on Raphtalia and Filo.

"Zweite Heal!"

But . . . What was going on? I felt the healing magic dissipate without ever actually taking hold, just like when Sadeena had blocked our magic earlier.

"Little Rock, there's something you need to know, so listen to me for a second."

"What is it?"

"The organizers are completely blocking our magic here inside of the arena."

"Does that mean it wasn't you that blocked the support magic I tried to cast?"

"No, that was me. But this is different. Right now, there are dozens of magic users all working together to completely obstruct our magic. They're casting counter-magic nonstop from several areas around the arena."

Their efforts to sabotage us just kept getting more and

more annoying . . . Whatever, if we couldn't use magic then I'd just apply the healing medicine I'd brought. We had two minutes left before the match started. We would just have to do what we could in that time. Besides, I had seen how strong Sadeena was. If she was fighting with us, we should be able to win easily.

"Another thing, little Rock."

"What now?"

"I'm guessing you probably suspected this while we were fighting, but the organizers had debuff magic being secretly cast on your team nonstop, during the match. On top of that, they were buffing me."

"What the hell?!"

"In other words, now that the organizers consider me an enemy, you shouldn't expect me to be as strong as I was earlier, okay?"

Damn it! Things just kept getting worse and worse! They went so far as to interfere with us healing our wounds, so we had to settle with the bare minimum of treatment. On top of that, the buff that had been applied to Sadeena had now been switched to a debuff.

If I made a big fuss in protest right now, would they listen? Most likely, they would just think I was making excuses and ignore me. It was the underground coliseum, after all. Maybe the very nature of the place made it a mistake to try and make a quick fortune there. I was starting to regret letting the competitive odds lure me into competing.

Plus, our opponent would be buffed. It was safe to assume that the purpose of this three-minute interval was to apply the buff. I had a feeling that my body felt even heavier now than it had earlier, too.

"You three were pretty impressive yourselves. I was pretty surprised during our fight, you know?"

"Yeah, but . . ."

I was one of the four holy heroes that protects the world from the waves. Normally, my strength was worlds apart from that of ordinary people. Damn it! If my stats hadn't been reduced by that curse, then a little debuff magic wouldn't have made a difference in the world!

Hold on . . . I'd gotten my hands on a shield in Kizuna's world that would probably be useful at a time like this. It had come from the White Tiger materials. I was pretty sure it had a support nullification special effect. That could be useful right now if a debuff counted as support magic.

I started messing with my shield but then paused. I didn't have enough materials on hand to power it up adequately. I tried using what I had and then checked the status screen. Hmm . . . It was really iffy. Since it was only partially powered up, it was far inferior to the Demon Dragon Shield, which was fully powered up. The difference was big enough that it would be a step down, even if I took the debuff into consideration.

"Ra—Shigaraki."

"Yes?"

"Weapons made out of the White Tiger materials may be able to nullify debuffs."

This time Raphtalia checked her status screen.

"My stats aren't high enough to handle the katana anyway, but there's no support nullification effect on the weapon."

Oh well. We would just have to keep using the same weapons we had been.

"In any case . . ."

Sadeena glanced over at the spectators and organizers before swinging her harpoon around lightheartedly and then giving me a wink.

"I guess we'll just have to do this, won't we?"

"Yeah."

"Yes. Let's overcome this obstacle and get the villagers back!"

"They won't beat meeee!"

Raphtalia and Filo agreed with us. Right around that time, the survey tally was completed, and it was officially decided that the exhibition match would be held.

Realistically, it would be impossible for us to use magic. We had powerful debuff magic being cast on us, and the enemy was buffed. What kind of bastards would make us to fight under such conditions?! I mean, I knew what kind of people they were already, but give me a break!

Should I order the slave trader and accessory dealer to crush them later? They could do that, right? If I exerted my influence as a hero as well, surely we could end them for good. Either way, I needed to focus on winning the fight right now. I'd just look like a whining loser if I tried to pick a fight with them after being defeated.

Something bothered me about how the organizer merchants turned around and left before the results of the survey had even been announced. We needed to finish the match quick. I was sure they were up to no good.

"And noooowww! Let the baaaaattle . . . BEEGGIINN!!"

The gong sound echoed out, and our fight with this Murder Pierrot freak began. Right now, our top priority was to quickly finish off this . . . puppeteer? The clickety-clack of the two puppets out in front as they quickly came running our way was just creepy.

"Let's do this! Aim for the one controlling them in the back!"

"Understood!"

"Here I go!"

Since we couldn't use magic under the circumstances, Sadeena didn't even try to cast any spells and just took off after Raphtalia and Filo while still in her animal form. She was fast . . . but yeah, not that fast. She tended to lag just one step behind

Raphtalia and Filo at her current speed. Watching Raphtalia and Filo dash out into the front made it obvious to me that she'd had support magic cast on her earlier.

My job was to stop these two puppet things!

"Ha!"

I leapt out in front and blocked the attacks of the puppets, which were brandishing swords and axes. I could feel the heavy impact travel through the shield and into my body. Still, it hadn't been enough to surpass my defenses.

". . ."

". . ."

The way they jerked around while making clickety-clack noises was seriously creepy. Murder Pierrot was holding a ball of thread and seemed to be using it to control the puppets.

"I harbor no ill will toward you, but I want to end this ludicrous match as quick as possible, so please don't hold it against me!"

"We're gonna win!"

"I'm sure it's no fun to get stuck cleaning up after a girl like me, is it? But we have our reasons, so don't hold it against us!"

Before I could even tell them to, Raphtalia, Filo, and Sadeena all brandished their weapons and rushed in to attack. Our opponent was supposed to be strong, but . . . surely they weren't strong enough to handle all of us. We'd gotten here by overcoming every obstacle that had been put in our way, no matter how great! Losing was not an option!

"Spider Net . . ."

"Wha—"

"Huuuh?"

"Oh?"

The three of them had tried to attack, but their weapons came to an unnatural halt right in front of Murder Pierrot. Huh? What was going on?!

"Something's . . . stuck to my weapon . . . Thread?!"

"It's stuuuuck!"

"Looks like things might get sticky, doesn't it?"

The thread that their weapons had gotten tangled up in suddenly came into view, as it wrapped around the weapons tightly. And then, as if it were alive, thread after thread shot forth and began wrapping around their bodies, as well.

Was it an immobilization attack? Was there seriously an attack that worked like a spider web?! We must have been dealing with some kind of therianthrope or something that had insect-like characteristics. Or maybe it was actually a monster that was using a human form like Filo did.

Murder Pierrot held the ball of thread out.

"Bind Wire"

Thread shot out of the puppets that I was holding on to with a hissing sound and came straight for me.

"Damn it! Let go!"

I yanked at the thread forcefully as it tried to wrap around me, and it gave easily . . . but it wouldn't break! I could have just written it off as being futile, since I wasn't able to attack by nature. But regardless of that, this elasticity was just unreal. What in the world was this?!

"Ugh! This thread!"

"Ewww!"

"Little Ra—Shigaraki! Little Humming! Let go of your weapons!"

Filo and Sadeena each let go of their weapons, but Raphtalia was holding a vassal weapon that she couldn't let go of if she wanted to.

"Little Shigaraki!"

"I know! But . . . Take this! Instant Blade! Mist!"

Raphtalia tried to force a skill to cut the thread, but it just resulted in sparks flying. No way! Just what kind of material was this stuff made out of to be able to take one of Raphtalia's skills and still not break?! Or was that it? Could we not cut it because the gap between our stats had been made so massive that this was all futile? If that was the case, I might just have to incinerate everything with the Shield of Wrath.

Using brute force, I overpowered the thread that was binding me down and placed my hand on my shield.

Due to interference, the shield may not be changed.

A message appeared in my field of vision. Huh?

"I won't let you."

Thread after thread wrapped around my shield. You couldn't even tell whether it was a shield or just a big jumble of thread anymore.

"Change Seal Wire"

"Damn it . . . What the hell . . ."

I knew that our opponent was supposed to be crazy strong, but even so, something about this just wasn't right! I couldn't imagine attacks like this coming from anyone other than a hero!

"Fire Paralysis Wire"

The thread in the area surrounding me burst into flames and started reaching out for me. Damn it! The heat didn't bother me, but the enemy was clearly trying to eliminate me, the leader of our team!

"Mr. Na—Mr. Rock!"

"Hurry up and put your katana away! Use your other weapon!"

"Un . . . understood!"

I needed to put some distance between us quick, while I could still move! That said . . . How could I do that? That's it! I'd repel them with Shooting Star Shield!

"Shooting Star—"

"Skill Seal"

The thread wrapped around my throat. It wasn't the least

bit uncomfortable. But . . .

"Wh . . . what?!"

I was trying to cast the skill, but for whatever reason I couldn't say the name of the skill!

"What the hell is going on?!"

This made no sense! This Murder Pierrot freak was blocking my skills! Not even magic could explain that! The fact that she was using status effects on me, despite my resistance to them, must have meant . . . there was a good possibility that they were trap-type attacks. It depended on the game, but sometimes traps could apply status effects regardless of resistances. I couldn't deny that such a thing might exist, and in all actuality, I must have been experiencing it right now.

"Take thiiiis!"

Filo ducked under the thread and rushed at Murder Pierrot to attack barehanded. I don't know if it was underestimating Filo because she was barehanded, or just being focused on me and Raphtalia, but Murder Pierrot threw up a web of thread, in what appeared to be a really half-assed attempt to guard against Filo's attack.

"How about thiiis!!"

Filo transformed into her filolial form with a loud boom and leapt high up and over the thread, kicking it as hard as she could. Murder Pierrot seemed surprised, turning to Filo and scattering several threads in her direction instantly.

"I'm not done!"

Murder Pierrot must have gotten careless after seeing how bulky Filo was in her filolial form, because the thread she'd scattered wasn't dense at all. Regardless of the magic interference, Filo changed to her human form, went into the accelerated state that she had learned from Fitoria, and squeezed between the threads. The instant of the attack, she switched back to her filolial form and delivered a swift kick.

"Ugh!"

Murder Pierrot took the full brunt of Filo's attack and was sent flying. But as if to dampen the force of the impact, the thread spread out and wrapped around Murder Pierrot. It formed a cocoon for an instant and then unraveled before Murder Pierrot landed on the ground, unscathed. The unraveled thread wrapped up into something like a cocoon and rolled off to the side of the arena.

"We're not finished!"

Raphtalia brandished her katana and prepared to deliver a follow-up attack.

"Spirit Blade! Soul Slice!"

"Useless . . ."

"Oh really?"

Raphtalia's katana passed right through the thread and cut into Murder Pierrot.

"—!?"

Murder Pierrot seemed to be saying something, but all I could hear was static. Why? What was that noise? Regardless, we had to keep going. Raphtalia had a katana that could be used to attack nonphysical entities, immaterial opponents like ghosts.

"Okay then . . . Next is . . ." continued Raphtalia.

"Mind Line"

Thread shot out rapidly, as if to protect against Raphtalia's next attack. The new thread wrapped around the katana that had passed through the previous thread.

"I'm still here, toooo!"

Filo followed up and tried to deliver another kick, but thread shot out across the whole area . . . Wait! Those puppets that I thought were near me had now suddenly appeared in front of Filo. Damn! I could barely even move!

"Next——y turn. Needle Shot!"

Now there were needles coming out of the ball of thread?! The needles had thread attached to them. All of these attacks made me feel like I was watching an instructional video about sewing!

"Little Rock! You okay?!"

Sadeena came over to where I was to check on me. If we had no weapons and couldn't use magic, we would have no way to fight . . . Was that it?

But wait, what happened to assistance being bought and weapons being thrown in to participants when the fight is too one-sided?! As the thought crossed my mind, I looked up and noticed that the thread had carefully intercepted all of the weapons that had been thrown in. The arena had turned into a mess of spider web and the weapons couldn't make it down to us.

As for magical support, I couldn't say definitively what was going on from here, but it was safe to assume that the organizers were blocking any attempts at that.

Damn it . . . If things kept going like this, Raphtalia and Filo could end up in trouble. I was being pulled by the thread, too. It was stuck to my limbs and was trying to force me to walk. Judging from the direction, it seemed like Murder Pierrot was trying to use me as a shield against Raphtalia's attacks.

I'd thought that Sadeena was about as formidable as they came, but I guess there's always going to be someone stronger. Then again, that's just how it felt to me now, and this might not have been a problem for us if we could use magic and didn't have the debuffs or curse effects.

"Big sis! Mmhem . . . Mmhem . . ."

Filo returned to her human form and took a few big steps back before clearing her throat several times. Then . . . for whatever reason, she began to sing.

"Why are you singing at a time like this?!"

I yelled at Filo. She looked at me and started signaling something to me with her hands. Umm . . . Judging from the hairdo and the way she posed with the imaginary weapon . . . Kizuna? And she was singing, so . . . Was it the ability she had gained in Kizuna's world? I knew she could do that when she had been a Humming Fairy, but did that mean she could do it in this world, too?! Now that I thought about it, I was pretty sure she had been saying something or other about lullabies earlier!

There was a pounding sound and the thread surrounding Filo began to shake. Moments later, the thread caught fire and quickly returned to the reel that Murder Pierrot was holding. I knew it! The thread must have been weak to magic-based attacks.

"Fire Sooong!"

I was pretty sure it was just Filo singing, but the song was echoing throughout the area. So it wasn't magic, then? In that case, they wouldn't be able to block it. After that, Filo took a deep breath, changed into her filolial form, and then held her wings up to her mouth like a megaphone and screamed.

"Air Block Voice!"

There was a loud boom, and then I saw something like a shock wave shoot out of Filo's mouth and toward Murder Pierrot. She had some pretty ridiculous secret moves. Why hadn't she used that on Kyo, for crying out loud?! Then again, I guess just using magic like normal might have been more effective.

"Thank you, Humming!"

Raphtalia was making her other katana appear and disappear as needed, while she slipped through Murder Pierrot's obstacles, in what appeared to be a graceful dance, and then closed in to attack. We were overwhelming the opponent . . . but how long would that last?

Ugh . . . The weight of the debuff magic had become noticeably heavier. Raphtalia and Filo were moving more sluggishly now, too.

"Little Rock."

Sadeena had been bound just like Filo, but she transformed to break free and came over to me. This thread I was wrapped up in had turned into a real flame war, but Sadeena reached out and touched me.

"What's up?"

"It's not that I forgot to mention this, but there is a way to use magic in a situation like this, you know?"

"Huh? How is that?"

"Have you not studied magic?"

I thought back to when I had been studying magic while we were peddling. Counter-magic was something that could only be used on an individual opponent, but it was possible for multiple people to cast counter-magic. But what if multiple people were performing a single incantation? Aha, so if it were several people casting cooperative magic, then it might just work. I remembered seeing Filo do it several times before.

Sadeena brought her mouth next to my ear and quietly explained.

"So you and I can work together to cast cooperative magic, little Rock."

"But they'll notice us chanting the incantation and just interfere, won't they?"

"Leave that part up to me, darling. I won't fail."

Sadeena winked at me and started focusing on the incantation.

"You focus, too, little Rock. I'll help you out. We're going to cast support magic."

Fine, whatever. I started to focus. I felt a flow of magic power coming from Sadeena . . . Strange. It was like the flow of power that I felt when casting magic with Ost . . . but something was different. I closed my eyes, and in my field of view, something that looked like a square block appeared. Next to it was a sculpture of some random shape? No, that wasn't it. It was a puzzle piece. What was going on?

"Is this your first time casting cooperative magic? Basically, we form the magic power into predetermined shapes."

Damn it. What she was asking me to do wasn't easy.

"Power of two, lend your strength to support them! Re-spin the threads of fate and turn their defeat into a victory!"

I could feel Sadeena rapidly forming the pieces of the puzzle and converting each one into the language of magic.

"Here, let me see that, little Rock. I'll help you with it."

She started working on forming the block that I had been trying to shape. Although, it wasn't going as smoothly as hers, since it was a section that would normally be up to me to complete. Still, what was this feeling? Something about what Sadeena was doing felt really similar to what Ost had done. When I thought about that aura, a blurry image of one of the pieces Ost had shown me came into sight for a split second.

"If you don't stop getting distracted and finish this soon, little Raphtalia will be in trouble, you know?"

Raphtalia and Filo were still putting up a good fight, but it was probably only a matter of time before that changed. I could see Murder Pierrot reeling in the weapons that had been thrown at us and trying to swing them around with the thread. Right now, I needed to focus on this magic, and after that we'd just have to figure out a way to overcome this opponent, even if by brute force.

"Dragon Vein! Hear our petition and grant it! As the source of your power, we implore you! Let the true way be revealed once more! Give us the power to overcome the obstacles before us!"

Sadeena completed the cooperative magic and raised her left hand into the air. Dark clouds began to form above us, and the sound of thunder echoed throughout the arena.

"Oh? So this is the magic we ended up with, is it?"

"Descent of the Thunder God!"

Without even trying, the name of the spell came out of my mouth at the same time Sadeena shouted it. A target icon appeared in my field of vision.

"Little Rock, I'm sure you know who we should target with the magic, right?"

"Yeah . . ."

Without hesitating, I chose Raphtalia. Sadeena must have agreed, because she pointed her finger at Raphtalia. The thunderclouds moved over to the air above Raphtalia and lightning came crashing down.

"Ahh!"

Raphtalia shouted out in surprise.

"Now . . ."

She had left herself open, and Murder Pierrot's thread shot out toward her. But the thread bounced off, unable to wrap around her. And that wasn't all.

"Ugh!"

With a loud crackle, Murder Pierrot received a strong electrical shock and reeled back slightly.

"What . . . is this?"

Raphtalia was standing there with a shocked look on her face. I couldn't blame her—I felt the same. Raphtalia's whole body was surging with electricity, after all.

"My stats have all skyrocketed!"

"Little Ra—Shigaraki! That's our powerful cooperative support magic, darling! Don't waste it!"

"Un . . . understood!"

"I won't lose."

Not to be outdone, Murder Pierrot shot out a barrage of threaded needles, but Raphtalia repelled every one of them and closed in on Murder Pierrot at a speed that made her earlier sluggishness seem like nothing but a bad dream.

"I can withstand any attack!"

Murder Pierrot shot a web out of her ball of thread and tried to put some distance between them.

"We'll see about that! Brave Blade! Mist!"

Raphtalia was dual wielding now. She faced Murder Pierrot and fired off her skill. Raphtalia's blades followed a cross-shaped trajectory that cut right through the web of thread and into Murder Pierrot.

"Ahhhh!"

As if to follow up her attack, lightning shot from the blades into Murder Pierrot, who was sent flying. Still not ready to give up, Murder Pierrot broke the fall and sprang back up, ready to fight.

"You can't beat ussss!"

Filo took a deep breath and fired off another Air Block Voice.

"Ughhhh . . ."

It hadn't seemed that powerful this time, but apparently it was still more than enough to create a shock wave that did some damage to our opponent.

"Now to finish this! Combo Skill! Blade of the Thunder Emperor!"

Raphtalia swung one of her katanas down hard. When she did, the blade was enveloped in bluish-white lightning that radiated outward brightly, and a rain of thunderbolts fell on Murder Pierrot.

"Gaahhh!"

The violent impact shook the whole arena with a loud boom, leaving a large crater in the floor. It was almost as if the ceremonial magic spell Judgement had rained down from the sky. The only thing left standing inside of the crater was Raphtalia.

We won . . . I think? It sure seemed like we had won, but Murder Pierrot's thread was still wrapped around me tightly. Raphtalia shook the blood from her blade and went to check to make sure that Murder Pierrot was incapacitated.

". . . ?"

Raphtalia looked closely at her katana and then used the sheath to roll the fallen Murder Pierrot's body over.

"This is . . ."

She poked at Murder Pierrot's torso lightly with her sheath, and it made a hollow sound. It sounded just like . . . wood? And then the ball of thread that Murder Pierrot had been holding started to roll along the floor. That's right. It went rolling off toward a pile of weapons that had been wound up in thread and tossed aside into a corner of the arena. I had a really bad feeling about this.

"Scape-Doll"

A pair of scissors appeared and cut open the cocoon of thread that had wrapped around the pile of weapons, and something came crawling out.

"I'm guessing that buff is——?"

A second Murder Pierrot was standing there right before us. Raphtalia raised her katana and readied herself.

"That won't be enough to———me. You're simply not strong enough."

"Huh?"

Murder Pierrot spoke so softly that I could hardly hear what was being said!

"You have to———no one can stand up to you. Otherwise, you'll be destroyed by other———. You shouldn't be struggling against someone like me."

What was this clown going on about?

"I've fought enough to earn my pay. Truthfully——— fight———th. Eventually——ssshhsssaa . . ."

Was it just me or was I hearing static again? I kept hearing crackling and hissing noises when this clown was talking to us.

"You have to work harder, or you'll die."

I heard Murder Pierrot clearly that time. And then, after waving to me, there was a small explosion and Murder Pierrot disappeared, leaving behind a cloud of smoke.

So . . . a ninja? It was pretty much exactly how you would expect a ninja to disappear. At the same time, the thread that had been strewn out all over the arena disappeared, too, along with the puppets that Filo had been fighting.

"What the hell was that?!"

Not only did I have no idea who she had been, but the way she talked made it sound like she had been testing us. And then she just up and disappeared.

"Murder Pierrot has vanished! We have a winner! Rock Valley's Party and Nadiaaaaaaa!"

What started out as just a few spectators clapping here and there quickly turned into a roar of cheers and applause. I guess they didn't actually care which side won in the end.

"We did it, little Rock."

"We won!"

"Filo wiiiins!"

"You mean Humming!"

I scolded Filo and all she had to say was "whoops!"

Jeez . . . It was just in one ear and out the other with that bird!

"But . . . what was that? That Murder Pierrot freak . . . When did she even switch places in the first place?"

"When the cocoon was formed, I'm guessing. Something

about it just didn't feel right, you know?"

"But she hid it super-duper good, right! Soooo, it wasn't magic, then?"

I had a feeling Sadeena and Filo were right. As far as I could tell, continuing the fight shouldn't have been a problem, but it was as if our opponent had achieved what she came for and just left. And that was after telling us we needed to get stronger . . .

I wasn't sure if Murder Pierrot was supposed to be our enemy or an ally. But no . . . Ally wasn't right. This was just a hunch, but there was something eerie about it all. It felt similar to when I first encountered Glass. I'd have to ask about that weird weapon next time we met.

But right now, we had to prioritize Raphtalia's fellow villagers. We waved as if to announce our victory and then quickly headed back to the contestants' waiting room.

Chapter Nineteen: Big Shots of the Underground

We asked the slave trader's assistant to retrieve our fight purse for us and dashed out behind Sadeena into the streets of the Zeltoble markets. After all, Sadeena had gone and done something completely different than what she had been asked to do by the crooked merchant.

It was easy to imagine what I would have done if I had been the merchant. I would confiscate the skyrocketing authentic Lurolona slaves and call it compensation. Then again, that may have been the plan from the very start. It would be a huge headache if that actually happened, which is why we were running in such a hurry like this.

"That debuff magic was quite powerful, wasn't it?"

"Yeah, it was."

After leaving the arena, my body felt light as a feather . . . so light that I almost flipped over at first.

"Little Rock, this way."

We went in the direction that Sadeena was pointing toward. Finally, we arrived at a building in a residential quarter of Zeltoble that had a bunch of hostile-looking thugs standing guard outside. It looked just like the kind of stone-built house that a merchant would prepare. Something about it resembled

Kizuna's house. In front of the house, there were several carriages lined up that looked like the kind they used to escort prisoners. It looked like my guess turned out to be right on the mark.

"We're currently in the process of collecting a debt inside of this building. Anyone not involved is unwelcome here!"

A group of mercenary types that were probably hired as protection were standing in front of the door to the house.

"Sorry, but we are involved, boys."

Sadeena began casting a spell and the mercenaries realized who we were.

"It looks like that bunch showed up just like they said they would!"

"I'm afraid we can't let you pass, lady. Be a good girl and come with us. Accept your punishment for going against the boss' wishes!"

And then, from out of who knows where, a whole bunch of mercenaries and whatnot, around forty men in total, appeared from all around and rushed at us to attack. It looked like they were nice enough to bring a few magic users, too.

If they thought they could overpower us with numbers, they were in for a real surprise. Had they even considered who their enemy was? Even if they thought they could bombard us with debuffs, this wasn't the arena. There was no way that Raphtalia and Filo were going to lose to a bunch of riffraff in a place that hadn't been rigged up beforehand.

"Here I goooo! Jingle-jaaangle!"

"Ugh . . . Uwaaaahhh!!"

Filo changed into her filolial form, attached the morning star to her leg, and began swinging it around, mowing down the mercenaries.

"You're in our way!"

"Gahhh!"

Raphtalia began cutting them down with her katana.

"Too bad, boys! Drifa Chain Lightning!"

Sadeena cast lightning magic that jumped from one enemy to the next, electrocuting the mercenaries as it went. They obviously didn't bring enough magic users to interfere with our spells. And then, as if to add the finishing touch, Sadeena thrust her harpoon into the gut of one of the mercenaries as hard as she could. She sent him flying into the other few still standing, knocking them over like bowling pins.

And just like that, the whole lot outside of the building were put to rest.

"Heh. In an area this cramped, they wouldn't stand a chance no matter how many they brought."

There were also some archers or something attacking us from a distance, but I had cast Shooting Star Shield and the arrows were just bouncing off without ever getting near us.

"Sadeena, are the villagers' slave curses not registered to the merchant, then?"

"Don't worry, I paid to have the slave curses removed, and I told them ahead of time to run away if anything happened."

"Wouldn't that mean that they already ran away from here?"

Sadeena glanced over at the building when I asked.

"Hmm?"

Filo had her head cocked to the side for some reason.

"Umm . . . The new big sis just made some kind of noise."

"Oh? I'm surprised you noticed. I was just checking to see how many people were in the building."

Sonar? That must have been it. I'd heard that dolphins, whales, and killer whales could use sonar to locate objects in the ocean. I guess she had some kind of ability like that since she was a therianthrope. That sure must have been convenient.

"It's okay. It looks like they got surrounded before they could run and are holed up inside."

"And what part of that is okay? Oh, whatever . . . Let's do this! Raphtalia!"

"Okay!"

The door had been locked from the outside to keep them from getting away. So Raphtalia cut the door down and stepped inside. I followed after her, and we made quick work of several thugs that were trying to capture the villagers.

"Gahhh!"

Behind them was the merchant that announced the exhibition match at the arena earlier. To think that he would go out of his way to show up at a place like this . . . That worked out just perfectly for us.

"Ugh . . . Nadia! You have a lot of nerve breaking your contract!" he screamed.

"What can a girl do? I got stuck with the wrong opponent. It's not like I didn't try, you know? Besides, this is something little Rock and I decided on together."

"And that's my cue. Thanks a lot for earlier. I'm not going to complain about that, since the match was decided by a vote, and you can never know what to expect at the underground coliseum. But this business here is different."

"The hell it is! Thanks to your little crew showing up, my profits are nonexistent! That's why I'm going to confiscate the precious cash cow of that contract-violating . . . woman that doesn't even bat an eyelash when her slave curse is activated!"

He seemed to realize that this wasn't his lucky day. The crooked merchant actually tried to explain his actions, all while glaring at Sadeena, obviously infuriated. What was all that about not batting an eyelash at a slave curse, anyways? I looked over at Sadeena and she pointed at her chest.

"Boobies!"

"Shut up! Just show me!"

I removed the sarashi cloth that she had wrapped around her chest, and sure enough, there was a slave curse right there, fully activated and shining bright as the sun.

"That's what you get for being stingy and using a cheap slave curse. A little thing like this isn't going to do diddly to a girl like me, you know?"

Filo had deactivated her own monster seal once, now that I thought about it. Maybe these kinds of things weren't as effective when the recipient was really good with magic?

"You should be writhing in pain with each step! How the hell are you able to stand there looking so smug?!"

"Obviously because it doesn't hurt that bad, right?"

Huh? Did that mean it wasn't actually fully disabled? Ahh, now that I thought about it, Filo's monster seal never actually activated. But Sadeena's slave curse was activated and running nonstop. So she was mitigating the effect, but that didn't mean it didn't hurt . . . She sure was something.

"You fools will regret this! Do you really think you'll get out of this alive?! I won't allow it! Even if you make it out of here, you'll have the underground guild on your tail no matter where you run!"

"Weapons merchant . . . I'm afraid that won't happen."

Just then a voice came from behind us. I turned my head to look, and standing there were the accessory dealer and the slave trader. Rishia had come with them and seemed to be trembling a bit. Raph-chan was there, too.

"I was really nervous watching your match!"

"Rafu!"

"I bet you were. Honestly, the combat aspect of it might have been more of a hassle than when we faced Kyo."

Sadeena did things like nullify magic and dodge skills and was a complete monster when it came to her sense of combat. I had plenty of questions for that Murder Pierrot clown, too, but . . . whatever.

"You . . . you're the accessory—" exclaimed the crooked merchant.

"We thought our presence might be required, so here we are. Yes sir."

The crooked merchant seemed to be genuinely shocked. He was pointing at the accessory dealer with his eyes wide and his mouth hanging open.

"Why?! Why are you here?! Still, that doesn't matter! There's no way that Zeltoble's underground merchant guild will allow this!"

"No, I'm afraid he's not someone the merchant guild can lay a hand on. If you had actually watched the fight at the coliseum earlier, weapons merchant, I'm sure you would have realized that."

He'd just shown up when something unexpected happened and improvised without having actually checked the situation himself and then ran off to confiscate the slaves.

"I represent my family when I say that we feel the recent issue at the underground coliseum was trivial, and we declare our opposition to the penalization of Rock Valley's Party. Yes sir."

"The accessory guild that I oversee declares its opposition, as well."

"What? Why?!"

"Because while you were working behind the scenes to decide who would win the competition, we were working behind the scenes as well. Yes sir."

"What are you implying?!"

"Let's see . . . First, you make a nice profit off of the tournament . . . and then you take the brats that Nadia was harboring and throw them into the auctions at the peak of the price bubble to make a nice profit there, too. Does that sound about right? After figuring out a way to kill off Nadia, of course."

"Sounds just about right to me. That's why I was being extra careful, you know. That's also why I used my underground connections to have the children's slave curses removed," Nadia chimed in.

Seriously? I could never quite understand what this woman was thinking. If she already knew what was going to happen, why hadn't she tried a little bit harder to do something about it?!

"Now then, let's talk business. Umm . . . weapons merchant, is it? We're going to win the tournament after winning tomorrow's match. The money that we'll get from that is pretty much equal to Nadia's debt. I'm going to use that money to buy Nadia's freedom, so the Lurolona slaves that you and Nadia were holding on to become mine."

"Hell no! Why would anyone give up a cash cow like that?! Do you have any idea how much those slaves are trading for right now?!"

Meh. I was fully aware that he wasn't going to agree to my terms, of course.

"How the hell did you get those two on your side, anyways?!"

Oh yeah . . . I hadn't introduced myself, now that I thought about it. I guess it would be difficult to figure out who I was, considering the company the slave trader kept, and the shenanigans of the accessory dealer, after all.

"Everyone at the coliseum has already figured out who Rock Valley's Party really is, you know? Whether they're the real thing or not is another thing, of course."

"Well, he might have heard and just laughed it off, figuring we were just imposters, so I'll go ahead and tell him."

I glared down at the crooked merchant with contempt in my eyes and jutted my thumb out in my own direction to accent my haughty self-introduction.

"I'm Naofumi Iwatani. I was summoned to this world as one of the four holy heroes—the Shield Hero. I entered your coliseum tournament for the express purpose of getting back the ridiculously overpriced Lurolona slaves."

"I really would have rather you not introduced yourself. You're going to hurt your reputation."

Raphtalia was over there moaning.

"Reputation? Who cares about that? I didn't have the luxury of being able to choose my methods if I wanted to get the overpriced Lurolona slaves back quickly."

"What?! Hogwash!"

The crooked merchant blurted out in response, as if I had said something unbelievable. So what? A self-introduction wasn't proof enough? What a hassle.

"If you think I'm lying, then how about I prove it for you? How about these? Air Strike Shield! Second Shield! Chain Shield! Shield Prison!"

I continued to change my shield repeatedly while showing off my skills.

"Surely you're not going to try to say I'm faking it with magic, since I haven't made a single incantation."

"In that case, allow me to provide irrefutable evidence. Yes sir."

The slave trader passed me a cluster of rucolu fruits. I guess I was supposed to eat one? I plucked one of the fruits off, dangled it in front of the crooked merchant's nose to show him that it was the real thing, and then gobbled it up.

"Oh my!"

For whatever reason, Sadeena placed a hand on her cheek with a dreamy look in her eyes.

"Do you still not believe me?"

"I can't . . . ugh . . ."

The crooked merchant hung his head in despair and flopped down onto the floor. Apparently, eating rucolu fruit, as if it were nothing, had become indisputable proof of identification as the Shield Hero. Then again, the method had still only really caught on in and around Melromarc and among a select group of merchants. There would be people that hadn't heard the rumors, but this merchant didn't seem to be one of them.

"So there you are. You ready to give up, now? Oh, and don't think that I've forgotten about your little stunt with the forced exhibition match, either."

"Wh . . . what do you want from me?!"

"Hmm, let's see . . . There may still be Lurolona villagers out there, so you'll notify me if you happen to come across any authentic ones. Whether it's installments or whatever, I'll pay for them. That said, I expect you to hurry up and crush this bubble and get the prices back to where they should be."

It was almost certain that this crook had exploited Sadeena's request and intentionally pushed the prices of the village slaves up. In that case, if we took care of the ringleader, then the skyrocketing prices should settle back down, too. The phenomenon may have already gained some momentum of its own, but we had an all-star cast of underground merchants right here. Surely it wasn't something they couldn't handle.

"For example, you could use what happened here to go spread rumors about the Shield Hero sending assassins after people with Lurolona slaves."

There were plenty of witnesses. I was sure the rumors would spread like wildfire.

"If you surrender and play nicely like those two merchants over there, you won't regret it. So what do you say?"

"Fine . . . I surrender . . ."

And so, finally, the curtain fell on the underground coliseum incident. Of course, it goes without saying that the following day's fight was essentially a throwaway match, and we ended it as soon as it started.

Epilogue: Come-On

There was a total of fifteen slaves that Sadeena had been harboring. It was questionable whether we would have been able to buy that many with the prize money from the coliseum. The Lurolona slave that Raphtalia had spotted at the slave auction turned out to be among them, too, by the way. The way they told it, Sadeena had been sending one of the Lurolona slaves to the auctions, with the merchant, to buy up the other villagers. You would have to be confident about being able to identify them for that plan to work, of course. Sadeena broke off her contract, too, and was happy to be free once again.

"Alright then. Did you finish talking to them, Raphtalia?"

"Yes. They all believed me. I also told them about your territory and how we're right in the middle of rebuilding the village there."

"Good, good. I guess all that's left is asking whether they want to become my slaves or not."

"About that . . . Would you mind waiting until we take them back to the village for that?"

Hmm . . . I guess she figured that Keel and the other slaves would serve as an example, and seeing them would make the new slaves decide they wanted to become stronger of their own accord. Raphtalia was pretty clever, after all.

"That's fine. Alright then, just ask them to join our party for now. I'll send them back to the village with my portal skill as it refreshes."

Under the guidance of Sadeena and Raphtalia, the fifteen slaves spent their time enjoying each other's company as I went about returning them to their home village with my portal skill. Experiencing the portal for the first time was quite a shock, but that soon wore off.

"How about we head back for now, too? I'm exhausted, to tell the truth."

"Agreed."

We used the portal to return to the village, and when we got back, all the original villagers—including Sadeena—seemed to be busy rekindling old friendships. Filo had gone to the neighboring town to tell Melty all about our heroic exploits in Zeltoble. I just hoped she didn't go blabbering about things best left unsaid.

"So, little Rock, I guess your real name is little Naofumi, then?"

"I see you're sticking with the 'little.'"

Like always, Sadeena was overly familiar with me and talked to me like I was a child.

"So, little Naofumi, tell me . . . How far have you gone with little Raphtalia?"

"Gone?"

"Sadeena!"

What was "gone" supposed to mean there? Raphtalia didn't like obscene jokes or topics related to that kind of stuff, and I was sure Sadeena knew that, too, since they were so close. In that case, she must have been asking how far away from here we had traveled.

"We went all the way to another world on the other side of the dimensional rifts. That katana that Raphtalia has is one of that world's . . . I guess it would be like one of the seven star heroes' weapons in this world."

"Oh my . . ."

Sadeena looked hard at Raphtalia.

"Wh . . . what?!"

"Is that true? Have you really only gone that far with little Naofumi?"

"Y . . . yes!"

"What's going on here, Bubba Shield?"

Keel called out to me. She was in a happy mood after being reunited with her fellow villagers.

"It's nothing, Keel."

"Oh really?"

"Just tales of Raphtalia's heroic exploits is all."

"Yes, your interpretation is just fine, Mr. Naofumi."

Huh? What was up with that wording? That almost made it sound like my first guess had been the correct.

"Well, in that case . . . you won't mind if I take little Naofumi for myself then, right, little Raphtalia?"

"What are you saying?!"

"What the hell, woman!"

"Huh? I'm totally serious about making little Naofumi mine, you know."

Sadeena replied slowly in a flirtatious manner and then hooked her arm around mine. Stop that! I wanted to throw up. I tried to pull my arm away from her, but it felt useless as she just kept trying to hook her arm back around mine over and over. Damn it! This woman was persistent!

"Don't you want a girl like me to tend to your every need?"

"Sadeena . . . Are you being serious?"

"I sure am."

Sadeena responded without hesitation. Damn it.

"Huh? You mean you like bubba? You're not the only one! Everyone in the village loves bubba, you know!"

"I'm a tyrannical moneygrubber! I'm not interested in making friends, and I'm not anybody's bubba!"

"Could you have come up with a line any less convincing?!"

What was that, Keel?! I knew it . . . This kid was slow in the head. Sadeena was just making brazen sexual advances at me because she knew I hated that kind of thing! You could tell by the way that she was acting that she was just trying to mess with me. This was the same woman that put my hand on her chest and said, "boobies!" Taking her seriously would only wear you out. Raphtalia was the really serious type, and she tended to especially dislike that kind of talk.

"Right? Okay then, little Keel, how about you and I go after little Naofumi together? I'm going to make little Naofumi my hubby!"

"Like hell you will, you spaz!"

Raphtalia's face was growing paler by the moment. She looked my way.

"Mr. Naofumi . . . Did you and Sadeena happen to . . . have a drinking contest?"

"Drinking contest? The first time we met, she had been drinking like a fish and she still made me drink with her. We drank the next time we met, too, but she never drank enough to get drunk."

"Oh, come on, you. For all intents and purposes, you stood up to me and you won!"

Raphtalia threw her head backward and covered her face with her hands, as if she had been completely horrified. What was going on?

"Mr. Naofumi . . . For as long as I can remember, there was always something that Sadeena used to tell the villagers."

"Huh?"

Keel was nodding knowingly. What the hell?

"She would say, 'My lifelong partner will be someone that

can hold their liquor better than me! If I ever find someone like that, there's no way I'm going to let him get away. You've all been warned!'"

"No one else in the village could drink like Sadeena! There was even a rumor that she won a territory drinking contest and then went drinking after!"

"Oh really . . ."

"The fact that Sadeena says you're going to be her future husband means that you must have beat her in a drinking contest, bubba. That's what all the villagers will think!"

"Huh?"

Now that I thought about it, Sadeena had given me a drink with a rucolu fruit in it. I had a feeling she'd started acting even friendlier with me after that. Huh? So that was why she wanted me to be her husband? I figured she was just messing with me, but . . .

I looked over at Sadeena. The woman switched back to her human form and started drawing on my arm with one hand, while holding her other hand to her cheek and blushing. It made me think . . . If this had been before Bitch tricked me, I'd probably be thinking "score!" thrilled that I was finally getting some attention from the opposite sex.

"Hey bubba, how did you manage to beat Sadeena, anyways?"

"I don't know if I beat her, but she started getting real friendly after I ate a rucolu fruit."

"That'll do it!"

Keel and all of the Lurolona slaves nodded in agreement. I got the feeling that Sadeena had been like a big sister to the village children, so maybe they all knew her well?

"People gave it to me every now and then, when we were peddling, right?"

"Huh? That was rucolu fruit? I thought it was just a token to show you were welcome there."

Having me eat a piece of rucolu fruit had become a popular way of making sure I wasn't just some fraud posing as the Shield Hero. Apparently, I was the only one out there who could eat rucolu fruit and be no worse for the wear. I liked to think of it as a sign of welcome that was also a punishment for imposters.

"So now you know I'm being sincere! Thank you, little Naofumi!"

"Blegh!"

Sadeena pursed her lips and thrust them quickly at mine. I turned my head away in a flash. Still, Sadeena's lips touched my cheek and she gave me a little smack.

"Aww, that's too bad. Next time it'll be the lips!"

"Go to hell!"

That was close! She almost stole my first kiss! Sorry, but I had no intention of starting a family in this world. As soon as this world became peaceful, I'd be returning to Japan without hesitation, after all!

Was it just me or had the air grown really tense? Raphtalia was glaring at me and Sadeena with a really aggravated look on her face. See! I told you that Raphtalia was serious and didn't like this kind of thing.

"Ra . . . Rafu . . ."

"Fehhh . . ."

"Sadeena!"

"Oh my! This is so much fun! Is it okay for me to be this excited about the days to come, I wonder?"

"As long as you behave yourself . . ."

"I have an idea! Hey, bubba! You should cook for everyone!"

"Cook for us!"

"Yeah, cook!"

"Coooook!"

"Shut up!"

Our plan to round up Raphtalia's fellow villagers had made good progress, I think. I wasn't sure if I could count them as part of our fighting potential yet, but I could still use the extra manpower.

But . . . was it just me? The saying "out of the frying pan and into the fire" came to mind. Sadeena changed from her human form to her animal form and was trying hard to get her arms around me, while I tried to pacify Raphtalia, who was aggravated because she was hypersensitive to that kind of sexual behavior. I couldn't help but think these two would be the death of me.

Character Design:
Nadia
サディナ

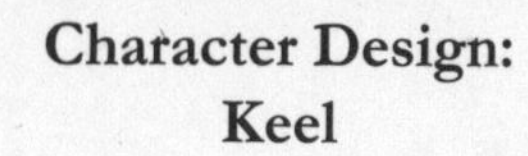

Character Design: Keel

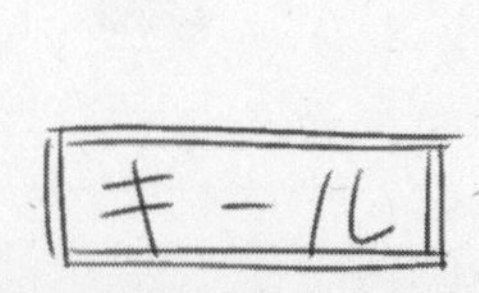

The Rising of the Shield Hero Vol. 10
First published by KADOKAWA in 2015 in Japan.
English translation rights arranged by One Peace Books
under the license from KADOKAWA CORPORATION, Japan.

ISBN: 978-1-944937-26-3

Written by Aneko Yusagi
Translated by Nathan Takase
Character Design by Minami Seira
English Edition Published by One Peace Books 2017

Printed in Canada

3 4 5 6 7 8 9 10

One Peace Books
43-32 22nd Street STE 204 Long Island City New York 11101
www.onepeacebooks.com